SNIPER'S JUSTICE

DAVID HEALEY

INTRACOASTAL

SNIPER'S JUSTICE

By David Healey

Intracoastal Media digital edition published March 2021. Print edition ISBN 978-0-9674162-7-4

BISAC Subject Headings:

FIC014000 FICTION/Historical

FIC032000 FICTION/War & Military

Revenge is an act of passion; vengeance of justice. Injuries are revenged; crimes are avenged.
— Samuel Johnson

PART I

CHAPTER ONE

January 1945, Vosges Mountains, France

WAITING IN AMBUSH, Caje Cole shivered in the freezing fog and snow but didn't take his eyes from the rifle scope. Any minute now, he expected to see a German unit come into view on the snow-covered road below.

All around him, the other squad members were ready. Vaccaro crouched at Cole's elbow, sighting down the barrel of his own rifle. Lieutenant Mulholland stood behind a tree, pointing his weapon down the slight incline in the direction from which they expected the Krauts to appear. Cutting through steep hills, the road seemed to pass through a tunnel of thick spruces and hemlocks arching overhead, adding to the winter gloom.

"You know what I've been thinking?" Vaccaro whispered.

"You thinking? That sounds about the same as you pulling the pin out of a grenade," Cole responded without taking his eyes off the road. "Give me a few seconds, so I can take cover."

"Very funny, Hillbilly. What I've been thinking is that it probably hurts less to get shot in cold weather. You're so damn numb that you can't feel it."

"City Boy, everybody knows it hurts more to get shot when it's cold," Cole said. "Take a hammer and whack your thumb in January and then whack it again in July. See which one you like better."

"What kind of test is that? I'm talking about getting shot."

"The thing is, you can only test it once when you get shot. Now with a hammer—"

"Quiet, you two," the lieutenant said. "Save it for the Krauts."

Cole grinned. Mulholland was getting antsy. Cole couldn't blame him. Their squad had been sent back along this road to intercept the Germans behind them. They weren't necessarily supposed to stop the Krauts, but to buy the rest of the unit some time.

With any luck, they might even lead the Germans right into a trap. Unfortunately, the squad would be serving as the bait.

The cause of the hold-up that necessitated this delaying action was the condition of the mountain roads. The trucks carrying the soldiers and supplies down the slippery, snow-covered roads were having a terrible time negotiating the hills and curves. The nimble Jeeps with their chain-wrapped tires fared somewhat better. Finally, one of the Studebaker trucks had slid sideways into a ditch and managed to get itself stuck.

The problem was that the truck now blocked the road, so they couldn't just leave it. It was a fact of life that any truck that got stuck instantly became crudely personified as a *stubborn bitch*. Half a mile behind them, every soldier in the unit, no matter how weary and frost-bitten he might be, was now pushing that truck, some of them hauling on ropes secured to the front bumper, trying to get *that stubborn bitch* out of the ditch.

From the other direction, they all knew that the Germans were coming. It was the squad's job to slow them down while the rest of the unit got the road cleared.

Everybody kept saying that the Germans were beaten, but apparently, the Germans in these hills hadn't gotten the message. Every time they ran into the Krauts, those bastards fought like hell.

"I wish those Kraut bastards would hurry up and get here," Vaccaro said. "Let's get this over with."

"Just keep your eyes open," Cole said.

If there was one thing that Cole had, it was patience. He tended to move slowly and deliberately, a perfect economy of motion without any wasted effort. When he did move in a hurry, it caught people off guard.

He was like a hawk floating easily in the high air that suddenly dives to strike its prey with vicious precision.

If Cole was a hawk, then Vaccaro was more like a junkyard dog. Nonetheless, they made a good team. Cole's nickname was Hillbilly, a nod to his Appalachian roots. As for Vaccaro, everybody called him City Boy, which fit his Brooklyn origins. Just about every soldier had a nickname, earned for some action or personality trait. As for the greenbeans in the unit, nobody even bothered to give them names. They tended not to last that long.

"Here they come," the lieutenant said.

Off in the distance, they heard the rumble of motorized vehicles. Mixed in was the distinctive sound of an enemy tank. It was funny how you could hear the difference between a Sherman and a Panzer. This Panzer was definitely coming closer.

If it was any consolation, the Germans would be having just as hard of a time navigating the narrow winter roads. In fact, they might even be having a harder time of it, considering that if the Krauts had a Tiger with them, those tanks were twice the size of a Sherman.

"That's just great," muttered Vaccaro beside him. "Tanks. Why does it have to be tanks?"

"We're just lucky, I reckon," Cole said.

"We'd be a whole lot luckier if we were about ten miles behind the lines, eating Christmas leftovers."

Cole didn't have an answer for that. Like the others, he knew that they weren't even supposed to be fighting any battles. After a hard fight across France, his squad had been scheduled for some well-deserved R&R over the Christmas holiday.

However, Uncle Adolf had made other plans for the holidays. The Germans had launched a surprise attack through the Ardennes Forest, forcing exhausted troops who had been looking forward to some rest back into the fight—Cole and Vaccaro among them.

The attack had been massive, with thousands of infantry and hundreds of Panzers. Most incredible of all, the Germans had staged their forces in complete secrecy, catching the Allies totally unawares. Nobody had expected troops to attack across that rugged terrain, lending to the element of surprise.

As a result, German forces had pushed the Allies back across 50 miles of hard-won ground, which was a bitter pill to swallow. Since then, the attack had faltered and the Germans had mostly been contained in what had come to be known as the Battle of the Bulge.

Once again, Cole and his fellow soldiers had hoped for some respite. During the battle, he had managed to defeat an enemy sniper known as *Das Gespenst* once and for all.

Cole had expected to have some time to savor his victory against *Das Gespenst* and catch up on his sleep. But then on New Year's Day, the Germans had gone and shown that they were by no means finished. To start off 1945, Hitler had masterminded Operation *Nordwind* through the Vosges Mountains to the south of the initial attack. Having rallied the forces pushed back initially by Allied forces, the second half of the Battle of the Bulge had begun. Steeped in myths and legends that spanned centuries, the Vosges region was dotted with small villages, valleys, and mountain peaks popular with hunters. This time of year, it was also wintry and frozen.

Cole had heard it said before that war was hell and life wasn't fair, and he agreed. He also thought that war in Europe was *cold*. Somewhere in the Pacific, his cousin Deacon Cole was fighting the Japanese. That sounded like a tropical vacation compared to this.

Trying to ignore the fact that he was shivering, Cole listened to the sound of the tank grow louder. He had taken off his gloves before getting set up with the rifle, and his fingertip felt numb on the trigger. Since that morning he had also noticed a scratchy throat coming on, and his bones felt achy. He tried to ignore that, too—the last thing he needed was to get sick out here. As if the cold and the fighting weren't bad enough, adding to the men's misery was the fact that the flu had been going around.

Right now, he had more immediate concerns than the flu. If there was one thing that any infantryman feared, it was the German Panzers. The tanks were not invincible—the GIs had certainly proved that by now—but against a Panzer, their individual rifles might as well be pea shooters. Their squad didn't have one of the new recoilless rifles or even a bazooka. After all, their orders were to slow down the Krauts while the rest of the unit got the road cleared.

Among the trees below, a snowy branch suddenly moved, despite the fact that there wasn't any wind. Then another branch slightly higher than the first one quivered. Clumps of snow fell. Beyond this localized disturbance, the rest of the forest remained still.

It was a curious phenomenon that could have been chalked up to some forest creature, but Cole knew better. He guessed correctly that it meant a German was climbing the tree, trying to get a glimpse of the road ahead.

For their ambush, the squad had picked a spot where they had a commanding view of a bend in the road. The Krauts weren't foolish enough to come around that bend right into any waiting guns. Always cautious, they had sent a scout ahead.

"Hey, twelve o'clock," Vaccaro whispered, suddenly deadly serious. "See that tree moving?"

Cole didn't respond, but pressed his eye tighter against the rim of the telescopic sight. The icy metal felt as if it was cutting into flesh, but he ignored it, willing his eye to see every detail of the forest below. Another branch quivered, then stopped. High in the tree, Cole caught a glint of something. Binoculars? Rifle scope? The German scout was looking right at them. They just had to hope that they had hidden themselves well enough to fool the scout.

Cole held his fire, although he could easily have picked off the German. He wanted the Germans to think that the road ahead was clear and that there wasn't any danger.

Seemingly satisfied that this was the case, the tree branches moved again, this time in the opposite order as the scout descended. Cole had to hand it to the Kraut. Other than the stirring of the branches, which would have been hard to notice if you weren't looking for it, the scout had moved silently and stealthily.

Meanwhile, the Germans came closer. They could hear them, but not see them. The clanking of the panzer treads on the hard-packed ice of the road became distinct. They heard a few commands shouted over the relentless engines—a few *Kübelwagen* vehicles along with the

Panzer. Even if the Allied planes had been flying, the Germans would have had good cover under the canopy of the evergreen forest.

"Here they come," Mulholland muttered. "Steady ... pick your targets."

There was no need for him to say it. After months of combat, these men knew the drill. All of them aimed their weapons, held their breath, intent on the targets soon to appear around the bend.

They didn't have to wait long. First to appear were a handful of soldiers wearing white winter camouflage smocks. In the old days, these would have been called skirmishers—sent out ahead of the main force to probe the presence of the enemy.

Still, the men around Cole held their fire, awaiting an order from the lieutenant. The Germans on the road below came closer. Now, the roar and clank of the Panzer sounded even louder. The stink of exhaust reached them like an affront to the clear mountain air. The tank took up most of the road. Despite its size and weight, the Panzer was having some trouble on the icy incline, lurching sideways on the road before straightening itself out.

Cole set his sights on the man in the turret of the Panzer.

"Fire!" Mulholland shouted.

The first burst of gunfire dropped three of the enemy soldiers. The others scattered into the ditches and trees. They knew better than to throw themselves flat on the road, right in the path of the Panzer, where they would be turned into German pancakes.

Through the scope, Cole could see the tank commander in the Panzer turret, pointing in the squad's direction. It was all too clear that the *Unteroffizer* was ordering the Panzer to target them. The barrel of the tank's gun swiveled toward them, the muzzle looking big and black as a pit into hell. Any second now, the Panzer was going to blow them all to Kingdom Come.

Not so fast, Cole thought. He squeezed the trigger. The tank commander slumped in the turret. Cole's squad had a temporary reprieve from the threat of the Panzer's main gun. That didn't prevent the tank's heavy machine gun from buzzing like a metallic hornet's nest.

More soldiers poured in from the sides of the tank, setting up an assault on the squad's position. Cole had seen it all before. You could count on the Germans to be efficient. After years of battle, they knew their business.

Then again, so did the squad. The soldiers around Cole poured a withering fire down the road. The squad had the advantage of being behind cover, while the Germans on the road mostly remained exposed.

Down on the Panzer, someone from below pushed the body out of the turret and the dead *Unteroffizer* rolled down the side of the tank and fell to the snow like a sack of grain. He noticed that unlike the infantrymen, the tank crew didn't wear camouflage.

Another man appeared in the turret, this one armed with a *Schmeisser*. He let off a burst in the direction of Cole's squad, then shouted something down into the tank. Once again, the big gun began to swivel in their direction.

"Ain't gonna happen," Cole muttered. He put his crosshairs on the soldier in the turret, and fired. The tanker slid back down into the hatch.

But this time, there was no stopping the Panzer from sending a round in their direction. The tank fired. The muzzle blast lit up the forest canopy with an orange glow, the shock wave from its big gun making the branches all around dance as if hit by a gust of wind. Snow showered down.

Traveling at nearly four thousand feet per second, the tank round *whooshed* over their heads and struck the road behind the squad, punching a hole in the icy road. They had dodged a bullet—a damned big bullet, at that—but the squad might not be so lucky again. Already, the Panzer's gun was angling lower.

"Fall back!" Mulholland shouted.

Nobody needed to be told twice. Their orders were to delay the German advance, not stop it. For that, they would have needed a lot more firepower.

Besides, the Americans up the road had a surprise in store for the Germans.

Cole slipped from behind the fallen log that he had been using for cover, even as a burst of fire from the Panzer's 7.92 mm MG 34 machine gun chewed up the bark. Time to go.

The squad began a running battle back to the rest of the unit. They stopped now and then to fire at the Germans who had outpaced the tank.

Cole threw himself down flat on the road, locked his arms into a prone position, and waited for the tank to come back into sight. He was disappointed that the tank crew had figured out not to put anybody back in the turret—either that, or they had run out of crew to sacrifice. Instead, a couple of soldiers had climbed onto the tank to serve as its eyes and ears as it navigated the road. While the Panzer had viewing slits and periscopes like any tank, it was easier to drive when somebody had eyes on the road. One of the soldiers leaned over the hatch to shout instructions down into the tank.

Cole picked him off.

Then he and the others were up and running again, back toward the main position.

"I hope they know we're coming," Vaccaro panted, laboring to run in the awkward pac boots. Though the rubberized boots kept their feet more or less dry, it was like trying to run with canoes strapped to your feet. It didn't help that the rubber soles slipped and slid on the hard-packed road.

"They'd have to be deaf not to have heard that Panzer," Cole said, chancing a look back over his shoulder. So far, the road was empty, but they could hear the enemy tank approaching with its steady *clank, clank* and straining engine.

Around another bend in the road, they found the rest of the unit. The truck had been pulled out of the ditch, and already the convoy was rolling on. But they had left behind an insurance policy in the form of a Jeep with a recoilless rifle mounted on it. The Jeep sat in the middle of the road, its weapon pointing toward the oncoming Germans. The gun had been sighted in on a crest in the road. All they needed was a target. From the shouts of the approaching Germans and the sound of the Panzer echoing through the forest, they wouldn't have to wait for long.

"You guys are a sight for sore eyes," Vaccaro panted.

"You know how to sweet-talk a guy," said the GI set up behind the recoilless rifle. The weapon fired a HEAT round that could spell trouble for a Panzer despite its thick armor—if it hit just the right spot. "Stick around and enjoy the show, why don't you?"

Sure enough, the Germans were coming up the road. Cole got behind a tree and brought his rifle to his shoulder. He was just lining up the sights when the Panzer came over the crest in the road and the recoilless rifle fired.

Again, the orange muzzle flash lit up the tunnel-like canopy of forest hanging over the road. The sound was deafening, like somebody had just stabbed his eardrums.

There was a white-hot flash as the round hit the Panzer dead-on.

The tank lurched to a stop, smoke and flames pouring from the hatch.

There was no need for a second shot, and no time for that, anyhow. Undeterred by the destruction of the Panzer, German troops stormed up the road.

"Hop on, boys," the gunner said. "Let's get the hell out of here."

The squad didn't need to be told twice. They scrambled onto the Jeep and hung on tight. The engine had already been running, and seconds later they were rolling. The Jeep wasn't exactly fast, not on that treacherous road, and it was now overloaded with men clinging to any available surface, but it was going in the right direction at least—away from the Krauts.

Cole looked back and had one last glimpse of the burning Panzer and the white-smocked Germans dodging around it. The scene was marred somewhat by the appearance of a burning figure crawling from the wreckage of the tank. He looked like a sausage that had caught fire on a grill. The burning man tumbled down from the tank and stood in the middle of the road, doing a terrible dance. Maybe he only imagined it, but Cole thought that he could hear the man screaming.

Cole raised his rifle. It was a long shot, taken from the back of a bouncing vehicle, but he quickly pulled the trigger and put the enemy soldier out of his misery.

The gunner from the recoilless rifle turned to him and angrily snapped, "What the hell did you do that for? That's a waste of ammo."

"Shut up," Vaccaro told him.

The gunner opened his mouth to say more, but Cole flicked his cut-glass eyes at him, and the man fell quiet.

Years later, it would seem like Cole could only recall bits and pieces of the war, like some half-remembered bad dream when you woke up the next morning. The older that he got, the more that the memories of the war became more like pictures in a scrapbook than a movie in his head. A movie that he had lived through.

He didn't know it then, but this scene of the burning Panzer illuminating the forest gloom would be engraved forever in his mind's eye. To him, it summed up the whole Battle of the Bulge.

"It's a hell of a thing," Vaccaro said, watching the scene fade into the distance.

Cole didn't ask Vaccaro to explain. He knew exactly what he meant.

CHAPTER TWO

Autumn 1991, Appalachian Mountains

COLE BENT over the knife blade, honing it to perfection. He loved the warm, buttery feel of the steel under his fingertips as he coaxed it into shape.

This piece of metal had come from an old farm implement on an abandoned property he had found while roaming the mountains. Cole had knocked the rust off with a grinder, then hammered it flat to reveal the perfect, gleaming metal underneath. He liked metal with character and a story, not to mention the challenge of making something old useful again. This old metal had some life in it yet.

As he bent over the knife, the cheaters he wore to see the close work were one of his few concessions to age. That, and some gray hair, though his hair was still thick. He wore it long now like some old mountain man, the hair in back touching his shirt collar.

The process of transforming a cold, rectangular bar of metal into a useful object never ceased to enthrall him. Cole had spent much of his earlier life destroying things and it gave him pleasure to do the opposite now.

Each knife was a journey. He started with a blank piece of metal and a rough idea, but the true knife was hidden somewhere within the steel. When he thought about it, his whole life had been much the same, a journey and a transformation, just as any good life was when you looked back on it.

That fall morning, Cole reckoned that his own journey was winding down. He was becoming an old man. Seventy was on the horizon. Age often made him introspective these days. Back in WWII or Korea, there were times when he hadn't expected to live until the next minute, let alone for several more decades. Many good men on both sides had not been nearly so fortunate. He had tried to live a good life for them.

Cole hoped now that when the end did come that it would be in his bed, or better yet, hunched over his workbench or hunting in the woods. You couldn't always choose how you went, but he could hope.

Meanwhile, the world kept changing. Color television. Games that you played on TV, instead of with a ball. Frozen dinners that came in an aluminum foil tray, eaten by a lot of people even up here in the mountains, where folks ought to know better. Then there was the politics. Cole hadn't bothered to vote for anyone until Eisenhower, who had been worth the effort of going into town and casting his ballot. An actor named Ronald Reagan had been president, then George H.W. Bush. Bush had been a pilot in the war, and he was from Texas, two things in his favor. There was talk of a young man from Arkansas running in the next election. Arkansas? The next thing you knew, there'd be a president from someplace like Delaware.

Cole turned back to his workbench and put all of the world's nonsense out of his mind.

Then came the knock on the workshop door.

"Gran sent me up here," announced his grandson, Danny, sticking his head cautiously through the door. He had learned the hard way that it was not in his best interest to startle his grandfather. Best to knock first. "She said a letter came special for you."

"Put it over there," Cole said, nodding toward the table.

"Aren't you going to read it?" Danny asked.

Cole gave the boy one of his looks, but he couldn't make it stick. He had too much fondness for the boy.

At sixteen, Danny looked startlingly like Cole had at that age, all arms and legs and sinew, but better fed. That wasn't the only place where the similarity ended. Danny had soft brown eyes and was popular with the local girls at school. *School.* Cole had made damned sure that his grandson learned to read and write, getting a better start than he had himself.

Where Cole possessed a natural-born ornery streak, he recognized kindness in the boy. Cole considered that to be a good trait, but it surely hadn't come from his side of the family.

Danny wouldn't even go hunting with his grandfather because he didn't like killing animals. Then again, Danny wouldn't starve if he didn't fill the stewpot as had been Cole's case at the same age. Times had changed for the better.

The boy could be nervous as a cat around the old man when Cole was in one of his moods, causing Danny to act a little scared of him. Cole was aware of his own rough edges and did his best to handle Danny gently. Cole's own daddy had whipped hell out of him, so he had promised himself that he would never raise a hand against any child. One glance from his cold, gray eyes was all the correction that was ever needed.

Cole took those eyes off the knife long enough to give the envelope a glance. It was in a square envelope made of fine, ivory paper, with his name written on it in script. Looked like a fancy wedding announcement. Some relative expecting him to put on a department store suit and give them a gift.

"Unless it's the electric bill, I ain't interested."

"Gran said you ought to open it right away because it's from Germany. C'mon, Pa Cole. See what it is."

"You open it, boy. Can't you see I'm busy?"

Danny gave a dramatic teenaged sigh. "All right."

"Here, use this."

Cole shed his eyeglasses, then handed his grandson the knife blade he was working on, which Danny used to slit open the envelope. Cole frowned when he saw that the knife had struggled a bit against the thick paper, so he took it back and returned it to the grindstone.

"It's an invitation," his grandson announced.

"I don't know nobody in Germany," Cole said.

"Maybe not, but they know you, evidently." The boy was always talking like a teacher, which secretly pleased Cole. "They're opening a WWII museum in Germany, and there's an exhibit about you and they want you to be there for the dedication. You're famous, Pa Cole."

Cole grunted. He didn't hold with any of that *Pee-paw* or *Mee-maw* silliness, or God forbid, *Pop Pop*. Danny called him Pa Cole and the boy's grandmother was Gran. As for the invitation, he could not imagine what sort of fool would put him in a museum.

He nodded toward the potbelly woodstove in the corner. "Throw it in the fire," he said. In Cole's mountain accent, the word sounded like *far*.

"No way! Aren't you even going to look at it?"

"Nope."

"There's a note in here from somebody named Colonel Mulholland. It says you ought to come." The boy's voice rose an octave with excitement. "All expenses paid!"

Mulholland. Now there was a name from the past. As a young man, Mulholland had been Cole's sniper squad leader in Normandy and beyond. What the hell did Mulholland want after all these years?

Curiosity finally got the better of Cole. Reluctantly, he put down the knife and held out his gnarled hand. "Give it here."

Danny hesitated, as if he worried that Cole still planned to toss the thing in the fire. Instead, Cole read the note from Mulholland. Years before, that would have been impossible because Cole had been illiterate. Growing up in the mountains during the Depression era had been about survival, not learning his letters. When he had finally returned from Korea, Cole had set about learning to read and write with a great deal of help from Norma Jean Elwood, who had become Norman Jean Cole in short order.

Grumbling, he shoved his cheaters into place and read:

> *Dear Cole,*
> *It's been a long time. Hope you are well. Like me, you are*
> *probably feeling the years pile up, but we are a lot luckier*
> *than many good men we knew, who never had the chance to*
> *live their lives. Recently, an opportunity presented itself to*

*honor their memory with the construction of a large new
war museum in Munich. As it turns out, I was asked to be
on the advisory committee for this museum. I can't take any
credit for it, but one of the museum exhibits is focused on
sniper warfare and you figure prominently.*

*When the museum board heard that we had served together,
they were very excited about the possibility of you coming to
Germany for the dedication of this museum. Of course, all of
your expenses for you and a guest would be paid. If you are
the same old Caje Cole, I know that your first instinct will
be to say no. However, let me tell you that the time has come
for us to put some things aside so that we can all heal from
this war, and more importantly, help future generations
remember and understand so that the mistakes of the past
are not repeated. Besides, I've got to say, I wouldn't mind
seeing you one last time. You and I are just about out of
ammo, my friend!*

Yours truly,
Jim

Colonel James Mulholland, US Army (retired)

"DON'T THAT BEAT ALL," Cole said. Mulholland had managed to touch upon duty and a heartstring at the same time. He always had been a smart SOB. Cole hadn't known that Mulholland had made a career of the military, but he wasn't all that surprised.

"Are you gonna go?" the boy asked.

"Hell no," Cole said, but he shoved the letter and invitation into a pocket instead of tossing them into the wood stove.

* * *

"You and Danny are going," Norman Jean announced at supper-time, once she heard the news. Of course, it was Danny rather than Cole who had spilled the beans.

Cole stopped chewing. "What?"

"It will be good for you. Hillbilly, you ain't hardly been out of these mountains in ten years." It was just like Norma Jean to call him by his old nickname. "Besides, it will get you out of my hair for a spell. My sister might come down from Baltimore to visit."

Norma Jean's uppity sister had moved north and married a steel-worker, and Cole got along with her about as well as magpies got along with hawks. Which was to say, not at all.

Cole felt like his wife and grandson were ganging up on him, so he found an excuse after supper to head back out to the workshop, where everyone would leave him the hell alone. If it hadn't been dark, he would have taken his shotgun and headed into the woods.

But Norma Jean wouldn't let him be. No more than half an hour passed before she came through the door. Unlike Danny, she never bothered to knock first.

"Can't you leave a man alone?" Through an unspoken rule, they had long-ago reached an understanding that the house was her domain and the workshop was Cole's. Both knew to tread lightly in the other's territory, which made for a long and happy marriage.

"We ain't done talking about this trip," Norma Jean said.

"All right. Say your piece, but I ain't going."

"You're only thinking of yourself," she said. "It will be good for the boy. He's never been anywhere. It would be good to have some experi-ence before he goes off to college."

"College?" Cole almost choked on the word. He shook his head. His wife had been pushing for the boy to get a real education, but Cole wasn't nearly as convinced that it was important.

"Times are changing, you dumb hillbilly. Danny can't stay on this mountain forever. The world's a big place and it's about time he started seeing some of it for himself."

"The army took care of that for me."

Norma Jean put her hands on her hips. "The army? You mean those folks who sent you halfway around the world to get shot at? Is that what you would wish on Danny?"

"No," Cole agreed. Besides, it was all too clear that Danny wasn't like him.

"You write back and tell them you're going, and that you are bringing your sixteen-year-old grandson."

Norma Jean went out and shut the door.

Cole grumped and muttered during the next several days, but Norma Jean ignored him. Gran had spoken, and that was that. Cole knew that he had gotten his marching orders. Sometimes, he thought that General Eisenhower or even MacArthur himself could have learned a thing or two from Norma Jean.

He wrote back to accept the invitation and sure enough, two plane tickets soon arrived in the mail.

* * *

THE WAY that Danny had come to live with them was a story in itself, and not an altogether happy one. Shortly after returning from Korea, he and Norma Jean had gotten married. They lived for a time in the small cabin that Cole had built, but when it was clear that a child was coming along, Mrs. Bailey had announced that she was moving into town with a maiden aunt and that the house near the knife workshop was the young couple's if they wanted it.

"A cabin ain't no place to raise a baby," Mrs. Bailey had announced.

Cole liked his cabin just fine, but in the mysterious ways that women often operate, between Norman Jean and Mrs. Bailey, he found himself moved into the modest two-story clapboard farmhouse. He couldn't even say exactly how it had happened. One of the two upstairs bedrooms had been done over into a baby's room—a nursery, as Mrs. Bailey proudly called it.

The house was very modest, with just the two rooms downstairs, two rooms upstairs, and a lean-to kitchen off the back. Hollis Bailey's father had built the place, using fieldstone for the foundation and logs for the floor joists. The house didn't have a lick of insulation, but worn braided rugs across the painted floorboards kept the worst of the cold at bay through the mountain winters.

Cole and Norma Jean's daughter, Janey, never had much liked the mountain life. No sooner had she graduated high school than she took up with a group of friends, traveling around to rock concerts and smoking dope. In the late 1960s and early 1970s, this was what a lot of young people were doing. Their daughter had gone hippie on them. It didn't seem to bother Norma Jean, who saw Janey as a strong young woman following her own path, but truth be told, it just about broke Cole's heart when Janey left the mountain. He missed the young girl he had once known who liked to run barefoot through the grass, catching June fireflies. But Janey had gone and grown up.

Then the news came that she'd had a child by some young man she wasn't married to. Cole had to be talked out of arranging a good ol' shotgun wedding. Even Norma Jean was not pleased by the situation. Janey promised to come by soon for them to meet their grandson, but the months passed. Whenever she called or wrote, she always seemed to be living in a different place.

It fell to the local sheriff to knock on their door one winter's night with the news that the car Janey had been riding in was in a terrible accident somewhere in upstate New York, sliding off the road during a snowstorm. Janey and her man both died in the crash, but by some miracle, the baby had been spared.

There was no question that Cole and Norma Jean would raise the child as their own. Janey had named him Danny. As for the last name, well, Janey had never married the boy's father, so as far as his grandparents were concerned, the boy's name was Danny Cole.

* * *

COLE AND NORMA JEAN had done the best they could for the boy, hoping that someday, things would turn out better than they had with Janey. The loss of their daughter nearly broke their hearts—the little boy was the only thing that kept them from being overwhelmed by grief.

Of course, Cole was always taking the boy into the woods, showing him all that he knew, from the names of the trees, to the shapes of the tracks beside a mountain stream, to the constellations in the winter sky. Cole had reached an age where he felt that it was important to pass things along. It was something he had not done with Janey, her being a girl and all, but Cole could see the error of his ways. If he had only spent more time with Janey, maybe things would have turned out differently. He didn't plan on making the same mistake twice.

When the boy was ten, Cole gave him an old single-shot .22 rifle, expecting that he would cut his teeth as a hunter on the local squirrels and rabbits. While the boy was responsible with the rifle and learned to be a crack shot, he never brought home any game.

"I don't like killing," he had explained to his puzzled grandfather. Danny made a joke of it. "If I could shoot a Snickers bar out in the woods, I'd be the best hunter ever!"

Just once, when the boy was twelve, Cole had taken him deer hunting. It had been nothing short of disastrous, and by an unspoken mutual agreement, they had never discussed it since.

For Cole, his fondest memories of childhood—and those were few and far between—had been waking early to go with his old man into the woods to go hunting. He had thought to share something equally as special with Danny.

Sure enough, Danny had been excited to head out into the woods before dawn. The late fall morning felt crisp as the sun slowly crept above the hills. Cole had already found a likely spot where a buck he had been scouting all summer liked to pass through on his way to forage for hickory nuts. They set up behind a fallen log and waited.

"There he is," Cole said quietly. "Aim just behind his shoulder, just like we talked about."

Danny put the rifle to his shoulder. The lever-action .30/.30 kicked like a mule, but the boy could handle it for one shot.

Across the clearing, the buck seemed to sense them, lifting his majestic head. The first rays of the morning sun caught the antlers, reflecting off the ivory tips. It was a sight that damn near took Cole's breath away. The buck was a ten-pointer and weighed more than two hundred pounds. Any boy ought to be proud to take an animal like that as his first deer.

Beside his grandson, Cole waited tensely. Seconds dragged by. Any moment now and the buck would be gone.

"Go on," Cole whispered.

But Danny refused to shoot. Slowly, he lowered the rifle.

"What's wrong? You've got a clear shot."

"I can't do it. I can't kill him."

The buck had not moved. Cole put his rifle to his shoulder, lined up the sights, and started to squeeze the trigger. He was about to kill again, just as he had done so many times before. He breathed out, breathed in, held it.

That's when he sensed Danny at his elbow, the boy holding his breath. He glanced at the boy and saw a stricken white face, the soft brown eyes filled with tears.

Cole lowered the rifle. The buck seemed to look directly at them, maybe catching their scent at last, then leaped away. The sun-dappled clearing stood empty. The buck that Cole had watched and waited for all summer was gone, likely spooked for good.

"You let him go?" Danny asked.

"I reckon we'll let him live another season and get even fatter," Cole said.

"I'm sorry, Pa Cole," Danny said, looking as if he might cry. "I know I let you down."

Cole worked through several emotions in the space of a few seconds, from anger to disappointment, then resignation. For better or for worse, Danny was never going to be like him. He reached down and squeezed the boy's shoulder, then managed to force a smile for the boy's sake.

"Ain't nothin' to be sorry about," Cole said. "Let me tell you, there are a lot of ways to disappoint someone, and letting that buck go ain't on my list. Besides, that buck ain't none too sorry!"

"But we came all the way out here this morning and we're going back empty-handed."

"There's no such thing as a bad morning in the woods," Cole said, taking a deep breath of the fall air that smelled of fallen leaves and frost. On mornings like this, when it felt so good just to be alive, he often thought of the dead who weren't there to enjoy it. He hoped that heaven was like the mountains on a fall morning. "Coming out here with you this morning is enough for me."

"What will Gran say?"

"What, about not shooting a deer?" Cole snorted. "She don't care about that. What Gran is goin' to say is, do we want buckwheat pancakes and bacon for breakfast, that's what. Now, let's head on back."

CHAPTER THREE

ALREADY, the trip to Germany was turning into an adventure. For starters, Cole had never flown on a massive, wide-bodied, Boeing 767. Each row of seats sat seven people, with groupings of two seats, then three seats, then two seats, separated by two aisles down the middle of the jet.

"Big as this plane is, I'm amazed the damn thing can take off," he said.

"I've got a window seat!" Danny exclaimed, fiddling with the shade. "Pa Cole, do you think we'll see the ocean from up here?"

"Gonna find out," Cole said. "Once we're in the air, look for a lot of blue water underneath us. That'd be the ocean."

"Very funny. I think I'll know it when I see it."

Danny's enthusiasm felt contagious. They hadn't even gotten into the air yet, but Danny bounced in his seat like a puppy, taking in all of the sights and sounds. He had never flown before and was excited about the experience.

Cole had to admit that he was pleased to see Danny so excited. He realized that Norman Jean had been right all along. If nothing else, this trip would be memorable for their grandson. Although they saw each other every day, this trip was a chance to spend some one-on-one time with Danny; soon enough, the boy would be heading off to college or all his attention would be focused on a girlfriend. Cole knew well enough that time passed and things changed, even when you were standing still.

Maybe he ought to get out more and travel, but he felt content at home in the woods and mountains, hunting, or working on his knives. At first, the hurly-burly of the massive airport, along with the crowded plane, felt almost overwhelming. But Danny's excitement helped him see the trip through the boy's eyes and made him realize that he was just being what Norma Jean would have called a grumpy old man.

Besides, Cole reminded himself that all he had to do was sit back and relax for the eight-hour flight to Munich.

Most of the passengers appeared to be well-heeled tourists, some of the women wearing skirts and the men in dress slacks and sports coats. This being the early 1990s, anybody who wasn't a college kid or teenager still dressed up to get on an airplane. His grandson had on jeans, a polo shirt with a little alligator on it that cost more than Cole's first pickup truck, and Nike sneakers. Gran had taken Danny shopping before the trip and bought God knows what else that the boy wanted.

Cole's needs were simpler. Hell, as a boy he'd gone whole summers without wearing shoes. He wore a dark brown corduroy sports coat with elbow patches that Norma Jean had found brand new at a thrift store, along with his best pair of Levis, freshly ironed, and sturdy brown shoes.

More than a few of his fellow passengers were Germans close to Cole's age. He found it jarring to hear them speaking in German, the sound of the guttural language taking him back to memories he hadn't visited in a long time. *More like dredged up*, he thought. He told himself that he had better get used to it. He'd be hearing a lot more German spoken during the next couple of weeks.

Cole's German consisted of a few phrases that were still stuck in his head, such as *Surrender* or *Don't shoot* or even his personal favorite, *Stirb, du Nazi-Bastarde*. Loosely translated, this meant, *Die, you Nazi bastards*.

Somehow, he didn't think those phrases would be a whole lot of use in the next few days.

He couldn't help but wonder if he had faced one or two of these German passengers from the wrong side of a battlefield. It was a strange thing to think about, but he reminded himself again that the world was always changing.

Several people had brought along books to read on the plane, including a World War II novel by Ken Follett called *Night Over Water*, which was a current bestseller. Appropriately enough, it was about intrigues during a transatlantic flight. The in-flight movie was going to be *Quigley Down Under*, a shoot-'em-up western starring Tom Selleck that was set in Australia, of all places.

Other passengers had newspapers and magazines with them to pass the time on the flight. Several of the headlines focused on the recent fall of the Berlin Wall. For more than forty years, Germany and Berlin itself had been divided. Western Germany operated as a free democracy. The people and the economy thrived in the post-war years. Eastern Germany found itself behind the Iron Curtain, as part of territory seized by the Soviets. There, people were forced to live under Communism, a highly dysfunctional system of government that treated the needs of its population as an afterthought.

That repressive system had finally collapsed under its own weight, helped in no small part by the efforts of President Ronald Reagan, who had been determined to win the Cold War for once and for all, famously declaring, "Mr. Gorbachev, tear down this wall!"

Prompted by many other calls for change from every quarter, the Soviet premier had listened. The opening of the border and the demolition of the wall were justifiably headline news. The Germany that they were visiting was being reunited for the first time in decades.

To Danny's delight, they caught a few glimpses of the endless sea before the jet climbed above the clouds. The sky darkened as the sun went down; this was an overnight flight and they would awaken in Germany the next morning.

Once they were well out into the Atlantic, the free drinks flowed. These tourists set about drinking like it was their job.

"Something for you gentlemen?" the stewardess asked.

Danny looked at Cole. "Can I have a beer?"

"No."

"I'm sixteen! The drinking age is fifteen in Germany."

"We ain't in Germany yet. Besides, if your Gran finds out I let you drink beer on the plane, won't neither one of us get any older." Cole looked at the stewardess, who had known better than to get involved in their beverage decisions, and said firmly, "Two Coca Colas, miss."

With a sigh, Danny accepted his plastic cup of soda. "Well, when we get to Germany, does that mean I can have a beer?"

Cole thought about that. He didn't intend for this to be one of those exhausting trips that parents and grandparents knew all too well, where Danny kept asking to do things or buy things, and Cole would be forced to say no. After all, his grandson wasn't eight years old anymore.

He knew that he had to let the boy off the leash sometime to make his own discoveries—and mistakes. Hell, Cole hadn't been much older when he shipped out for the war. But he had been a different person. Danny seemed a whole lot younger in Cole's eyes, even a little naive. As for allowing his grandson to drink beer, Cole himself mostly steered clear of alcohol, knowing what it had done to his father. It wasn't a habit he wanted to encourage in his grandson, but he knew that forbidden fruit always tastes sweeter.

"You know what?" Cole finally said. "You are sixteen years old. I ain't gonna hold your hand every minute of this trip. You may want to go off on your own and explore, and that's all I'm gonna say about that."

Danny nodded, grinning. His grandfather hadn't come out and given him permission to hoist a tankard, but he was saying that Danny could make some of his own decisions.

"That's a deal. Just so long as I don't have to keep *you* out of trouble," Danny said.

"I'm an old man. What kind of trouble would I get into?"

"Gran told me not to let you shoot anybody."

Cole snorted. "Your gran always had what I'd call a dry sense of humor, ever since she stole my clothes from that swimmin' hole on Gashey's Creek."

"Huh? I never heard that story."

"You ask your gran about that sometime when she's acting high and mighty."

Since Danny had taken the window seat, Cole found himself directly across the aisle from a fellow who looked to be about his own age. Like Cole, the man had opted for soft drinks and Cole couldn't help but notice that he had a slight German accent. Finally, he caught Cole's eye and said, "Hello. Have you been to Germany before?"

Cole nodded. "A long time ago," he said. "During the war."

The other man nodded and offered his hand across the aisle, "Hans Neumann," he said. After Cole had introduced himself in turn, his fellow passenger continued: "I, too, was in the war, but I suspect that I fought for the other side. You see, I was a soldier in the Wehrmacht. But not for long, thank goodness. I was captured and sent as a prisoner to Ohio."

"A POW, huh?"

Hans smiled. "It was the best thing that ever happened to me. I felt like I had gone to heaven! The people were kind and I was just a boy really, who didn't have much choice about going into the army."

"Nobody had much choice," Cole agreed.

Hans nodded. "No, and that is why I was glad to be out of the war. There was plenty to eat in Ohio. There were pretty girls. I ended up staying there for the next forty years, ha! I found a wife and bought a farm and raised a family. I became an American citizen, which was my proudest day. But you see, I still have a few relatives in Germany, so here I am on this plane."

Cole appreciated that Hans had summed up his life story in a few sentences, like the summary on the back of a book. Cole doubted that he could do the same; his life was a little more complicated.

"Good for you," was all he said.

Hans smiled. "Good for me, indeed. This may be my last time going back. I have a bad heart, you see. Growing up, we were always told to eat lots of cheese and butter. It's good for you, we were told! Well, the whole time it was clogging up my arteries."

Cole snorted. "Yeah, don't get me started. No salt, no sugar—"

"No fun!"

Cole found himself taking a liking to Hans, the Wehrmacht soldier-turned Ohio farmer. They were now just a couple of old codgers, bitching about the things that all old codgers bitched about. At this point in his life, he liked that just fine.

Cole had felt some uncertainty beforehand about this trip, but now, talking with Hans, he was finally starting to relax. Maybe Norma Jean was right that he was always too worried about what could go wrong.

"You hit that on the head, Hans. It's no fun getting old."

"You are from the south?" Hans asked. "I can hear it in your accent."

"Born and raised. Got me a little place in the mountains and couldn't be happier."

Hans nodded agreeably. "Look at us, having survived that nightmare, we are here today. We are blessed, my friend." Hans raised his glass of soda in salute and Cole did the same. "Is that your grandson with you?"

"That's right," Cole said. "We're taking a tour of Germany."

"He is a good-looking boy," Hans said in a tone of grandfatherly approval. "I have three grandsons myself. I am so glad that your grandson is going as a tourist and not as a soldier, as we had to do."

"Amen to that."

"Listen, I am going to put my head down and take a nap. All this traveling has made me tired and like I said, my heart is not what it used to be." Hans took a pen from the pocket of his blazer and jotted a phone number on a cocktail napkin. "This is my telephone number and the address where I am staying in Munich. I still have many friends there and many family. If you and your grandson need anything while you are in Germany, you get in touch. You never know when you will need a friend."

Cole took the napkin and nodded his thanks. "Much obliged, Hans."

Left alone now, with Danny wrapped up in gazing out the window at the play of fading light across the pillowy clouds, Cole found himself lost in reflection.

Cole thought about his own arrival in Europe aboard a landing craft at the Normandy beachhead. There had been lots of training in England, of course, but nothing truly prepared anyone for the horrors they had experienced on that beach. On that beach, Cole had picked up an abandoned sniper rifle and his real career as a soldier had begun.

Consciously, he knew that he should be saddened and filled with regret at all the lives lost and the killing that he had done. But a deeper, raw part of Cole that he sometimes thought of as "the critter" hadn't minded at all. In fact, that part of him missed it. He missed the excitement and even the camaraderie of fighting alongside good men.

Maybe these weren't the best realizations to be having thirty thousand feet over the Atlantic. He let his mind wander to other things, and soon Cole managed to drift off.

He awoke to the gentle chiming of the seatbelt light and the pilot giving a weather report.

Next stop, Germany.

Cole felt butterflies in his stomach, but he told himself that it was just from the jet changing altitude.

CHAPTER FOUR

AFTER THEY DISEMBARKED from the plane and went through customs, with a bored official waving them through without even looking at their passports, they emerged into the busy international arrivals terminal to see a uniformed driver holding a sign that read, "Herr Cole."

"I reckon that's us," Cole said.

Much to Cole's embarrassment, the driver insisted on carrying their bags to a shiny black Mercedes. The uniform was simply that of a chauffeur, but deep down, it made Cole uneasy. He had some experience with uniformed Germans, and it hadn't been good.

However, this German was friendly and pleasant. He spoke perfect English, and explained that he had been a school teacher before retiring and deciding to keep busy by ferrying important passengers around Munich.

"Last week, you would not believe that I met Jim Palmer. A famous American baseball player! I even got his autograph. Are you famous?"

"Not for anything that you'd want to know about."

The driver laughed good-naturedly, then whisked them from the airport to the hotel. On the way, he explained that the hotel near the airport was popular with travelers from all over the world and was much larger and modern compared to the traditional hotels within the city itself, which were more like *Gasthäuser*—guesthouses. "I know you Americans like everything the bigger, the better," he said.

In the lobby of the massive Hilton hotel, Cole was taken aback by the shiny glass doors, the gleaming trim, the expansive veined marble. He gave a low whistle.

"This sure ain't the Apple Blossom Motel," he said. "It's kind of fancy."

"We're just like rock stars," Danny said happily. "Or country music stars, at least."

"Don't get used to it."

But things kept getting better. Cole was half-convinced that they must have been dropped at the wrong hotel, but sure enough, the clerk had a reservation for them, along with a voucher for meals.

"We even get our own rooms," Danny said. "We don't have to share."

"It's something, all right," Cole agreed, still amazed by the lavish surroundings. Not for the first time this day, he realized that he was a long way from the ramshackle cabin where he had grown up in Gashey's Creek. Back then, he'd been lucky if he got some biscuits to go with his squirrel stew. He had slept on the bare wooden floor of the loft with his brothers and sisters, body heat alone keeping them warm on winter nights. When he had gotten older, there had been a mattress stuffed with corn husks. During the war, he mostly slept on the cold, hard ground and hadn't minded.

After washing up, they'd come back down and had a massive breakfast in the hotel restaurant, with the waiter squeezing fresh oranges table-side for their juice.

Sated, they made their way back up to their separate rooms. Danny was excited to give the cable television a whirl to watch the German version of MTV. Cole was more interested in a nap before they had to meet Colonel Mulholland that afternoon.

He closed the door, took off his shoes, and tried to get settled on the enormous bed. However, he just couldn't seem to relax. The soft mattress kept threatening to swallow him whole. So much luxury felt overwhelming. After a while, he gave up and pulled some of the blankets onto the floor. Just like old times. With the reassuring feel of the hard floor beneath him, Cole finally slept.

* * *

COLE AWOKE to the sound of somebody pounding on the door. Annoyed with himself, he realized that he had overslept. Traveling had taken a bigger toll than he had expected. *Not as young as I used to be.* He glanced at the Timex on his wrist. He was supposed to go down and meet Colonel Mulholland in just half an hour.

Through the peephole, he saw that it was Danny knocking. Cole unlocked the door.

"I can't believe I had to wake you up," his grandson said. The boy noticed the blankets and pillow on the floor. "Pa Cole, did you fall out of bed?"

"Something like that," Cole replied. "Just give me a minute. I'll be ready. Don't you worry about me."

He slipped into the bathroom. A shower would have been nice to help him wake up, but he settled for putting on a fresh shirt and splashing some water on his face, trying to get rid of the groggy feeling. It felt like his head was packed full of wool. Well, that was jet lag for you. Back home, it was close to his bedtime. At the moment, his bones felt every one of his years.

He emerged from the spacious bathroom feeling only marginally refreshed. However, seeing Danny bubble over with enthusiasm was better than a cup of coffee.

"Here, you better take my extra key," Cole said. "Just in case I don't wake up next time."

"Why wouldn't you wake up?"

"Because I'm dead, that's why."

"That's a terrible thing to say!" Danny replied, but he was grinning. He had gotten used to Pa Cole's dark sense of humor over the years. "Do I have to give you my extra key?"

"What, are you worried I might walk in while you are entertaining some cute young *Fräulein?*"

Danny's face turned the shade of a mountain sunset. "No, that's not—"

"You hang onto your keys," Cole said. "C'mon, let's go down."

Danny looked him up and down. "You look kind of nice, Pa Cole. You're wearing your sports coat again."

"I reckon it's best to look nice when you're going to meet a ghost from the past."

They took the elevator to the lobby, not saying much. Like a kid, Danny kept wanting to press all the buttons, making stops at each floor. Cole told him he could ride the elevator on his own time. There was that fluttery feeling in his belly again, which Cole was quick to blame on the elevator ride.

In the lobby, Colonel Mulholland was already waiting. Cole had wondered if they would even recognize each other after all these years. Cole still saw himself as a young man, but knew that the mirror said otherwise. To his surprise, Mulholland hadn't changed all that much. He was still tall and lean, except for a bit of a paunch that hinted at good living. He wore eyeglasses with a bluish tint. Mulholland's back was straight as a ramrod. In fact, from his posture to his close-cropped haircut, Mulholland looked very much like what he was, which was a retired Army officer.

"Caje Cole, as I live and breathe," his old officer said, grinning ear to ear. "I'll be damned if it's not my favorite hillbilly."

"Colonel Mulholland," Cole said, gripping the man's hand.

Mulholland laughed. "I'm just Jim these days." He turned his attention to Danny. "This must be your grandson that you said was coming with you."

"Nice to meet you, sir," Danny said politely.

They spent some time catching up. It turned out that there was a Mrs. Mulholland, who would not be accompanying them today.

"She has heard enough about the museum," Mulholland said with a laugh. "Of course, she will be coming to the museum opening. It's going to be quite a party."

For Mulholland, there were children and grandchildren, too. They all lived back in the U.S.

It was funny what you remembered about someone, Cole thought.

The Mulholland that he remembered had been a decent officer, both courageous and fair, even if he and Cole hadn't always agreed on how to fight the war. As a very young man, he had led Cole's squad across much of Europe.

The one time that he and Mulholland had really clashed had been over a French Resistance fighter named Jolie Molyneux. The young lieutenant had set his sights on Jolie, flirting with her in his polite manner and his high school French, seeming to think that she would naturally gravitate toward him as an officer who was superior to a mere enlisted man, but it had been Cole who caught her eye.

There never had been anything polite about Cole. A brief and fiery wartime romance resulted. That affair prompted some tension between the two men until Jolie had been wounded during Cole's fight with the sniper known as *Das Gespenst* and she been forced out of the picture.

Of course, that had been a lifetime ago. Cole wondered if Mulholland had ever told his wife about his infatuation with a lusty French Resistance fighter. He sure as hell had never said a word to Norma Jean. A smart man didn't reminisce about old girlfriends and flings in front of his wife. Cole liked his head just fine without it being flattened by an iron skillet.

Mulholland turned his attention back to Danny. "I'm glad you're here representing the next generation, although I'm sure you are sick and tired of hearing your grandfather's war stories."

"He's never said much of anything to me."

For the first time, a troubled look crossed Mulholland's face. Both he and Cole knew that there were some war stories better left untold. He forced a smile. "Well, over the next few days, we'll see if we can share the ones that matter," he said diplomatically. "If you're all set, let's head over to the museum. It's not open to the public yet, but considering that you are one of our VIPs for the grand opening, we can give you a preview."

* * *

To Cole's surprise, Mulholland was driving himself around Munich in a silver BMW. He explained that he had been stationed for so long in Germany that he had gotten a driver's license, a car, and even an apartment where he lived except for trips back to the U.S. to visit relatives.

"At least we're on the right side of the road over here," Mulholland said. "Driving in England is a whole different story, believe me."

"At least there aren't any landmines this time around."

Mulholland laughed. "You've got that right."

Looking out the car window was a strange experience. Cole kept expecting to see bomb-damaged buildings and German POWs marching past with their hands in the air. However, the scars of war had long since healed. He could not think of a small city that looked more prosperous than Munich. By far, the broad streets and well-kept buildings put any grungy American city to shame.

At the wheel, Mulholland seemed to sense Cole's bewilderment as the old soldier synced his memories with the modern Germany presenting itself beyond the windshield. "Now you see why some people joke that the Germans won the war, after all. Impressive, isn't it? However, if you're looking for monuments or historical markers, you'll be disappointed," he said. "The Germans have done all that they can to minimize recognition of the war."

"Back home, there's at least one monument to some war in every courthouse square and you don't have to go far to find a historical marker on the side of the road. I think there's one for every skirmish from the War Between the States. There might even be some markers for where the Yankees stole some chickens."

"Yankees? The War Between the States? You must mean Union troops? The Civil War?" Mulholland laughed. "I know you Southerners have a different view. Didn't we decide that we had relatives on opposite sides back then?"

"I reckon we did."

"It's funny, but Americans seem to tolerate Confederate monuments. There may come a time when they get pulled down. Who knows?"

"Wouldn't be right," Cole said. "It's our history."

"History has a way of getting swept under the rug," Mulholland said. "Anyhow, here in Germany, that's already been done. There's almost nothing to recognize that most of the country became a battle-field. There aren't any monuments, not even to the thousands, make that the hundreds of thousands of Germans, who perished during the Allied bombings."

Cole looked around at the pristine buildings, but what he still saw in his mind's eye were the ruins of war.

"The closest you're going to get around here to a war memorial is Dachau," Mulholland said.

Cole was familiar with Dachau, one of the original and most noto-rious Nazi concentration camps, which happened to be located in the suburbs of Munich. Looking at some of the older pedestrians they passed on the sidewalks, Cole realized that it was entirely possible that some of them had lived here when the concentration camp was in full operation.

Cole shook his head. "Dachau. It is hard to imagine the evil that people allowed to be done to one another."

"Awful," Mulholland agreed. "But there's a small museum that recognizes what took place there. The barracks and other buildings where the prisoners languished are being allowed to fall into slow disrepair because no one was interested in preserving that horrible and troubled past."

"They ought to have bulldozed that place."

"Maybe. The one museum that Munich is known for is the massive Deutsche museum. There are some exhibits to the aircraft industry that include the development of Messerschmitt fighters, but aside from that, you won't find much military history. It's mostly about transportation and science."

From the back seat, Danny spoke up. The two men had almost forgotten he was there. "Transportation and science? Ugh. Sounds like a place for school field trips."

"You're probably right. That reminds me. I brought you some-thing." Keeping one hand on the wheel, he reached into the glovebox and took out a chunk of concrete about the size of a baseball, then handed it back to Danny.

"A piece of concrete," Cole said. "That's right generous of you."

Mulholland laughed. "It's not just any chunk of concrete. It's a piece of the Berlin Wall. That's the real deal. I picked it up myself."

"Wow!" Danny said. "I've seen the Berlin Wall all over the news."

"This is a truly eventful time in Germany," Mulholland said. He was referring, of course, to the fall of the Berlin Wall that had divided free Berlin from East Berlin. "Needless to say, the German people are elated to finally be reconnected with old friends and family that they had not been able to communicate with for more than forty years."

They had all seen the news reports. The economy of East Germany was far behind that of the West, which had flourished under the capitalist system enabled by the Allied victory. The beautiful city around them was evidence of that success.

Mixed with the elation that the wall had finally come down was the growing concern that the former Communist territory might be a drag on the economy. These Germans would need jobs and decent educations. Germany had a lot of work to do ahead of it in finally reuniting the country. In some ways, the reunification was the closing chapter of the war era. Although Germany could fit neatly inside the state of Texas with room left over, it was geographically large for Europe. It was no small task to combine the two sides into a single modern nation of nearly eighty million people—equivalent to one-third of the current U.S. population. Back during WWII, Germany's population had been closer to one-half the size of the United States, which had grown exponentially.

"All of the excitement about the Berlin Wall has overshadowed the museum opening somewhat, but I won't complain. There's such a thing as too much attention. Our museum board has faced some controversy about opening a museum. Considering the way that Germany has downplayed the war, that's not surprising. But we need to tell the story of the war before those of us who remember it are all gone."

In the backseat, Danny hefted the chunk from the Berlin Wall. "This is really cool. Thank you."

"If you think that was cool, you haven't seen anything yet."

Mulholland drove past a soaring ultra-modern building built of stone and huge sheets of glass. With the sunlight glinting off it, the building looked like the tip of an iceberg exploding from the ground. This building made it clear that it had something to say.

The BMW pulled into a long entrance road, freshly blacktopped, that led to a parking area.

"Whoa," Danny said. "Is this the place?"

"Welcome to the World War II Museum of Europe. Or to put it another way, *Das Museum des Zweiten Weltkriegs in Europa.*"

As Mulholland parked the BMW and they got out of the car, Cole said, "Quite a place."

"Ha, you haven't even seen the exhibit hall yet," Mulholland said. "You're one of the stars of the show."

Cole wasn't sure that he liked the sound of that. Just a few minutes before, Mulholland had mentioned that there was such a thing as too much attention. Cole agreed.

He stood for a moment, taking in the monumental grandeur of the building, and then slowly followed Mulholland and Danny toward the entrance. He didn't know what to expect, but he suddenly dreaded the memories that this museum was dragging up.

CHAPTER FIVE

THE MUSEUM grand opening was to be held in two days, which left them time to explore the city. Cole wasn't one to sit in his hotel room. If he and Danny had come all this way, they were going to get out and see something. Plus, he wouldn't mind tracking down some more Bratwurst, which he had sampled at dinner. Grilled, garlicky, and served with Sauerkraut ... the stuff was that damn good. He didn't remember eating any Bratwurst during the war, most likely because there hadn't been much of anything to eat in Germany back then.

"You know, I've got an idea," Cole announced the next morning over breakfast, once the waiter had finished squeezing their fresh orange juice again. He pulled out the cocktail napkin on which the old German soldier he had met on the plane had written his telephone number. To his surprise, he had found himself thinking about their conversation. Several things that Hans said had resonated with him and left a positive impression. "I think I would like to invite Hans to the grand opening. I think he'd appreciate it."

"Sure."

"I'll need your help to call him. I don't know how to work these damn German phones."

"We don't even need to use the phone," Danny said. "We'll just ask the hotel concierge to call him for us."

"The what?"

"You'll see."

Cole shook his head. Danny was learning fast. Cole felt like he was getting left in the dust.

They finished their breakfast, eggs and fried potatoes with ham, with lots of hot German coffee, then headed over to the concierge, who obliged by placing the call and handing the phone to Cole. He could handle this part. Not only did Hans agree to attend the museum dedication as Cole's guest, but he also invited Cole and Danny to meet him in the city later that day.

That afternoon, they met Hans at a coffee shop not far from the Marienplatz, a wide cobblestoned square in the heart of Munich. Expensive shops and restaurants lined the surrounding streets. The city itself dated far into ancient times and was known as the capital of Bavaria. Loosely interpreted, *München* as it was known in German, translated to "The Monk's Place" in reference to the ancient monasteries around which the city had grown.

"There you are!" Hans said as they came through the door. He shook Cole's hand vigorously, smiling. The old man's grip was strong. "Forgive me, but I already feel as if we are old friends."

"Us old-timers need to stick together," Cole said.

Hans turned to Danny and shook his hand enthusiastically as well. "It is good to see you helping your grandfather. Who knows, you may even learn something from him?" The old German turned to indicate a pretty teenage girl at his elbow. Cole had to admit that he hadn't paid attention to the girl when he had first entered the shop. However, he could see that Danny's eyes were riveted on her. "Allow me to introduce my niece, Angela. My grand-niece, actually. Like Danny here, she is keeping an old man out of trouble."

It was clear that Angela instantly had Danny's full attention. From the stunned look on Danny's face, it was evident that his grandson had taken one of Cupid's arrows right through the heart.

"Uh hi," Danny said.

"Hello," Angela said. It was obvious from her bright smile that meeting a young American her own age was an unexpected benefit of escorting her great-uncle around town.

Hans winked at Cole, who thought with amusement that the old German knew exactly what he was doing. Like Danny, his grand-niece had likely expected a boring afternoon keeping her aged uncle company, but Hans had set the stage for something else.

More coffee arrived, along with a plate of pastries, and after some polite exchanges among the four of them, the table divided into two conversations, one between Hans and Cole, and the other between Danny and Angela that seemed to focus on music.

"I want to thank you for inviting me to the museum dedication," Hans said. "I am truly honored. I am also curious. I must admit that we Germans have mixed emotions about anything to do with the war."

"That's understandable," Cole said.

"Of course, the people of Munich have an even more difficult relationship to the war, considering that the Nazi party got its start in the beer halls here. Berlin may be the capital of Germany, but Munich is seen as the capital of the old Nazi party."

"Not the proudest history."

Hans shrugged and sipped his coffee. "But you know, the Nazi party involved relatively few people here, especially at first. It is the end of the war that many people have the bitterest memories of. That's when the Allied bombings took place and so many people died. People in my own family. Women and children. What did they have to do with the war? Nothing, really. Many see those bombings as retribution. It was revenge, pure and simple."

Cole nodded. He had no love for Nazi Germany, but he had to admit that the thought of the many civilian deaths in the air raids made him uncomfortable. "The war wasn't fair," he said.

"It left many people bitter," Hans said. "Also, here in Munich at the end of the war, many Germans saw us as giving up too easily when the first Allied troops arrived. There was very little fighting except by a few die-hards."

"Maybe most people had the good sense to know when to call it quits."

Hans nodded. "If only they had called it quits much sooner. We might all have been spared a great deal of sorrow."

The conversation moved to more pleasant topics, which was just fine by Cole. Already, he was having some misgivings about the big museum opening tomorrow. The war had ended decades before, but some wounds took a long time to heal. The museum was intended to help that healing process, but Cole couldn't help but feel that the museum was still managing to pour salt in some of those wounds.

As the afternoon moved toward evening, with the shadows lengthening outside and after-work crowds beginning to fill the street, they started to say their goodbyes for now. Cole was starting to think about his supper and maybe trying the Schnitzel tonight.

But to Cole's surprise, Danny announced, "Hey, Pa Cole, Angela invited me to the Hofbräuhaus with her friends after this. If it's all right, I mean."

"I reckon I can find my way back to the hotel."

Hans said, "I certainly won't get lost, either. I've known Munich my whole life. You two go along and have a good time with friends. It is what young people should do." He looked at Cole. "Agreed?"

"Agreed," Cole said.

Danny and Angela headed for the Hofbräuhaus. Hans melted into the crowds flowing home. Cole returned to the hotel and ate alone, which was, well, *lonely*, but the food was good.

Much later, back in his room, he heard Danny return. His grandson was out in the hall, fumbling with the door to his own room. He seemed to be having some trouble fitting the key to the lock and getting it open.

Cole went out and found his grandson reeling a bit, but smiling happily.

"I guess someone had a good time," Cole said.

"*Probst!*" Danny replied, then hiccuped. "I had two beers! I feel a little dizzy."

"Oh boy," Cole said. In his experience, a German beer was a large stein of strong lager. "Let's get you to bed."

He got the door open, helped Danny get his coat and shoes off, then tumbled him into bed.

Danny fell asleep instantly.

Shaking his head, Cole decided to stay and keep an eye on his grandson. The damn fool boy. He sat in a chair by the window, where he could look out and see the lights of the city. From time to time, a plane took off, bound for New York City or maybe London or Paris. His thoughts wandered across the years, strung out like beads of dew on a spiderweb. He dozed. At first light, reassured that Danny was fine, he slipped back into his own room.

* * *

"I'll never drink another beer as long as I live," Danny stated miserably.

They were having a late breakfast at the hotel restaurant. Danny sat slumped with his head in his hands, looking miserable.

Cole had to laugh. "If I had a nickel for every time I heard someone say that the next morning, I coulda bought Rockefeller Square."

"You're making fun of me," Danny said.

"No, it's just something to keep in mind when you feel better tonight and you have an urge to visit that beer hall again. I ain't gonna lecture you. Hopefully, you learned your lesson."

Danny just groaned.

Cole gave him his fresh-squeezed OJ. "Don't worry. You'll live."

"I did have a good time, though. Angela was nice. Her friends were fun. She said I ought to come back and visit this summer."

Cole surprised himself by saying, "Something to think about."

By the time the hour arrived to get ready for the museum opening that evening, Danny was fully recovered and back to his usual chipper self. That was youth for you, Cole thought, along with some help from a nap and an afternoon swim in the hotel pool. In fact, it was Cole who felt himself dragging after he had put on his suit, freshly pressed by the hotel staff. Sure, part of it was the damn jet lag. But another part of him was simply dreading the opening and all of the old wounds it might open.

* * *

COLONEL MULHOLLAND PICKED them up promptly, pulling up in his BMW in front of the hotel.

"Ready?" he asked.

"Ready as I'll ever be," Cole said, slipping into the front seat while Danny got into the back. "I haven't felt so nervous since D-Day, but I've got to say, this car is a lot more comfortable than a landing craft."

"Here we go then," Mulholland replied, pulling away crisply from the hotel.

The museum was just a few minutes away. When they arrived, Cole was amazed to see soldiers, Jeeps, and a couple of German *Kübelwagen* pulled up on the lawn. Pup tents dotted the grass. Some of the troops wore vintage WWII GI uniforms, some had on the sheepskin coats favored by aviators, but most had on Wehrmacht uniforms.

"Who the hell are they?" Cole asked. "Actors?"

"They're WWII reenactors," Mulholland said. "You know, like Civil War reenactors back home? Over here, reenacting WWII is becoming a popular hobby. Of course, you're going to see mainly German reenactors. Nobody wants to be the bad guys."

"Bad guys?"

"Us," Mulholland said. "Americans."

"That's the damnedest thing I've ever seen," Cole said.

"They go out on the weekend to shoot blanks at each other, and maybe camp out," Mulholland said. "It's also an excuse to drink, pee in the woods, and get away from their wives. They were more than happy to come out for this event."

Cole shook his head, not sure what to say. Who wanted to play at being a soldier? He'd had enough of the real thing.

They continued to the parking lot, only to discover that more of these reenactors stood along the sidewalk leading to the entrance.

"Looks like we have an honor guard," Mulholland said.

"You do see that these are Germans? Should I put my hands up to let them know we surrendered?"

Mulholland laughed. "I think we'll be OK."

Inside, there was quite a crowd already. Almost everyone looked to be older, and well-dressed. Drinks flowed from an open bar and servers offered trays of fancy hors d'oeuvres. Cole didn't know what some of the things were, so he stuck with the miniature sausages on tooth-picks. The delicious smells of food and tangy champagne filled the air, mixing with wafting cologne and perfume.

One thing for sure, Cole thought, was that tonight was all a long way from the mud, the stink of open latrines and death, the shivering in the chill air or sweating in the heat, that all soldiers had known back then.

Cole heard a lot of English being spoken, sometimes in British accents, with only a smattering of German. It made sense that most of those in attendance seemed to be American or English because from what he had seen during the preview, this museum celebrated the Allied contribution to winning the war. Most of the pictures of Germans showed them with their hands up. Most of the photos of Germany showed the devastation wrought by the Allied bombing.

To his relief, he spotted Hans strolling around the exhibit hall. His pretty grand-niece accompanied him. The old German smiled when he spotted Cole. The girl wore a big smile as well, but it wasn't for Cole.

"Hello," she said to Danny.

"Hi!"

The two young people drifted away, leaving Cole and Hans to explore the exhibits together. Cole had seen some of them before, but it was all somewhat overwhelming. Everywhere he looked, there were life-size images of soldiers. Many had been black-and-white photographs originally, but were now colorized. Physical artifacts that ranged from rifles to grenades to helmets were on display.

"It's a strange thing, isn't it? Back then, who would have thought that all this would be in a museum. I mean, they've got ration cans and old packs of cigarettes on display. Stuff we threw away. Hell, we were mostly just trying not to get shot."

Hans smiled sadly. "Difficult memories," he agreed.

They came to the exhibit focused on sniper warfare, and the reason for Cole having come all the way from the United States for the museum opening. The exhibit briefly explained tactics, and a battered rifle with a telescopic sight was on display in a glass case. The worn wooden stock had several notches carved into it, and while just about everything else in the museum was explained in detail, no explanation was needed for what those notches meant. This was not Cole's actual rifle from the war, but there was no doubt that this sniper rifle had seen use during the war.

A large photograph featured an American GI hunched over a rifle with a telescopic sight. The young man's face looked gaunt, the single eye that was visible looked startlingly intense.

"You," Hans said.

"Yep," Cole said. "That's me when I was a whole hell of a lot younger."

"Ha, we were all younger then, my friend," Hans said, then grew serious. "You must have been an accomplished sniper to be featured here."

"The truth is, I made the mistake of letting them write a story about me way back then. A famous reporter named Ernie Pyle wrote it. They even took my picture." Cole pointed to a copy of the news clip, which had been reproduced here.

"He would not have written a story about just anyone," Hans said. "You must have been a very good sniper to be noticed."

"I'm not proud of it," Cole said, although he knew he wasn't entirely telling the truth. He *was* proud of what he had done. Hell, he was proud of what every last soldier had done to win the war. "I was just doing what I was supposed to do. Doing my duty."

"Then you should take pride in that," Hans said. He straightened. "We all should."

For a split second, Cole felt an old warning vibrate within him. It was that sixth sense that had kept him alive, warning him of danger. He had not felt that in a long, long time.

Behind them, a deep voice spoke, heavily accented, "I wonder, did you have the father or grandfather of someone here tonight in your crosshairs when that photograph was taken?"

Cole realized that it was a good question.

He turned to find himself staring into the face of someone he had not seen in decades. It didn't matter how many years had passed—he could still recognize those features and those cold eyes. Back then, the face had been magnified some distance away in his telescopic sight. It was not a face that he had ever wanted to see again, that was for damn sure.

Cole stared. The man smiled back at him, but there was no warmth in his expression. Neither man spoke, both of them tense, waiting to see what the other would do next. It was as if two old rival wolves had suddenly crossed paths in the forest.

Standing in front of Cole was *Gefreiter* Hauer, the German sniper that Cole had known as *Das Schlachter*.

The Butcher.

PART II

CHAPTER SIX

January 1945, Vosges Mountains

GEFREITER HAUER SCOWLED at a man who had stepped on a brittle branch buried under the snow, the sharp crack sounding like a gunshot in the stillness.

"*Dummkopf*," he muttered. "Do that again and I will cut your throat."

"Never mind him, Hauer," whispered the *Oberleutnant* nearby. The officer had grown more anxious as they approached their objective, a mountain village that they were to capture. "Do we have a clear way forward?"

Acting as the spearpoint of the German advance, Hauer turned his attention to the forest ahead, rifle at the ready.

Nothing moved, so he glanced at the *Oberleutnant*, who signaled for the company to advance.

Behind Hauer, a great mass of troops moved through the wintry hills, their passage muffled by the freezing mist and snow-laden boughs of the conifer forest. Orders passed quietly from man to man in order to avoid any shouting. Their goal was to advance as far as possible under the very noses of the enemy. Success depended upon surprise.

The road proved to be narrow and winding, forcing the lead Panzers and the convoy of trucks to move slowly. Crowded out of the road, many of the men had taken to the forest, where the footing was better than on the icy, snow-packed road.

Hauer was among those leading the troops through the forest.

He stopped to study the landscape ahead through binoculars.

"What do you see, Hauer?" asked the *Oberleutnant*, who had come to depend on the sniper as his eyes and ears in the forest. Where other men let their attention wander, distracted by the cold, Hauer was also sharply attuned to their surroundings.

"The village is just ahead," Hauer said, lowering the binoculars. He pointed. "Do you see the smoke through the trees?"

The *Oberleutnant* squinted. When he looked closely, he could see smoke gently rising against the patches of sky visible through the trees.

"There it is. Good work, Hauer."

Hauer nodded and moved out, keeping ahead of the rest of the troops, his rifle with its telescopic sight slung across his back. Across his front, he carried a submachine gun on a leather sling, just in case they ran across any unexpected enemy troops. But from the clear road they had experienced so far, it seemed that the Americans suspected nothing.

As the shadows lengthened and nightfall approached, there was new urgency to the movement of the troops. Soon, the officers would have to call a halt.

These hills were challenging enough to navigate by daylight for advancing troops because it was difficult to maintain communication. The peaks and valleys limited radio signals. Maintaining any kind of sight contact remained impossible, meaning that individual units like the one to which Hauer was attached moved at their own pace through the hills.

While the terrain was not ideal, it also meant that the Americans did not expect an attack from this direction. All of their attention was to the north, where what the Allies called the Battle of the Bulge still raged in the Ardennes Forest. The second prong of the German advance was now coming at the southern end of the American position. Not so much as a single enemy plane had appeared in the winter sky, thanks to the dismal weather. Their luck was holding.

More than anything else, the Germans feared the planes that could appear out of nowhere to strafe and bomb their ground forces. Even a Tiger Tank didn't stand a chance against the American planes. As far as the Germans were concerned, bad weather was their friend because it kept the enemy planes grounded or, at the very least, helped to screen their movements from the air.

It was January 3, 1945. Winter fog had moved in, but the new year had begun with clear, crystalline skies and bitter cold, although those had not lasted. Celebrations of the new year had been few and far between because no one wanted to dwell too much on what this seventh year of the war might bring. Circumstances had changed a great deal since those exciting, heady days when the war began in September 1939 with the crushing invasion of Poland, when the war machine of Hitler's Third Reich had seemed invincible.

Hauer recalled those early days of the war fondly. He had been working as a butcher when the war began. He had resisted becoming a soldier at first, but the demand for troops made keeping out of the war impossible before long. Any able-bodied young man was expected to fight. He had soon found that he had many talents and a natural ability as a soldier.

Hauer heard footsteps behind him, crunching with too much noise across the snowy forest floor, and a moment later, Krauss was walking beside him.

"The Leader has thought of everything!" Krauss announced, panting heavily from the effort of catching up to Hauer. "We will take the Americans by surprise and smash them!"

Hauer glanced at the young *Soldat*'s ruddy cheeks and saw that he was serious. "Keep your voice down, or you will let the Americans know that we are coming," Hauer said. "You could lose the war for us. Wouldn't that disappoint The Leader?"

Looking mortified, Krauss fell silent, much to Hauer's relief. At first, when Krauss had begun following him around like a puppy, Hauer had been annoyed. Krauss had seemed to be awed by Hauer's reputation as a sniper, and couldn't take his eyes off Hauer's rifle. But then, Hauer had found it useful to have someone willing to fetch things for him or carry messages. Krauss might think that he was currying favor, but there was only one man that Hauer looked out for. Himself.

Hauer shook his head at the *Soldat*'s praise of Hitler's strategy. Soldiers did what they were told, of course, but even a private in the ranks had his own ideas about military strategy. Some thought that it would have been better to man a defense at the fortifications that made up the Siegfried line, which had been built at enormous expense, while others believed that the war was already hopeless. But if they were smart, they didn't say so.

"What do you think?" Krauss asked.

"About what?"

"The war, of course! Do you think that we can finally win it now?"

"What do I think?" Hauer shook his head. "I think that we are soldiers, Krauss. Let the generals determine the strategy. For us, we need to survive one day at a time."

He quickened his pace to leave Krauss behind. He was done talking for now.

Surely, the Americans knew about the massive Operation *Nordwind* counter-attack by now, but with their forces spread thin and hampered by the intense cold, they had been slow to send reinforcements or to bolster the defenses of the small towns that they currently held and occupied in Alsace-Lorraine.

As darkness fell, the officers called a halt. There was no point continuing along the treacherous road in the dark. For the troops spread out through the trees, moving through the forest at night was equally as pointless due to the logs, boulders, and other natural obstacles. Some slumped against trees and fell asleep instantly. They had been on the move constantly since first light, with little or no sleep the night before.

Each soldier received half a loaf of bread, and jars of jam were passed around. The jam began to freeze as soon as it was spread across the bread, but no man complained.

Hauer would have like some coffee, but no fires were allowed because that might cost them the element of surprise, or worse yet, make the entire battalion a target for an artillery barrage.

"This is it," the *Oberleutnant* announced. "This is the last food you will receive. If you want to eat tomorrow, you must capture enemy supplies."

Hauer picked a few pieces of sawdust from his ration of bread, wondering if this was truly all of the food, or if this was simply another tactic to get them to fight even harder. Then again, it was no secret that food was in short supply, even in the Fatherland itself, as the enemy pressed from all sides. What food could be found was being sent to the front, leaving the civilian population to survive as best it could.

"I hear the Americans have chocolate," Krauss said. The young soldier had settled into the snowy forest floor near Hauer. Like Hauer, he gnawed at the rapidly freezing bread.

"If we capture any chocolate, you can have mine," Hauer said. Krauss was hardly more than a boy; it wasn't surprising that he dreamed of chocolate. Hauer did not care for sweets. As a former butcher, what he longed for was red meat. Steaks, roasts, ham. That was proper food for a soldier. When was the last time they had eaten any meat other than sausage? He grunted, shaking his head. "Now better eat your bread and get some sleep, or you won't be good to anyone."

* * *

THE GERMANS WEREN'T the only ones on the move through the frozen hills and mountains near the border with Germany. Caje Cole and his squad rode in the back of a truck, enduring yet another bone-jarring jolt as the truck moved along the snow-covered road. The truck was open, lacking even a canvas covering to block the wind.

"Happy New Year, boys," somebody said.

Those who bothered to reply told him to go to hell.

"At least we ain't hungover," the soldier pointed out.

They should have been enjoying some R&R, hot food, and booze. Instead, New Year's Eve had come and gone in the back of this truck, with nothing more potent to drink than canteen water.

By now, the truck ride felt endless. It was slow going. The road wandered and the convoy had to slow at every curve to keep the vehicles from sliding off the road. Every couple of miles, one of the trucks in the convoy found itself spinning its tires helplessly, trying to climb a hill. The soldiers had to get out and push.

Just when it seemed like victory in the Ardennes Forest was going to signal a good start to this new year of war, the Germans had done the impossible and launched a fresh attack to the south. Once again, the Germans had shown that they were not necessarily defeated and in retreat. The soldiers in the truck were among those who had been rushed to reinforce the gaps in the thinly spread American lines. There were supposed to be some French soldiers joining the fight, but so far, nobody had seen any. There were even rumors that the Germans intended to re-capture Strasbourg, the largest city in the region.

Cole sat right up against the cab, glad for whatever shelter it offered from the wind. He sagged on the bench seat and bent over in a coughing fit.

"Hillbilly, you look like hell," said Vaccaro. "You ought to be in the infirmary."

"Do you see an infirmary around here?"

Vaccaro looked around the bouncing interior of the truck as if he might find one hiding in the corner. "Nope."

Cole grunted.

"Then let me at least get you another blanket." Vaccaro looked around the truck again, his gaze settling on one of the new soldiers who had been sent to fill their ranks after the decimating fighting since before Christmas. "Hey, Tawes. That's your name, isn't it? Give me your blanket a minute."

Private Tawes did as requested. Vaccaro tucked the blanket around Cole's shoulders. When he caught Cole's raised eyebrows, Vaccaro said, "What, you didn't think I was going to give you *my* blanket, did you?"

A few seats away, Tawes started to protest. "Hey, that's my blanket. Give it back!"

"Aw, stuff a sock in it, greenbean. You got to earn this blanket. Anyhow, they say shivering is good for you. It keeps you warm."

Sullenly, Tawes dipped his head lower between his shoulders, looking like a cold turtle trying to stay warm.

Cole tugged the blanket tighter around his shoulders, shivering uncontrollably. He had started feeling poorly a couple of days ago and now had a fever and chills. His body ached all over. Truth be told, all that he wanted to do was crawl into a hole somewhere and sleep. Sick and weak as he felt, the truck ride was pure agony.

"Do you think we'll get to fight the Germans?" Tawes asked, running his hands up and down his upper arms to keep them warm.

"I'll tell you what, Tawes. If you're so anxious to see the Germans, we'll let you have first crack at them."

The men rode on gloomy silence, each bounce of the truck threatening to shake loose something important and mechanical—like maybe the motor. The troops in the back of the lurching truck had no choice but to grin and bear it.

Finally, the convoy stopped while a fallen log was cleared from the road. The driver of the lead truck explained that there had been a sharp crack sound, and then the upper third of the tree had come crashing down from the hilltop. He had slewed the truck to the left, bracing himself for incoming artillery, but there was no attack. It was deduced that the sap within the tree had frozen and chosen that moment to suddenly burst the trunk. The driver still felt spooked.

"Everybody stay on the trucks," Mulholland ordered. "If you've got to take a leak, do it out the back."

Vaccaro spoke up. "Lieutenant, we need a medic over here, sir."

"What's going on?"

"It's Cole, sir. He's sick as a dog."

The lieutenant looked annoyed at the mention of Cole's name. Cole seemed to have a talent for ticking off officers. "All right," Lieutenant Mulholland said. He looked around, spotted a medic riding in the next truck, and shouted in his direction. "Doc, get over here and take a look at Cole, will you? And hurry it up."

Medics were not actual doctors, but "Doc" was their almost universal nickname. This one wore a large red cross on his helmet and another on his arm, the hope being that this might keep him from being shot at on the battlefield. It didn't help much. The Germans didn't target medics—that wasn't it at all. It was just that in the confusion of the battlefield, the red cross offered little protection.

The medic came over, his rubber-soled boots slipping and sliding on the icy road. If he had taken the time to notice, he might have seen that some of the tracks he passed in the snow had been made by German soldiers, who had passed this way not so long ago. The enemy footprints were easy to distinguish because the Germans still wore leather-soled boots with hobnails. The boots were old-fashioned and not nearly as waterproof as the Americans' pac boots, which had a rubber sole and leather upper, but the hobnails offered more effective traction in the ice and snow.

The medic climbed up in the truck and gave Cole a quick examination.

"It's the flu, all right. It's been going around. You've got a fever of one hundred and two. We need to move you into the cab of one of the trucks, where you'll be out of the wind, at least."

"Hell no," Cole said, his teeth chattering. "Just throw another blanket over me."

"I figured you'd say that," the medic sighed. Of course, the unheated cab of a Studebaker truck didn't offer much in the way of comfort. He handed Cole some pills. "See if those help any. Meanwhile, stay as warm as you can. You're pretty sick, so this is nothing to mess with. Next thing you know, you'll have pneumonia if you're not careful. I'll check back on you the next time that we stop."

"Thank you kindly, Doc."

The truck motor turned over, signaling that the column was getting ready to move out. The medic patted Cole on the shoulder, then moved toward the tailgate, the men making way for him without complaint. Medics had universal respect among the men not only for their dedication, but also for their courage under fire.

As the truck got rolling again, every bone in Cole's body seemed to ache and he felt awful. He swallowed the pills, hoping that they would help him sleep, if nothing else.

He closed his eyes, which felt like they had sand in them, opening them only when, to his surprise, he discovered Vaccaro tucking another blanket around him.

"Sleep tight, Hillbilly," Vaccaro said. "You heard the medic. We've got to keep you healthy so the Germans can kill you later."

"Thanks a hell of a lot," Cole mumbled, then dozed as the truck kept rolling through the mountains.

CHAPTER SEVEN

FOR TWO DAYS NOW, the soldiers of the 179th Infantry stationed in Wingen sur Moder had been hearing machine-gun fire in the distant hills, always creeping closer. *Ratatatat.* At night, they sometimes saw the flashes from artillery and mortar fire. Something big was happening, that was for sure.

It was no longer any secret that the Germans were on the move, headed in the direction of the town. The only question that seemed to remain was how long before the Germans got there.

And yet, their officers had not insisted on digging in or otherwise preparing for an attack.

"There aren't any Germans in this sector," their lieutenant had said nonchalantly. "Besides, what would they want with this place? No, the Krauts will be looking for bigger fish to fry."

But no matter what the officers said, it was hard to ignore the shooting growing ever louder in the mountains beyond the town.

"I don't like the sounds of that one bit," muttered Tony Serra, looking off into the hills. It was impossible to see anything happening in the tree-covered hilltops, but the two headquarters company clerks walking down the village street could hear the fighting taking place in the distance. "All that shooting makes me nervous. Did you hear the lieutenant this morning? He tried to say it was nothing but hunters. Since when do hunters use machine guns?"

"Maybe the Krauts won't come in this direction," Joey Reed replied. "They might go around us. That's what the lieutenant says, anyway."

"Yeah, and Betty Grable might show up for lunch."

"The whole unit is supposed to be relieved in a couple of days. It's going to be someone else's problem."

"Just who is going to relieve us now? Joey, use your head. With these hills crawling with Krauts, they're going to need every soldier. And that means *us*."

Reluctantly, Joey had to admit that he secretly agreed with Tony. He couldn't quite relax. No matter what their officers said, there was the distant chatter of gunfire. German forces were definitely in those hills.

It was true that they were supposed to be relieved, but that looked unlikely now. What they were coming to understand was that everyone was a front-line soldier. Currently, there were nearly four hundred troops and several officers scattered throughout the town.

The two clerks were part of the headquarters company. Joey had spent more time with a typewriter than with his carbine, which he hadn't cleaned since arriving in France. That was all right by him; he wasn't eager to mix it up with the Germans.

Like many of the units currently serving in Europe, the 179th had its roots as a National Guard unit. Most of the soldiers hailed from Oklahoma, which designated the buffalo as its state symbol. Considering that most of the young men in the unit had never been out of sight of the sweeping plains and red-dirt fields back home before the war began, the snow-covered mountains just didn't look right.

New Year's morning had dawned crystal clear and bitterly cold, a crisp start to 1945 and what everyone hoped would be the last year of the war. What they hadn't counted on was starting the new year with a fight on their hands.

The quiet of the new year had been shattered by a Luftwaffe attack on the railroad bridge just beyond town. Bombs had fallen and wiped out the bridge, but thankfully, the German planes had spared the village.

When it was clear that the Luftwaffe was targeting the bridge, Billy and most of the other soldiers in Wingen had come out to watch the show. Huge columns of smoke and debris spiraled upward with each bomb detonation.

"Happy New Year!" Serra shouted. "This is better than fireworks."

"Stuff a sock in it, Serra," the lieutenant said. "Anyhow, I thought the Germans weren't supposed to have any planes left to speak of. I guess somebody was wrong about that."

Finally, American planes appeared overhead to chase off the enemy, but by then, the Luftwaffe aircraft were long gone.

If it hadn't been for the war, it would have been easy to get lost in the picture-postcard beauty of the remote village. There were two churches, one Protestant and one Catholic, both modest and not in any danger of being described as cathedrals.

Along with the usual shops, the town had two hotels, which before the war had catered to hikers and other tourists, but now served the officers stationed in town. While other towns in France had been devastated by the fighting and even reduced to rubble, the local economy was thriving through commerce with the Americans.

All in all, it was pretty soft living for the soldiers stationed here compared to the front-line troops fighting to the north in the Ardennes Forest. Even enlisted men enjoyed comfortable quarters staying in homes throughout the town. Nobody was sleeping in a tent or foxhole.

Until a couple of days ago, the war had been going on to the north, leaving this region out of it.

However, the German's launch of Operation *Nordwind* was waking up the sleepy villages and hills. The offensive had failed to the north, but now, the Germans were trying again.

The two soldiers walked up the winding main street, both lost in their thoughts. They were interrupted by the appearance of Sister Anne Marie, carrying a basket of food.

"Happy New Year, Sister," said Corporal Serra, acknowledging the nun with a nod. He was Catholic himself.

"Happy New Year," she said, smiling pleasantly.

Both men brightened. "Happy New Year to you!" Joey heard himself singing out, pleasantly surprised that the nun spoke English. Like many of the people in the village so close to the border, she was also fluent in French and German.

Although Sister Anne Marie wore a nun's tunic, and also a shawl on this cold morning, her pretty face was plain to see. Even the tunic did not manage to completely disguise her shapely figure. Nun or not, there was no doubt that Sister Anne Marie was a looker. More than one young soldier had remarked that it was a damn shame that she'd gone and become a nun. The Lord worked in mysterious ways, that was for sure.

"I hope the new year brings us good things," she said. "Speaking of which, please help yourselves. I have some baked goods here headed for the priest's kitchen, but he won't be the wiser if there's a bun or two missing."

The two soldiers didn't need to be told twice. They both eagerly reached for a bun when the young nun pulled back the cloth covering the basket.

"Thank you, Sister," Joey said gratefully, nodding his thanks.

As the nun went about her errand, Serra gave her an appreciative look over his shoulder. "Now, that's a shame right there. A pretty girl like that deserves better."

"Better than what? She's a nun."

"My point exactly," Serra said, then sighed with delight as he bit into the warm bun. His next words were said around a mouthful of fresh-baked bread. "Why settle for being a nun? I'm telling you, that girl ought to be a saint."

* * *

IT SNOWED DURING THE NIGHT, just a light dusting that the men guarding the perimeter of Wingen sur Moder could feel against their exposed cheeks and necks. The chill sent shivers down their spines.

"See anything?" asked Corporal Wojcicki, peering out into the dark woods.

"Darker than the inside of a cow out here," replied his buddy, Stan Barnes, standing a few feet away.

Wojcicki had heard that one before, but he didn't comment. He was too worried about the dark woods being filled with Germans. The impenetrable shadows among the trees left a great deal to the imagination. He and the rest of B Company were on a hill overlooking the town, the idea being that the position offered a two-fold benefit. They overlooked the twinkling lights of the village and could get down the hill in a hurry to reinforce the troops there. Also, the position on the hilltop meant that they would likely be the first to encounter any approaching Germans, thus warning the soldiers in the town.

Up here on the hilltop, Wojcicki felt alone and exposed. They did have self-propelled 75 mm guns to provide some heavy hitting if needed—in other words, if the Germans arrived with Panzers.

Wojcicki wasn't totally unprepared. He had made a white smock for himself out of a bedsheet. He figured that it would provide some camouflage in the snow.

"Shouldn't we dig in?" Barnes asked.

"Nah, the lieutenant said not to bother because there aren't any Germans coming around. Besides, you'd damn near need a chisel to get through this frozen ground. Maybe even a blow torch."

So they stared out at the dark woods, their ears straining, waiting for something to happen. Shivering.

After an hour, the lieutenant came by and ordered Wojcicki and Barnes to scout ahead of the company. "Wojcicki, you ought to blend right in with that smock. Let's see if these woods are really empty."

"Yes, sir."

Corporal Wojcicki wasn't a big fan of the idea, but orders were orders. As they headed out, Barnes whispered. "Yeah, got to hand it to you for wearing that smock. You got us both sent right into the lion's den. If you get any more bright ideas, check with me first."

"Yeah, yeah."

Still, they were glad to move, because it helped them keep warm. Slowly, they worked their way from the clearing where the company was spread out into the deep forest. Wojcicki could barely see his hand in front of his face. He kept walking into trees.

In fact, Wojcicki was so intent on avoiding the trees that he was utterly surprised when he fell into the hole.

"What the hell!"

"You OK?" Barnes asked.

"Got your flashlight? I fell into a hole or something. Banged the hell out of my knee."

Barnes switched on the light, which was equipped with a red lens to help prevent them from losing their night vision. Briefly, in the strange red glow, they saw a freshly dug foxhole, and then another. Someone had lined the rim of each foxhole with rocks and logs. Nobody in Company B had dug these holes, which could only mean one thing.

The Krauts had already been here and dug in.

But where had they gone?

"Shut it off," Wojcicki said nervously, worried that the dim red light might give them away. "We've seen enough."

What Wojcicki and Barnes couldn't know was that the Germans had slipped out of the foxholes and were already sweeping around to flank the company. If it hadn't been so dark, they might even have seen the Germans moving through the trees. The gently falling snow had muffled the sound of movement through the forest.

"Let's get out of here," Wojcicki said, as Barnes finally snapped off the light and helped him out of the foxhole. "This place might be crawling with Krauts."

They hadn't even made it back to the company's position when they heard the indistinct shouts in the woods behind them.

Running faster, they made it back to the company, practically shouting the password so that they wouldn't get shot by their own guys. Quickly, they found the lieutenant to warn him. Wojcicki's smock, which had once been a pristine white, was now smudged with dirt from the foxhole that he had fallen into.

Around them, the shouts in the woods grew louder and more distinct.

"Hey, Mueller!"

"Wake up, Schmidt!"

Nearby, Private Schmidt raised his head and shouted back, "What? Who wants me?"

Wojcicki felt his blood run cold. Those shouts were coming from the woods, which could only mean one thing. "It's not us, dummy! It's the Germans!"

"Hello, Schmidt!" Laughter drifted from the forest. "Your old friends are here to see you, Schmidt!"

The Germans called a few more names at random. Wojcicki realized they were simply shouting out common German surnames to rattle the defenders. It was weird to think that some of the GIs might be about to fight their distant cousins.

He had to hand it to the Krauts—the tactic had sure worked. The soldiers of Company B were now apprehensive and confused. Judging by the occasional laughter from the woods, the Krauts were having a good time messing with the Americans.

From the woods, they began to hear banging and rattling. It sounded as if the Germans were using their mess kits to make a racket, as if it was New Year's Eve all over again.

"Hang Roosevelt!"

"Heil Hitler, my friends!"

The Americans gripped their weapons, trying to get a glimpse of anything in the dark forest surrounding them.

So far, nobody had opened fire, but that was about to change.

* * *

LEADING the rest of the German unit, Hauer moved silently through the dark woods. A few flakes of snow still reached him, and he felt invigorated by the cold and snow. This was proper German weather!

They had dug the foxholes earlier, fully expecting the Americans to attack. However, the Americans didn't seem to know they were there.

Instead, the Germans had launched an attack of their own.

At first, Hauer was annoyed when his comrades started calling out names. But when the Americans actually answered, clearly confused, he joined in the laughter. Were the Americans such *Dummköpfe*? It must be an inexperienced unit that they faced.

Now, Hauer took the game to a new level. He found a tree at the edge of the clearing and rested his rifle against it. He looked through the rifle scope, which gathered what light there was, and intensified it. He could see a few vague shapes outlined against the backdrop of the night sky. Incredibly, the Americans weren't even dug in.

"Go ahead and shoot, Americans! It will make you better targets!"

He picked out one of the vague shapes visible against the backdrop of snow, settled his sights upon it, and squeezed the trigger.

Instantly, firing erupted all around him. From the shelter of the forest, taking cover behind trees, the Germans shot at the Americans caught in the open. The Americans seemed to be shooting back without aiming. The battle-hardened German troops picked their targets carefully. As Hauer had warned, the muzzle flashes of the Americans only provided a better target.

Before the heavy guns could even open fire, a squad rushed from the woods and overwhelmed the crews of the 75 mm guns. Some of the Americans fled down the hill toward the village, while the rest were quickly rounded up and taken prisoner.

With the others, Hauer helped relieve the prisoners of their rations and wristwatches. Already, he had four watches strapped to his left wrist. They were useful to trade for bottles of schnapps with troops who hadn't seen any fighting yet.

A few bodies lay scattered in the snow, evidence of the Germans' more accurate fire. One of those bodies was still moving, dragging himself away from the Germans. Unlike the others, this soldier had on a white smock. Badly wounded, the soldier was leaving a dark trail of blood against the white ground as he tried to crawl away.

Hauer rolled the wounded soldier over with his boot, prompting a groan of agony, then looked down at him and asked, "Schmidt?"

The soldier looked up. "No, I'm not Schmidt. The name is Wojcicki. Go to hell, you damn Kraut."

Hauer put him out of his misery.

CHAPTER EIGHT

HAVING OVERWHELMED the ill-prepared American defenses, the Germans moved into the village below, the lights like a beacon. The sky above the hills to the east was getting even brighter as the winter dawn approached. A pinkish glow managed to light the underbelly of the low snow clouds. Even in the midst of the attack, a few soldiers still managed to note the surreal beauty of the scene.

It seemed a tragic moment in which to die, given the promise of a new day. They did their utmost to make sure that it would be Americans who died, rather than Germans.

To their surprise, the defenders did not open fire. In the darkness and the snow, the Americans didn't want to shoot their own men, some of whom were still straggling in from the debacle on the hilltop.

However, the German attackers had no such qualms. They opened fire at any defenders who dared to shoot at them, overwhelming them with rifle fire and machine-gun fire. They had tried to bring down some of the self-propelled 75 mm guns right into the streets of town, but a lone Sherman tank had managed to knock out those guns before being destroyed itself.

The fight for Wingen sur Moder seemed to be over almost before it had started. As the daylight grew and the last of the flakes from the departing snowstorm drifted down, the village found itself firmly in German hands.

* * *

BEFORE THE ATTACK, around three dozen soldiers in the service company had bedded down in the cellar of a house near the Catholic church. The upstairs of the spacious house had mostly been taken over as office space and sleeping quarters for some of the officers.

Joey Reed slept soundly, despite the crowded space. He didn't mind too much because the body heat kept the stone basement warm.

Before daylight, the sound of gunfire woke Joey up.

This shooting wasn't taking place in the hills. This was right outside. In the village streets.

"What's going on?" he asked.

"We're under attack, that's what," Serra said. "It sounds as if the goddamn Krauts are right outside the window!"

Both men reached for their weapons, but they weren't exactly eager to join the fight. Neither man had fired his weapon since training back in the States.

"Hey, you've got to put bullets in it, dummy!" Serra shouted, pulling Joey back from the window and shoving an ammunition clip into his palm.

Joey had to think for a second about how to load the carbine. On top of that, the weapon's action was caked with mud from when he had dropped it a couple of weeks ago and never bothered to clean it. In a headquarters unit, combat readiness was not emphasized as much as the importance of filing paperwork correctly.

He finally figured out the carbine, got it loaded, and joined Serra at the window. Beside them was another soldier, Private Paul Sampson, hunched over his own weapon. Quite unlike the mighty Biblical Sampson, this soldier was skinny and wore thick glasses with heavy black frames that dwarfed his bony face, but had somehow managed to enlist.

"Should we start shooting, or what?" Sampson wondered.

"No, we might hit our guys. Let's wait for orders," Serra said.

Joey stared out through the cellar window. Although it was dark, in the flashes of light from the shooting going on, he caught glimpses of men running here and there. He had assumed they were other soldiers from the 179th, mounting a defense of the town. Some must have been fighting back. But then he also saw troops wearing white smocks and the distinctive, square-shaped *Stahlhelm* of German troops. His blood ran cold.

"Holy cow, those are Krauts out there!" Joey said.

"You catch on fast," said Serra. "How good a shot are you with that carbine?"

"Not very good."

"That's what I was afraid of. And you're not the only one. We're all a bunch of clerks, for chrissakes. If I were those Krauts, I wouldn't exactly be shaking in my shoes."

As dawn gave way to the gloomy morning, the scene in the street only worsened. White-clad Germans went past with *Schmeissers* hanging from leather slings, herding groups of American POWs with their hands in the air. A few prisoners were in their underwear, despite the cold—the fact was that they had been surprised in their beds.

It seemed almost inexplicable that the Americans hadn't been more prepared, but the average GI couldn't be blamed. The capture of Wingen sur Moder reflected some serious shortcomings on the part of the unit's commanding officer.

Some of the Germans passed so close that the men hiding in the cellar could hear them conversing. The smell of cigarette smoke drifted in. The Krauts were smoking cigarettes that they had captured from the Americans.

They could see German machine-gun teams setting up at key positions down the street, unleashing overwhelming fire whenever someone shot at them from one of the houses in the village.

"Holy cow," Joey muttered over and over again. He felt a growing sense of desperation. What were they supposed to do?

The only real holdout against the Germans seemed to be a rifleman in the church steeple next door, who kept the Krauts scrambling for cover whenever one of them entered his line of sight.

It all felt surreal to Joey, like he was watching a real-life pageant or something. So far, nobody had noticed the clerks hiding in the cellar—possibly because they were all being quiet as church mice.

"Anybody got any ideas?" Serra whispered.

"The Krauts haven't spotted us. We've got that much on our side, at least," a sergeant said. Although he held the highest rank of anyone in the cellar, he didn't seem eager to take charge.

"Any ideas?"

"What we ought to do is sit tight until dark. We can try to slip out of here then and the Krauts won't see us."

"Dark? That's a long time to wait. You think we can hide out that long?"

The sergeant shrugged. "You got any better ideas? Maybe you want to go out there and take on the Krauts with that rusty rifle of yours. Nah, we can wait. It's winter. It gets dark early."

However, waiting was much harder than any of the men expected. Each minute dragged out for an eternity. They all seemed to hold their breath countless times as the enemy came within spitting distance of their hiding place. How was it possible that they had not been detected? Each cough threatened to give them away. They had no food or water. A corner of the cellar was turned into a makeshift latrine. Meanwhile, it wasn't getting any warmer in the cellar.

Through the window gratings, they kept watching the German soldiers, who looked bulky in their winter gear and square helmets, carrying their deadly submachine guns. As the hours went by, the Germans seemed to grow even more ominous in their imaginations.

Not far from anyone's thoughts was what had happened last month, at the crossroads town of Malmedy. German troops had captured nearly one hundred soldiers when their convoy had been cut off and surprised by Panzers. The Americans had taken cover in a roadside ditch as the Panzers made short work of their vehicles. In the end, they'd had no choice but to surrender. They had come out with their hands up and found themselves to be POWs.

No one was exactly sure what had taken place next, whether the shooting was a direct order or a terrible mistake, but the Germans had opened fire on the unarmed prisoners. When the shooting stopped, more than eighty Americans lay dead. Only a handful managed to escape.

"Think about what happened to those poor bastards at Malmedy," Serra said, as if reading Joey's thoughts. "We shouldn't be too quick to give ourselves up."

"That's for sure," Joey agreed.

At first, there had been bursts of gunfire throughout the village as pockets of defenders tried to turn the tables on the Germans. The gunfire had been sporadic at best. Eventually, the shooting stopped entirely, except for single shots here and there. It was all too clear that the village had fallen.

"That's the Germans mopping up," Serra said.

The only opposition that remained was the soldier up in the church steeple. At this point, the best that he could hope for was to be a thorn in their side, picking off any enemy soldiers careless enough to show themselves on the street directly in front of the church. From time to time, the Germans would unleash a burst of machine-gun fire at the steeple, but minutes later, the lone rifleman would be back at work. So far, the Germans hadn't brought up any heavy weapons to deal with the sniper—or maybe they didn't feel like he was worth the effort.

Finally, it appeared that the Germans had had enough. An officer appeared on the street, shouting up at the steeple from behind the shelter of a ruined car.

"Hey you, come on down from there!" the German officer called out in English. "The town is ours, so why keep fighting? You will be treated OK."

The drama playing out on the street held the rapt attention of the soldiers in the cellar.

"Do it, buddy," the sergeant muttered. "Give it up. You're dead meat, otherwise."

"No way," Serra said. "I wouldn't trust those Krauts as far as I could throw them."

As far as Joey could tell, the sniper in the church steeple seemed to agree with Serra, because seconds later the sniper fired a shot that hit the vehicle giving cover to the German officer.

"Last chance!" the officer shouted.

Again, another shot made the officer duck.

Now, another man ran to join the officer. He looked even sturdier than the other Germans. A big guy. He carried a rifle with a telescopic sight.

"Uh oh," Serra said. "That guy's a sniper!"

Soon, the sniper had set up beside the officer, aiming his rifle at the church steeple, waiting for his chance.

Joey looked down at his rusty weapon. It was loaded and ready to fire—at least, he thought it was. If he had an ounce of courage, he'd stick that thing right out the window and shoot that sniper in the back. What was he, less than a hundred feet away?

He might have done it, if he'd thought that he could hit the German sniper from here. During training, he hadn't been the best shot. Then again, Joey knew that if he opened fire, whether he took out the sniper or not, he'd be signing the death warrant of every man in that cellar.

How had he gotten into this mess?

For the answer to that, he thought, he'd have to go all the way back to December 7, 1941, when the Japanese had launched their sneak attack on Pearl Harbor. Every boy in Joey's school—and more than a few girls—had been eager to get into uniform and do what they could to get back at the Japs and Germans.

However, Joey had been too young to join up. He'd have to wait until he finished high school. Back then, the main concern that he and his schoolmates had was that the war would be over before they were old enough to fight.

How wrong they'd been. Now it was 1945 and the war was still going strong.

Joey had enlisted the day after graduating from high school. Basic training had been fine, but one thing was soon clear—Joey was not destined to be a front-line soldier.

Studious and gentle, solidly in the middle of his group of recruits, and with the rare skill among men of being able to type thanks to a high school business class, he had found himself assigned to be a clerk.

It didn't much matter to Joey whether he was armed with a rifle or a typewriter, and no one else seemed to mind, either. He was on the front lines with everybody else, doing his part, which was all that mattered.

He had dreamed about fighting the Germans, yet when the time came, here he was, hiding in a cellar.

The soldiers of the service company had mostly been issued M-1 carbines, which looked puny compared to the full-sized rifles. No matter—they never had any use for them.

But now, he did regret that he hadn't made some effort to keep his carbine cleaned and oiled. He should have at least fired it once in a while. Truth be told, combat readiness was lacking in the service company.

But now he held the carbine in his hands. The question was, what was he going to do with it?

A moment passed, and Joey didn't stick his weapon out the window. Come to think of it, neither did anybody else.

Another shot fired from the steeple hit the vehicle sheltering the two Germans. The officer ducked again, but the sniper did not so much as flinch, his eye never leaving his rifle scope.

A moment later, he fired.

The steeple went silent.

Whoever that sniper was, he knew his business, that was for sure. None of the other Germans had been able to take out the American in the steeple, no matter how many shots they fired at him.

Now, the Germans moved freely about the street. The final resistance in Wingen sur Moder had fallen. All that Joey and the others were able to do was peer out the cellar windows and watch it happen, wondering what their fate would be.

CHAPTER NINE

FOR THE SERVICE company men hiding in the cellar, the waiting game finally became too much.

"I've had enough of this," a soldier said. "I'm making a break for it."

"Me too."

"You'll get us all killed!" Serra complained. "This place is crawling with Krauts. Think about it."

An argument broke out in hushed tones. Some were all for getting out now. Others wanted to follow the original plan and wait for nightfall. The sergeant tried to order them to sit tight, but the sergeant's orders didn't hold a lot of weight.

"Do what you want, Sarge, but we're making a break for it."

"You'll never make it. You can't get past all those Krauts."

"We'll sneak out the back door of this place. From what we've seen, the Krauts are all out front."

After checking their weapons, the two men headed up the cellar stairs. Briefly, their footsteps sounded on the floorboards above as they made their way to the back of the house. The men below held their breath. They heard a slight *clunk* as the back door opened.

With no windows in the back cellar wall, they couldn't see what was happening.

Seconds later, they heard a shout, then two quick bursts of gunfire. So much for trying to escape.

"I told those dumb bastards to wait," Serra said. "The sarge was right. We've got to wait for dark."

However, they didn't get the chance. Several pairs of boots appeared at the window grating, followed by the muzzle of a submachine gun.

Inches away, Joey felt his insides turn to liquid.

"Come out, *Amerikaner*," shouted one of the Germans. It sounded like the same officer who had tried to negotiate with the sniper in the church steeple. "Come out or we will toss in a few hand grenades and see how you like that."

The men in the cellar looked at one another in desperation, but it was clear that they didn't have much choice.

"You saw what happened to the guy up in the steeple," Serra said. "I think we'd better give up."

The sergeant moved closer to the window and yelled, "OK, we surrender. You can't shoot prisoners."

"We will see," the officer shouted back. "You are only prisoners if you come out with your hands up. You have one minute."

Quickly, the men dropped their weapons. Most of the men were empty-handed, but a few grabbed blankets or spare clothes. Joey followed their example and grabbed his blanket.

They filed up the stairs and out the back door. Nearby lay the bodies of the two soldiers who had tried to escape, sprawled in the street with blood flowing from them. Joey felt sick to his stomach, but he kept moving, hands held high.

All around them stood German soldiers, submachine guns at the ready. Joey studied their faces, trying to determine if the Germans were about to shoot. Some of the Germans wore self-satisfied smiles, pleased that they had captured yet more American POWs, while others looked grim. Up close, the Germans had several days of stubble on their faces. The camouflage smocks that looked so white from a distance were actually flecked with mud and even blood.

The officer approached, the German sniper they had seen earlier trailing a few feet behind him.

"Smart *Amerikaner*! Very smart."

Some of the soldiers stepped forward and quickly searched their new prisoners. Joey had expected them to be on the lookout for weapons, but aside from a small pocketknife or two—which the Germans kept—the Americans were unarmed. To Joey's surprise, they took their wallets and money, chocolate bars, and wristwatches. Joey hadn't known quite what to expect as a prisoner, but he sure hadn't expected to be robbed.

A soldier looked at Joey's wrist and nodded, so Joe had no choice but to unbuckle the strap of his watch and hand it over. He felt a pang of resentment because his parents had given him that watch as a high school graduation present, right before he had signed up.

The German sniper who had eliminated the man in the steeple was among the soldiers looking on. He stepped forward and grabbed Serra's hand, then shucked his Timex off his wrist with such force that it seemed like he might take Serra's hand along with it. He then started to pull off Serra's gold wedding band, but Serra jerked his hand away. The soldier raised his rifle.

"Enough!" the officer said. "You have his watch, Hauer. Leave the man his wedding ring."

The soldier looked as if he might shoot Serra anyway, but then he lowered the weapon. With a smug grin, without taking his eyes off Serra, he slipped the watch onto his own wrist.

Serra glanced at the officer and said quietly, "Thank you."

If the officer heard Sera, he didn't show any sign of it. Instead, he turned and shouted orders to the soldiers.

Joey didn't understand a word of German, so he still wasn't sure whether or not the Germans were going to shoot them.

Having been searched—and looted—the prisoners were marched toward the church a short distance away.

It all felt so unreal, like a bad dream. Never in a million years had Joey expected to be taken prisoner. Killed, maybe, but not taken as a POW. Their training hadn't focused on being taken prisoner—maybe it wasn't something the Army wanted to encourage by preparing you for it. All he knew was that they were only supposed to tell the Germans their name, rank, and serial number. That response had been drilled into them. The funny thing was, the Germans hadn't even bothered to ask for that information. Maybe they didn't think the Americans were worth the effort.

The sights they passed in the street were not encouraging. Germans appeared to be everywhere, setting up machine gun nests at key points and fortifying positions. There were a hell of a lot of Germans. For weeks, there had been rumors that most of the German soldiers were now kids or old men, but that was not the case with these troops. They looked battle-hardened and went about setting up their defenses with the efficiency of men who had done it all before.

Clearly, from the effort being put into the defenses, these troops weren't just passing through. It appeared that they planned to stay for a while.

"Hands up! No talking! *Schweigen!* Keep moving toward the church."

Lined up at the edge of the street was a row of bodies. Dead American soldiers and a couple of villagers who had maybe been caught in the crossfire. Joey tried to count the bodies, but he couldn't seem to get his mind to work right. Counting past ten was more than his addled brain could handle. Anyhow, there were at least a dozen dead bodies, if not more.

It wasn't his first time seeing a dead man in the war zone, but the sight of the bundles lined up indifferently on the ground was upsetting. Just a few hours ago, these dead men had been very much alive.

At gunpoint, they were marched right up to the Catholic church. Most of the townspeople were nowhere in sight, except for a few who seemed to welcome the arrival of the Germans with open arms, bringing the soldiers baskets of food and bottles of liquor. That should be no surprise—this close to the German border, there were bound to be a few Nazi sympathizers.

As they approached the church, the priest was nowhere in sight. He hadn't been seen in days. Rumor had it that he had fled the town along with the village constable.

But to Joey's surprise, Sister Anne Marie stood at the foot of the steps leading to the church. She was apparently not intimidated by the presence of the Germans, but watched with concern as the captured Americans were marched toward the church.

Joey felt like he was in the presence of a guardian angel. Surely, even these tough-looking Krauts would find it hard to shoot down the prisoners in the presence of a nun. Joey caught her eye, and she gave him a reassuring nod. That small gesture gave him new strength.

As they reached the steps, one of the Americans at the front of the group bent down to tie his shoe. It was Sampson, the skinny kid with the glasses. Without warning, the German sniper shot him dead.

"Keep moving!" the officer warned.

Joey and the others had no choice but to step over the dead man's body. Joey saw Sampson's blood wetting the steps and felt sick.

Sister Anne Marie moved to Sampson's side, but he was far beyond any help. She made the sign of the cross and began praying over him.

Still stunned, Joey spent a moment too long taking in the scene. The next thing he knew, a soldier had clubbed him in the side of the head with the butt of a rifle. When he staggered, the soldier shoved him back into line.

"Into the church!"

The Americans had no choice but to obey. Joey's head rang and he felt warm blood running down over his ear, but he didn't dare to stop. The rifle butt had cut a gash into his scalp and any head wound bled profusely. He supposed that he should feel lucky that he hadn't ended up like Sampson, shot dead on the church steps.

Inside the church, they were herded toward the altar at the north end of the space. There was a door to one side that he supposed led up to the steeple where they had seen the sniper earlier. There was no other way in or out of the church that Joey noticed, except for the door that they had just walked through, now guarded by two soldiers with submachine guns. The stained-glass windows were narrow and high, decorative rather than functional, which would have made it quite difficult to crawl out of them.

Like many of the old European churches, this one had no pews, but only a flagstone floor that was cold and damp. The church had no source of heat other than the bodies it now held. All in all, the church made a perfect pen in which to hold the POWs.

To their surprise, another group of prisoners was already there, slumped on the floor or against the stone walls. Due to those thick stone walls, the church looked larger and more substantial from the outside. Inside, it felt more like a chapel than a full-sized church. With the influx of new prisoners, the interior became quite crowded. One of the guards dragged a bench around so that it separated the last third of the church closest to the door. The guards waved their weapons at the bench and then the soldiers, and though they didn't speak English, the meaning was clear enough—anyone who passed the line would be shot.

The guards soon grew bored and slouched against the wall, smoking cigarettes—but with their nasty submachine guns slung within easy reach.

Another soldier came in and placed a couple of buckets along the wall. The buckets were going to serve as their latrine. Clearly, the Germans intended to keep them here for a while.

The prisoners looked around, getting their bearings, and talking in low voices.

Serra approached Joey and looked at him with concern. "Jesus, kid. Your head is bleeding like a stuck pig. How you do feel?"

"Dizzy, but better than poor Sampson."

"Yeah, I can't believe those bastards shot him for tying his shoe."

Joey felt himself swaying. "I better sit down."

"Let me take a look at that head," Serra said. "I'm no nurse, that's for damn sure, but maybe I can bandage it up."

The guards had taken anything sharp that could be used by the new POWs as a weapon, but Serra managed to use his teeth to get a tear going in a shirttail. Once he had ripped off a rough strip, he wrapped it around Joey's head. "That's the best I can do," he said. "There's some other wounded guys in here from that first batch of prisoners, some of them shot up pretty bad, but we don't have any kind of medical supplies. The Germans took everything."

"Figures," Joey said. "Anyhow, thanks for putting the bandage on my head. I feel better already."

"You're a lousy liar, Joey, you know that? But at least it stopped the bleeding," Serra said.

"I sure am thirsty. Does anybody have something to drink?"

"Not that I can see. Not so much as a canteen."

"I'm sure not gonna ask those guards for a drink. It looks like they wouldn't mind using those *Schmeissers*."

"Hang in there, kid. I hate to say it, but from the looks of things we might be in here for a while."

CHAPTER TEN

THE BATTLE HAD BEEN swift and one-sided. Caught by surprise, the American force had been quickly overwhelmed. The officers had made the fatal mistake of ignoring the gunfire in the hills, insisting on putting their faith in intelligence reports that there were no substantial enemy units in the sector, rather than believing their own ears.

For the most part, the people of the village had hidden away during the brief fight, cowering in cellars or simply fleeing into the night ahead of the German advance. Worried for the church and the safety of the congregation, Sister Anne Marie had stayed. Where else would she have gone?

The young nun had watched with a growing sense of trepidation as the Germans quickly moved to take over the village. Just a few days before, the war had seemed all but over, with the village safely in American hands. Now, circumstances had changed considerably.

She watched the Americans being marched into the church. At first, she had worried that the Germans would shoot them all. Instead, they had killed just one prisoner, but his death on the church steps had been harsh and brutal.

It had been the German sniper who had done it. They had all seen him eliminate the American soldier in the church steeple as well. The man was a brutal killer.

She had seen another young soldier clubbed in the head for not moving fast enough. However, even she had to admit that for the most part, the majority of German soldiers had not mistreated the POWs. As for the villagers, the Germans seemed content to let them go about their business. Many villagers spoke German and a handful had even welcomed the Nazi troops with open arms.

"This is awful!" said one of the villagers, who had joined the nun near the church steps. "What are we to do?"

"Why don't you check on some of the older parishioners and see how they are doing?" Sister Anne Marie said. "They may be afraid to go out."

The other woman nodded. "Yes, that is a good idea. What about you?"

Sister Anne Marie had already made up her mind that while the church might be expected to remain impartial, her focus would be on helping the Americans. In her mind, they fought on the side of right-eousness, unlike the troops of the Third Reich. Besides, the Germans had their own medics and medical supplies. What did the Americans locked in the church have? *They have me*, she thought.

"I am going to tend to the wounded Americans in the church."

"But the guards—"

"You let me worry about the guards," she said, sounding more confident than she felt. "Before you go to check on the villagers, come help me make some bandages."

The two women went to the priest's small house next door to the church. The rectory was modest, no more than a small kitchen, a study where the priest conducted church business, and a bedroom. The interior felt cold and empty.

"Should we be in here?" the woman asked. "This is Father Jean's home, after all."

"If he did not want us in here, then he should not have run off."

In the bedroom, Sister Anne Marie found a chest with spare sheets and blankets. She fetched scissors from the study, and the two women got to work turning the sheets into strips of bandages. She chided herself for taking a small amount of delight in turning the absentee priest's sheets into bandages.

She looked at the growing pile of homemade bandages, then compared that in her mind's eye to the number of soldiers locked in the church, many of whom were wounded. "It's not enough," she said, and stripped the sheets off the priest's bed as well.

"Father Jean is going to get quite a surprise when he returns and finds that all his sheets are gone. We'll have some explaining to do."

Sister Anne Marie said in an innocent tone, "What is to explain? The Germans took them, obviously."

"Sister!" the other woman said, scandalized that the nun would make up a lie. But then she smiled. "Those Germans will stop at nothing!"

"You finish up the bandages and I will see what else I can find that will be useful."

As the shepherd of a relatively small flock, Father Jean lived modestly. He was not a bad man, but a weak one, having fled rather than staying to guide his flock. His greatest extravagance, besides a shelf filled with beautiful old leather-bound books, was an open bottle of brandy in the study. The books were useless, but Sister Anne Marie took the brandy—if nothing else, the alcohol might serve as an anti-septic. The kitchen provided a block of cheese, some stale bread, and a bowl containing half a dozen of the small and bitter local apples.

"Unless Jesus arrives to perform some miracle, this won't be enough," Sister Anne Marie said, gathering the food into a basket.

The other woman opened her eyes wide, indicating that she was a little shocked by the comment. Her expression seemed to say, *first a lie, now blaspheme!*

Sister Anne Marie smiled gently. "Thank you, Madame Tolétte. You have a good heart. Now, if you will go to check on the villagers, I will take the bandages and food to the church."

"Do you want me to go with you?" she stammered.

Sister Anne Marie shook her head. "If there is trouble with the Germans, I don't want you to be hurt."

"Aren't you afraid?"

Sister Anne Marie considered the question. Of course, she felt frightened. Who would not? However, her fear was outweighed by her sense of duty. She smiled. "What should I fear, when I have God?"

But left alone, crossing the short distance to the church, Sister Anne Marie knew that her words had been bravado to put the other woman at ease and perhaps to bolster her own spirits. Having cut the parish priest's sheets to ribbons, however, there was no turning back now.

The door to the church stood open. Sister Anne Marie called to the guards before stepping inside. They had lifted their weapons, but lowered them when they saw her nun's habit.

"What do you want?" one of the guards asked.

"I have come to tend to the injured Americans," she said.

"Go away!"

"But please—"

"We have orders to let no one in, not even a nun."

She could see that there would be no arguing with the stone-faced guard. She reached into her basket and took out the bottle of brandy. Madame Tolétte had seemed to think that Sister Anne Marie was already on the road to hell, so what was one more transgression?

"I wasn't just thinking of the Americans," she said. "I brought this for you."

The guard took the bottle and smiled, his glance lingering on her face. Although she had turned her back on such things, the sister was not immune to the fact that men found her attractive. She managed a smile in return that bordered on flirtation, but what harm would that do if it helped get her inside? With relief, she saw that her bribe, together with the smile, might just work.

"All right, go ahead. But be careful. I would not trust any of them."

"Bless you," she said.

The guard lifted the bottle in salute.

Once inside, she moved among the POWs. Seeing their wounds and injuries, some of them still barely dressed and shivering in the chill inside the church, she suddenly felt overwhelmed. What had she gotten herself into? Perhaps Father Jean had the right idea, after all. She stood stock-still for a long moment, not sure what to do.

"Here, Sister. Let me help you," said a soldier, reaching to assist her with the basket.

"Thank you," she said.

"I'm a medic," he said. "It looks like you brought us bandages. Thank you. We can use them, that's for sure."

"These are just bedsheets. I have a small bottle of mercurochrome and some ointment."

"That's great. I've got to say, I didn't think those Kraut bastards were going to let you in." He seemed to catch himself. "Sorry, Sister. What I mean is—"

"I know what you mean," she said. "We are all God's children."

"If you say so, but the jury is out on the Krauts, if you ask me, especially that Kraut sniper. Did you see how he shot that kid on the church steps? That wasn't war. That was murder."

She shuddered. She had witnessed the shooting. It was not a sight that she would forget anytime soon. "What is your name?"

"Corporal Moore."

"All right, Corporal. You are a medic, so why don't you take on the worst cases? I can assist if you need it. Meanwhile, I will help the less severely wounded."

Moore nodded. "Sounds like a plan to me, Sister."

One of the first soldiers that she moved to help was the one who had been clubbed in the head outside the church. The rifle butt had opened up a nasty gash in the young man's scalp. Most of the bleeding had stopped, leaving behind an ugly wound.

"Let me help you," she said. "I am Sister Anne Marie. What is your name?"

"Joey Reed."

"Well, Joey, let us bandage that head of yours."

"Thank you, Sister."

Although she was not a trained nurse, it was not unusual for her to help the sick and injured of the parish. Her experience so far ranged from helping with childbirth to assisting the town doctor in setting broken bones and putting in stitches. She had prayed at more than one deathbed as well. As a result, she was no stranger to pain and suffering.

The best that she could do was wrap strips of cloth around the soldier's head. The first layer soaked through with blood, so she added another, then another. She wanted to wash away some of the blood drying on his face and neck, but there wasn't any water.

That's when the sister had an idea. She went to the altar and returned with a small, ornate vessel. This was holy water that the priest had blessed to be used for religious purposes. He would have been aghast at using it for any other purpose.

She said a quick prayer under her breath, hoping that God would understand, then poured some of the holy water onto a strip of cloth, which she used to bathe the soldier's face.

"Sister, do you think I could have a sip of that water? I'm so thirsty."

"Here." She handed him the vessel, and he drank.

"Wow, that was good."

"Of course it is good," she said. She smiled. "It is holy water."

She gathered her bandages and vials, ready to move on to the next soldier. However, the young man surprised her by saying, "Sister, will you take a moment to pray with me?"

She touched his bandaged head gently. "You pray for both of us. I am going to do what I can for the others."

The young soldier nodded, got to his knees on the hard stone floor, and closed his eyes. Soon, his lips moved in silent prayer.

Sister Anne Marie shot a glance upward, in the direction that she imagined the soldier's prayers to be ascending. And then she moved on. Prayer had its place, she thought, but so did *action*.

After a couple of hours, the bandages and the small bottles of medicines had taken care of the more immediate needs of the captured soldiers. Fortunately, there were no grievous wounds.

But as it became clear that the POWs weren't leaving the church anytime soon, there were other concerns.

"Sister, do you think there's any way you can get some food and water in here? Maybe some blankets?"

Looking around at the suffering men, she nodded. The cramped quarters had not done much to increase the temperature. Some men huddled together for warmth.

"I will see what I can do," she said. "There is not much food, but

I'm sure that I can get water and blankets. The hardest part will be getting past the guards."

"Try finding another bottle of booze," suggested Corporal Moore, the medic. "That seemed to grease the wheels last time."

Sister Anne Marie nodded her thanks at the guards and returned to the village streets. Outside, the scene had not changed all that much. The Germans had settled in, ready to defend the town.

So far, no other Americans had appeared to contest the German occupation, but she had a nagging thought. Was Wingen about to become even more of a battle zone? The thought frightened her.

But she had more immediate concerns. The soldiers needed food, water, and blankets. They needed better medicines if there were any to be had. Where would she find these things?

The village shops were closed, but that had not stopped the Germans, who had broken the locks and ransacked the premises. She went from shop to shop, hoping to find something, anything, that the American POWs could use, but the shops had been cleaned out.

In the end, she turned to the parishioners for help. She went from house to house like a beggar, with the villagers sparing what they could. On Corporal Moore's advice, she also secured two bottles of liquor. Schnapps, this time.

Loaded down, she headed for the church, her mind already whirling with thoughts about where else she might be able to locate supplies.

She had not gone far when a gruff voice interrupted her thoughts.

"Where do you think you are doing?"

Sister Anne Marie looked up from her basket to see a large German soldier blocking her path. With a trill of fear, she realized that it was the same German sniper who had shot the prisoner on the church steps.

"I am going to the church," she said. "I have supplies for the prisoners."

"All that is for the Americans?" He sneered. "What are you doing to help our good German soldiers?"

"They are not locked inside our parish church."

"Whose fault is that? Surely their own," the sniper said. "They are the ones who allowed themselves to be captured. Why do they deserve anything? If I'd had my way, they all would have been shot. That would have saved us a lot of trouble. Who knows, maybe I will still get my way?"

She looked around for the German officer. Last time, he was the one who had kept the sniper in check. However, he was nowhere to be seen.

"Let me see what you have for the Americans," the sniper said.

He reached into the basket, tossing neatly folding blankets into the snow. He took out a can of food. "Why waste food on men who are as good as dead?"

The sniper didn't seem to expect an answer from her. He put the can into his coat pocket. Next, he grabbed one of the bottles of schnapps, which went into another pocket. He tossed a precious vial of mercurochrome away.

"Please," she said.

"Hauer! What are you doing?"

They both turned to see the officer heading in their direction. Hauer scowled, while she felt relieved.

"I am inspecting these items she is taking to the prisoners," Hauer said.

"Stop pestering that nun. Let me worry about the prisoners. I need you up in the church steeple. There are reports of American troops headed this way. You and your rifle are going to help hold them off."

"Yes, sir."

The sniper gave her one last glare, then moved toward the church so that he could take the stairs up to the steeple.

The officer turned his attention on Sister Anne Marie. His flinty glare softened. She could see that he was younger than he looked at first, and that his face was tight with exhaustion. "Don't mind him, Sister. Go on and take that to the prisoners."

She took a few minutes to pick up the blankets, shaking the snow off them as best she could.

As she moved toward the church, the officer shouted a warning. "Look out! *Achtung!*"

She froze. An instant later, a dark bundle flew through the air in front of her and hit the frozen ground with a resounding *thud*.

To her astonishment, she realized that a body had just crashed to the ground directly in her path.

She gasped, staring down at a dead soldier wearing an American uniform. She realized that it must be the body of the soldier who had been in the steeple earlier; this was the man that the German sniper had shot.

She looked up at the steeple and saw Hauer leering down at her. He had tossed the dead body out of the steeple, clearly intending for the corpse to drop on her head. If it hadn't been for the officer's warning shout, she would have taken another step and been crushed by the falling body.

The German sniper had just tried to kill her.

For once, Sister Anne Marie did not offer a prayer of thanks, but a silent curse directed at the sniper above. It was only with a powerful act of sheer willpower, brought about by reminding herself that she was a nun and should act accordingly, that Sister Anne Marie managed not to shout the ugly words that came to mind.

Behind her, the officer had no such compunctions. He cursed at the soldier in the tower, who looked down and shrugged, not looking chastened in the least. Then the sniper disappeared from view as he took up a position with his rifle.

Shuddering with suppressed fear and anger, she hurried into the shelter of the church.

CHAPTER ELEVEN

BY THE TIME Cole and the rest of his unit finally rolled up on Wingen sur Moder, the town had fallen and was firmly in enemy hands.

"It's a hell of a thing," Mulholland said, having gathered the platoon around. "The Germans have taken this village and we can't let them keep it. You know what that means."

"Yeah," Vaccaro said. "It means that we're going to get our asses shot off."

"That about sums it up," Mulholland said. "Happy New Year."

"New year, same old story," Vaccaro muttered.

The lieutenant turned his attention to Cole, who sat nearby, wrapped in blankets. He shivered with fever. "Cole, how are you holding up?"

"I reckon I'll live," Cole said, his voice raspy.

"You sit this one out," Mulholland said.

"Like hell I will, sir."

"That's what I thought you'd say. I won't order you to stay put because we can use every man. Just don't make the medic carry you back." Mulholland looked around the assembled men. "Any other questions?"

A soldier raised his hand. "Sir, I feel the flu coming on."

"Me too, sir. Can I sit this one out?"

"Very funny. You want to be as sick as Cole, go right ahead. Doesn't look like much fun to me. Anyhow, he said he's coming along."

Several men nodded. Sick or not, they were glad to have Cole along. "Yes, sir."

"Word is that this is a small unit in the village. Not much more than a squad. We should make short work of them."

Lieutenant Mulholland's prediction would soon fall into the category of "famous last words," but the squad had no way of knowing that just yet. It would turn out that there were a lot more Germans defending the village than anybody knew.

Quickly, they got organized for the attack. The Americans had approached on the main road through the mountains, which meant that the most direct way into the village was through an underpass that carried the road beneath a set of railroad tracks.

"The Krauts will be expecting us, sir," the sergeant pointed out. "We could go around the village and attack from another direction."

Mulholland shook his head. "Don't think I didn't already suggest that, Sarge. The CO informed me that skirting the town would take too long. He wants this town captured as fast as possible. Our orders are to attack head-on. If someone had their facts straight and there really aren't that many Germans, it shouldn't be a problem."

The plan of attack was simple. A handful of men would advance through the underpass and see if anybody shot back.

The lieutenant led the way himself. He had been in enough scrapes since coming ashore back in June that his voice quavered a little as he whispered orders to the men accompanying him. Nobody said anything about it. They knew the lieutenant had plenty of sand. More than a few of them also shook with more than the cold.

Cautiously, the lieutenant moved forward, flanked by two soldiers, Bigelow and Carpenter. For a change, Cole and Vaccaro hung back instead of leading the attack.

At first, it seemed as if the village might be deserted. They emerged from the underpass and started down the road into the village, feeling more confident with every step.

Suddenly, the dreaded rip of an MG-42 machine gun shattered the quiet. The weapon had been nicknamed "Hitler's Zipper" for the way that the machine gun seemed to tear the air. The Americans' sturdy Browning machine guns didn't come close to the same rate of fire. There was nothing like the sound of Hitler's Zipper opening up to turn a man's insides to water.

The burst kicked up snow and ice from the road, then caught Private Carpenter and spun him around like a top. Mulholland and Private Bigelow had a split second to dive for the roadside ditch just before another burst filled the air.

From inside the tunnel, the men fired back. More shots came from the village. Bullets pecked at the stones, forcing the men to keep their heads down. It was hard to say just exactly where the Germans were hidden. The buildings of the village offered too many hiding places.

"Get Cole up here!" the sergeant shouted. "We need to take out that machine gun."

* * *

HAVING BEEN CALLED upon to put his rifle to work, Cole crept forward into the increasing fire. Bullets whacked against the stones around him, ricocheting inside the tunnel. Other bullets kicked chips from the icy road.

If he hadn't been so sick, he might have paid more attention to the fact that he was advancing when the rest of the men were falling back.

As it was, he felt dizzy. It was hard to focus, too, as if he was crawling through the middle of a dream instead of a snowy road. Every bone ached as if he had already been hit with the slugs coming from the German machine gun. His head throbbed. And yet, he was expected to fight a battle. It was a hell of a thing. It was only the sheer adrenalin of combat that kept him in the fight.

"Tell me what you see, City Boy."

"You got it, Hillbilly. But I've got to say, I don't see much. Just a bunch of houses and shops. Brooklyn, it ain't."

"We ain't here to write a travel guide. Just tell me if you see any Germans."

"Oh, I see them, all right."

Now, they could both see activity in the village streets as German troops moved forward to meet the attack. The Germans also seemed to have a couple of mortars lined up on the American position.

"Mulholland said he was told that there was only supposed to be a squad of Krauts in the village. That's a whole hell of a lot more than a squad. Look at 'em all."

Cole managed to get his rifle to his shoulder. He could see lots of Germans, though most were behind cover. "I think we just kicked the hornet's nest," he said. "Where the hell is Mulholland, anyhow?"

"He's pinned down in that ditch over there."

"All right, let's whittle these Krauts down to size."

Cole tried to aim, but he had to admit, his eyes felt like someone had taken sandpaper to them. He felt too weak to hold the rifle steady. He fired and missed. Missed again.

Vaccaro gave him a target. "Hey, there's a sniper in that church steeple!"

Just as Vaccaro spoke, a bullet that seemed more precise than all the others pecked at the stone near his head. They both ducked.

Cole searched the church steeple, but couldn't detect any sign of the enemy sniper. Although Cole couldn't see him, there was no doubt that he was there, all right. Another bullet came in and hit the new greenbean soldier firing from the tunnel entrance. Private Tawes fell dead, hit square in the head, a neat round bullet hole in the front of his helmet.

Vaccaro swore. "Dammit, I knew I shouldn't have bothered to learn his name. These new guys never last a week."

His comments sounded unfeeling, but hardening your heart was sometimes the only way to get through this madness.

The sniper was taking a terrible toll, but Cole was too feverish to be able to focus enough to take him out. He could barely hold the rifle steady. He lowered the Springfield rifle and slumped against the tunnel wall.

Vaccaro looked at him with concern. "You hit?"

"I feel like a truck hit me, if that counts."

"That dead greenbean looks livelier than you do, Hillbilly. Don't make me carry you back."

The squad would have withdrawn, but they couldn't—not with Lieutenant Mulholland and Private Bigelow still pinned down in the ditch. Between the machine gun and the sniper, trying to make a break for it would have meant certain death.

"We can't leave Mulholland out there," Cole said.

"There might not be much choice," Vaccaro said. "Whoever thought there was just a handful of Germans in the village was wrong —dead wrong."

"There are a few of them," Cole agreed.

"We had better pull back. If they put a round from one of those mortars into this tunnel, we're all goners."

Behind them, they heard the clank and rumble of approaching tanks. From the engine noise, they knew that these were Shermans. That much was good news.

"Those look like ours!" Vaccaro said. "I never thought that I'd be so glad to see tanks."

So far, they hadn't seen any sign of German armor, which would have spelled trouble for any Sherman tank, which was equipped with a gun that was no match for the more heavily armed Panzers prowling these mountains.

The tunnel under the train tracks was just wide enough for the Shermans to pass through, once the dead greenbean's body was dragged out of the way.

"Poor bastard," Vaccaro muttered, helping to lift the body onto the back of a tank. "He'd barely been in the field long enough for his socks to get wet. Speaking of socks, that reminds me."

Vaccaro went through the dead soldier's pockets and liberated a chocolate bar and a pair of dry socks. The way that Vaccaro saw it, he could put those to good use, but the socks and chocolate wouldn't do the soldier much good considering where he was headed—the local graves registration unit.

Quickly, the tankers hatched a plan to free Lieutenant Mulholland from the ditch. The lead Sherman would pull out of the tunnel entrance and head down the road just past where the lieutenant lay. The armored behemoth would create cover for Mulholland and Bigelow, giving them a screen. After all, the Germans could fire all the machine guns they wanted at the Sherman, but the bullets wouldn't so much as dent the metal.

Once Mulholland was out of the ditch, the tank would reverse back toward the tunnel entrance, giving the infantrymen cover all the way. The second tank would hang back in reserve and provide any covering fire.

"You ought to let those Krauts have it," Vaccaro said. "Jam a couple of shells down their throat."

"I'd like nothing better," the tank commander said. "But there might be people in the village. I don't want to kill any civilians. We'll have to rely on our thirty for suppressing fire."

"Sounds like a plan to me," Vaccaro said. He shouted down the road, hoping that Mullholland could hear him. "Lieutenant, we're coming for you!"

It soon became apparent that the plan was going to be complicated by the fact that the Germans had started to advance toward the tunnel, clearly intending to push the Americans back.

"If we're gonna do this, we need to do it soon," Vaccaro pointed out. "Those Jerries mean business."

"No time like the present," the tank commander said. He pulled the tank hatch shut, sealing the crew within.

The tank started down the road toward the village. At the last second, Vaccaro fell in behind it.

Cole couldn't believe it. Vaccaro wasn't one to stick his neck out. Like Cole, he had seen all too often how that usually turned out.

"Where are you going, City Boy?"

"You sit tight, Hillbilly. We'll be back with the lieutenant in a jiffy."

From the village, the Germans redoubled their rate of fire. Machine-gun bursts and bullets hammered against the armored skin of the tank. Although the bullets couldn't pierce the armor, it must have been more than a little nerve-wracking to hear them pelting the metal. Cole had grown up in a shack with a tin roof, so he could well imagine that the inside of the tank must have sounded like the sleeping loft in the shack during a summer hailstorm.

If the tank commander had dared to leave the hatch open, the

German sniper in the church steeple might have tried to pick him off. However, the tank was buttoned up tight.

But the tank wasn't just a punching bag. The Sherman could punch back. Its machine gun blazed, making the Germans who had been advancing toward the tunnel scramble for cover.

Still, the Sherman was fighting with one hand behind its back, considering that it couldn't use its main gun for fear of civilian casualties. The lack of fire also emboldened some of the Germans, who crept closer, using outbuildings and ditches for cover.

With the tank hatched closed and the limited field of vision that the machine gunner had to work with, it was hard to see the Germans approaching or the fact that two of them carried *Panzerfaust*, their anti-tank weapon. Unseen by the Americans, one of the Germans set up behind a shed with the weapon, planning an ambush, waiting for the tank to come into range.

As the tank rolled closer, the German settled the sights of the weapon on the American tank. He was aiming for the sides of the Sherman, where the armor plating wasn't as thick.

The tank passed the spot where Mulholland and Bigelow lay in the ditch, then stopped. From the shelter provided by the back of the tank, Vaccaro waved at the two men. "Come on, sir! It's time to go!"

"Vaccaro, I never thought I'd say this, but you're a sight for sore eyes."

Mulholland didn't need to be invited twice. He didn't attempt to get to his feet, but rolled out of the ditch and behind the tank. The soldier followed his lead. In the lee of the tank, the lieutenant stood.

"We ought to try to advance into the village," he said to Vaccaro.

"I don't know about that, sir. There's a hell of a lot of Germans. The plan is to back this puppy back to the mouth of the tunnel and regroup."

"All right. Let's do it."

The tank crept forward, still firing, and the soldiers behind it didn't have much choice except to follow it or be exposed to enemy fire.

"Where's he going?"

"They're blind inside," Mulholland said. "They can't see that we're out of the ditch."

The lieutenant used the butt of his rifle to give the tank two quick whacks. The forward motion of the tank stopped. They heard gears shifting, and then the tank began to reverse. The reverse speed was faster than expected and the three men had to trot to keep from being run over.

Down the road, the German with the *Panzerfaust* saw the tank starting to retreat, and figured it was now or never. He lined up the sights and fired.

There was a tell-tale whoosh of smoke and flame, so fast that there was no time to dodge the deadly *Panzerfaust* round. The subsequent explosion made the tank shudder.

Whether it was a lucky shot or skill, the German's *Panzerfaust* round had scored a crippling hit.

Mulholland and the others just had time to throw themselves flat in the snow. Lucky for them, it was the right front quarter of the tank that took the brunt of the explosion. Nonetheless, Bigelow cried out as a splinter of shrapnel caught him in the leg.

To their horror, the wounded tank came to a halt, engine clanking and shuddering. Thick, black smoke began to pour out of the Sherman.

Unfortunately, the security offered by the tight steel confines of the tank also turned it into a death trap. Exiting a tank filled with roiling, choking smoke was no easy task—if any of the crew had even survived the initial blast.

"Those poor bastards!" Mulholland shouted. "We've got to help them!"

Without thinking, the lieutenant scrambled onto the back of the tank, headed for the hatch.

On top of the tank, the hatch started to open, then fell shut again. Whoever was in there seemed to lack the strength to lift it from within.

When the hatch started to open again, Mulholland was there, getting his fingers under the lip and yanking it open. A soot-stained face appeared, coughing and choking on the thick smoke that boiled out.

Mulholland started to help the tanker, who suddenly slumped lifelessly in the lieutenant's arms. From the village, they heard the solitary crack of a rifle. A shot from the sniper in the church steeple had finished the work that the *Panzerfaust* had started. Mulholland had no choice but to let go of the dead weight, and the body slid back into the smoking maw of the tank.

"Anybody else in there?" he shouted.

He waited a moment, bullets slicing the air around him, but no one else emerged. Flames began to lick upward from the interior of the tank.

Vaccaro had climbed up on the tank and grabbed Mulholland by the back of the belt, trying to haul him down from the top of the Sherman, where he was a target.

"Sir, it's no use! They're gone!"

It took another forceful tug from Vaccaro, but Mulholland finally got the message and slithered down off the tank, keeping low. Heavier smoke now poured from the crippled Sherman, helping to screen the soldiers from the gunfire in the village. It was as if in death, the crew of the defeated Sherman tank was making one final act of defiance against the Germans.

Benefitting from the bulk of the wrecked tank and the smoke-screen, the three soldiers were able to run back to the cover offered by the tunnel.

Finally safe for the moment, Mulholland punched the air in an angry gesture. "Son of a bitch! They were just trying to save my ass and I got them killed."

"Wasn't your fault, sir. You didn't kill those boys. The Jerries did."

Mulholland knew it was true, but it wasn't much consolation. He shook his head. He seemed to notice Cole slouched against the tunnel wall. "Hillbilly, are you hit?"

Cole raised his head, but didn't seem to have the strength to respond. Whatever energy that he had managed to summon earlier was gone. His eyes looked glassy and bright with fever.

"He's just sick, sir."

"I'll be damned. All right, let's get out of here. Somebody grab Cole. It's going to take more than our squad to capture this town."

They pulled back, leaving the dead to be collected later. Bigelow was wounded, and they carried him out. Vaccaro draped Cole's arm over his shoulder and dragged him out of the tunnel as the sound of German firing increased. Cole felt like dead weight.

So far, it had been one hell of a fight and it hadn't gone well. They had lost two men, along with a tank and its crew. As for Cole, it looked as if he was out of commission for the time being.

On the other side of the tunnel, the rest of the company had set up a defensive line, reinforced by the second Sherman tank. Now, the tables had turned. As the Jerries advanced through the tunnel, the Americans opened up with a withering fire. The tank fired directly into the mouth of the tunnel with a white phosphorous round, resulting in a blinding explosion. A single German soldier emerged, hands in the air, screaming as burning phosphorus consumed him.

Vaccaro fired, and the screaming ended.

It wasn't the first time that he had shot someone, but even if he was just putting that poor German bastard out of his misery, it wasn't something that he'd ever get used to.

He turned to look at Cole, who sat in the bottom of a foxhole with his eyes closed.

"Hillbilly, I hope you get better soon," Vaccaro said. "You're a whole lot better at this than I am."

CHAPTER TWELVE

NIGHT RETURNED, along with the bitter cold. The fresh snow that had fallen previously turned crunchy underfoot. Troops did what they could in their foxholes to stay warm, liberating tarps from the trucks and huddling together, but it wasn't enough. Everybody was shivering and miserable.

Adding to his misery was the fact that Cole was still fighting the flu, the night passing for him in fitful dozing. His head ached. His bones hurt. Vaccaro gave have him some lukewarm instant soup that he had begged and borrowed, which was about the best that could be hoped for in these conditions. Vaccaro also brought him some hard candy to help with his sore throat.

"I swear I could have heated up that soup on your forehead, Hillbilly. You want me to get the medic? Maybe he can give you some more pills."

"Don't worry about me," Cole said. "I'll be all right in the morning."

"If you say so."

Cole finished the soup, sucked on a piece of candy, and slept.

Vaccaro had given Cole his own blanket, so he tugged his coat as tight around him as he could, shivering. They had been in a lot of tough spots, but even he had to admit that this night was a new low point. It was freezing cold. Cole was sick. The Germans had halted the attack on the village, killing the greenbean and one of the squad veterans, wounding Bigelow, and destroying a tank in the process. All that they could do now was sit in the snow and lick their wounds.

From the village, he and the other soldiers heard the sound of singing. The Germans occupying the houses were sheltered from at least some of the cold. They started fires in the fireplaces, breaking up furniture to burn because most of the firewood was gone. Still, with the windows open to shoot out of, awaiting another American attack, the conditions were hardly cozy. But from the perspective of the shivering American troops dug into the frozen ground, the enemy was enjoying the lap of luxury.

"I hate those Kraut bastards," Vaccaro said. "They're all nice and warm in those houses, drinking schnapps and eating sausages, while we freeze our asses off out here."

"Why don't you stroll on in there and see how you like it," the sergeant suggested. "Maybe the Jerries will welcome you with open arms."

"Yeah, right. What are they singing, anyhow?"

"Sounds like more Christmas music. Has a nice ring to it."

The Germans must have gotten carried away with their attempts to keep warm, because one of the houses had caught fire and was burning merrily, casting a glow across the snowy village. They could see the shadows of enemy soldiers moving in the light cast by the flames, but nobody made any effort to put out the fire.

Dug into the cold ground, surrounded by snow and trees, all that the American troops could do was watch from a distance, wishing they could have some of the warmth from the fire.

For the next twenty-four hours, the American troops sat in their foxholes and shivered.

"What are we waiting for, sir?" Vaccaro asked Lieutenant Mulholland.

"Word has it that we're supposed to get more tanks. They're on the way."

"It's fine by me if they take their time getting here."

Everybody understood what he meant. Once those tanks showed up, they would have to attack the village again. Nobody looked forward to going up against fortified enemy positions.

It soon became clear that the American prisoners in the village were going to complicate the attack. Refugees from the village began to enter the American lines, carrying news of the POWs.

"The Germans are holding more than two hundred men inside the Catholic church," explained a villager named Madame Lavigne, who had fled the village with her elderly mother and a young niece. They were pushing their meager belongings in a wheelbarrow. Madame Lavigne owned a shop in town and looked formidable as a Panzer with her hefty build and winter coat, but the slim young niece attracted the attention of the soldiers. When they decided to camp with the Americans rather than take their chances on the road, several soldiers volunteered to help the niece set up a tent.

"How are the prisoners being treated?" Mulholland wanted to know.

"Some are wounded and there is not much food in town," Madame Lavigne said. "Not all of the prisoners are in the church. Some are being held in basements here and there."

From the sounds of it, a large portion of the infantry regiment that had been occupying Wingen had managed to get itself captured. This wasn't good news, because it meant that the tanks would not be able to unleash their guns on the Germans, for fear of hitting the Americans held in the village. When the soldiers attacked the village, they would be fighting with one hand tied behind their backs. If the weather cleared enough for the planes to get back in the air, it meant that they couldn't be used against the village, either.

If Wingen sur Moder was to be taken back from the Germans, it was going to be up to the soldiers to wrest it away using nothing more than rifles and machine guns.

"I've heard better news," Mulholland said. "This is shaping up to be a bloody fight."

* * *

WHILE THE STALEMATE between the Americans and Germans dragged into a second day, Cole used the time to sleep as his fever slowly ebbed. He woke from time to time in confusion, his fever dreams mixing with snatches of memories.

One memory had to do with Christmas. He supposed that his feverish sleep, along with just coming off the holiday season, had prompted the memory. Growing up in the mountains during the Depression, money had been scarce. They never had anything like a Christmas tree or any presents. When he heard the other soldiers wax nostalgic about their own childhood Christmases, Cole sometimes had to wonder if he had grown up in the same country as these other men. The closest that the Cole family ever got to celebrating Christmas was that they ate a big meal with nobody going to bed hungry for a change. His ma would even save up sugar, butter, and eggs so that there was enough to bake a pecan pie. Everyone got one slice. Cole usually collected the pecans himself before the snow fell, harvesting them from a patch that grew in a mountain clearing.

His pa always got drunk at Christmas, but then again, his old man never needed an excuse to get drunk. If the sun rose and set that day, that was usually enough reason for his pa to drink the moonshine that he cooked up in the hills. He might even have made some money with that endeavor if he hadn't kept drinking most of what he produced.

Once when Cole was a boy, his pa had arrived at the cabin on Christmas Eve just before dark, clearly pleased with himself and grinning from ear to ear. Weaving as he walked, he was drunk as a lord.

"I been to town and done bought you all a stick of peppermint for Christmas," he said grandly.

He reached into his pocket and brought out ... nothing. Puzzled, he patted his other pockets. Empty.

"Pa, where's the candy?" one of Cole's younger sisters asked. The thought of a peppermint stick was such a rare treat that she was close to tears.

"Dang it," he said, reaching into his pocket again and staring at his empty hand. "Didn't eat it, did I? I reckon I must have dropped all that candy."

Cole's mother had heard enough. She was usually too afraid of her husband to speak up. They were all afraid of him. There was no meaner drunk. But Christmas had made her bold. "You drunken fool," she said sharply. "It ain't right to tease the children so. You go on inside. Go on."

His father shrugged and made his way toward the shack.

Cole's mother gathered them around. "I reckon he done dropped that candy along the way. If you walk back along that road, you'll find it," she said. "Stick by stick. Hurry up now, before it gets dark."

When Pa said that he'd gone to town, he meant the lonely cross-roads that had a country store and another building with a gas pump. From their shack, it was six miles down dirt roads to that crossroads. Walking with sharp eyes, they found four sticks of candy along the road. The snow was late coming this year, so it helped that the colorful candy stood out against the drab ground. These were penny sticks, striped red, nearly as thick around as a cornstalk. None of the Cole children had ever had such a thing as a stick of candy. It was an unimaginable luxury. Finding each one was like discovering treasure. The candy sticks were a little dirty, but the dirt brushed off easily enough.

Where the fifth peppermint stick had gone was anybody's guess—if pa had even been sober enough to actually buy five sticks.

As the oldest, Cole had gone without. His little sister had cracked an end off her stick and tried to give it to him, but he wouldn't take it.

"Gone on now, I don't need it," he'd said, curling her hand back around the candy and giving her fingers a gentle squeeze.

Candy was for children and he was eleven years old. Cole couldn't ever remember thinking of himself as a child. In a way, he had been born old.

In the foxhole, Cole shivered. Now, why had he remembered all that, he wondered? It was because of the candy that Vaccaro had given him.

He slept again and woke in the dark, men snoring around him. He noticed the stars glittering above and realized that he felt better. His fever had broken.

And none too soon. In the distance, a machine gun chattered. Cole might have slept, but the war had not.

* * *

IN THE CENTER of the village, Sister Anne Marie hurried toward the
Eglise Saint-Félix-de-Cantalice, carrying a heavy basket. The church
near the village center looked small but sturdy, a bastion of red brick,
like a bulwark of faith and hope against sin. The stucco exterior gave
the structure a vaguely Tudor appearance. Because it looked as if it had
been there for ages, many were surprised that the church had only
been built in 1914. This morning, she thought that perhaps the *eglise*
was truly an island in a turbulent sea, considering that the village had
found itself caught in the storm of battle. There was no shooting at the
moment, which meant that they were in the eye of the storm.

As she walked up the street, instead of the usual handful of pedestrians and bicycles, she passed knots of German soldiers. They had
thrown together sturdy defenses by turning carts on their sides or
carrying out heavy furniture from the houses.

Soldiers were dragging an old bathtub out of a house to add it to
the defenses. The sound of the cast iron scraping across a bare patch in
the cobblestoned street grated on the ears, sounding unnaturally loud
in the still air.

The sight of armoires and sofas—and now, a bathtub—bristling
with machine guns and mortars was a strange one, to say the least.
However, the village was not currently under attack since the attempt
by the Americans had failed the day before. Even from here, the young
nun could see the burned hulk of the American tank near the railroad
overpass. Of course, no trains had run in many days due to the fighting. Looking more closely, she could see a body hanging half out of the
turret, badly burned. More bodies lay scattered in the snowy road,
their drab uniforms in stark contrast against the snow.

If her hands had not been full, she would have made the sign of the
cross. Instead, she whispered a prayer.

The Germans that she passed in the street smoked and laughed
with one another. Some leaned against the walls of the houses, looking
all the more bulky menacing in their heavy winter coats.

Judging by their laughter and their easy conversation, they seemed
to be old hands at the business of war. Most ignored her, but a few

gave her a polite nod and said, *"Guten morgen, Schwester."* Good morning, Sister.

"God's grace to you," she replied sincerely.

A few of the looks she received were lascivious, however, and she tugged her shawl tighter around her shoulders and face. God forgive them, she thought. Were men so weak that they could lust after a nun?

If nothing else, she felt a sense of relief that the German sniper who had tried to drop a dead man on her head was nowhere to be seen. A glance up at the church steeple confirmed that he wasn't up there, either.

Above the surrounding hills, the winter sun shone pale and watery through the gauzy clouds. They would find no warmth there this day. The sunlight wouldn't even reach into the shady places in the village, leaving the ice and cold to tighten its grip.

Most of the villagers who remained stayed out of sight, keeping to the shelter of cellars and the sturdy stone houses. But Sister Anne Marie knew that she could not hide or flee town as the priest had done. That was not why she had answered the call of her faith and become a nun. Her duty lay here. She had not grown up in this village, but in one that was somewhat larger. Still, there were not many options for a poor girl—even a pretty one. Her choices were to become a spinster schoolteacher or nurse, a wife to a young man who was equally as poor, or if she was lucky, to marry some middle-aged merchant who would treat her like a servant.

Instead, the church had offered another choice. She received an education and a certain independence of mind that becoming a wife would never allow. Also, she received some measure of respect when she had donned those habits.

Although the decision had mystified some of her friends and family, she gladly became Sister Anne Marie.

Did she love God? Of course—and she had come to love Him more deeply in the short time that she had been a nun.

On this morning, as war raged, there was nothing that she would rather do than serve God by helping others. This was the truth that kept her warm despite the cold.

Again, the door to the church stood open, although the entrance remained guarded. The guards barely gave her a glance as she came in. They were used to her coming and going by now.

She crinkled her nose against the smell that greeted her inside. The church always had been old and damp, but now she smelled the overflowing latrine buckets against the walls, the musky smell of unwashed male bodies crowded together, and an undercurrent of rotting meat from wounds that desperately needed treatment.

"Hello, Sister," said the young soldier named Joey, eagerly greeting her. He offered to take the heavy basket from her, but she declined, fearing that as weak as he looked, it might knock him down.

She reached up and touched the bandage around his head. The scalp wound had bled freely and now the cloth was stiff as tree bark. "How is your head?" she asked.

"Oh, I'm fine," he said. "A lot of these guys are worse off than me."

Unfortunately, Sister Anne Marie knew that to be true. "Let me see what I can do," she said. "Will you help?"

"Sure I will."

The basket was stuffed with as much as she had been able to forage. A few bottles of water and a few tins of things like canned sausages. She looked around at the more than two hundred men crowded into the church. What she had brought was not enough. What she needed was a miracle, but she was no saint. She dreaded the thought, but she might have to go to the German commander to see if he could help with supplies.

"You there!" shouted a deep voice from the doorway.

Sister Anne Marie turned, and her heart sank to see that it was the German sniper whom she thought she had avoided. "What do you want?" she demanded, realizing that she did not sound very sisterly just then.

"I want to see what's in that basket."

Beside her, she sensed Joey starting to take a step forward as if to intercept the German, protecting her. She was sure that would not end well. "No," she whispered to him, and the boy hung back.

The big soldier strode toward her, his deadly rifle with its telescopic sight slung over one shoulder. The guards had no intention of interfering. In fact, they seemed intimidated by the sniper. One of them intently studied the roof beams.

"There's nothing here that you would want," she said. "It is only supplies for the soldiers."

"Supplies for the *American* soldiers," the German pointed out. He reached into the basket and withdrew a jar of blackberry jam. "They do not deserve such luxuries. I will share this with the *German* soldiers."

Sister Anne Marie tried to lock eyes with the sniper, hoping that a stern look from a nun might help, but his face remained hard and unmoving. "Whatever you say," she said.

"I know," he said. "You are lucky that I am letting you keep any of it for *diese Schafe*." *These sheep*. "You know what sheep are good for, don't you? Mutton and chops. Sheep are not soldiers."

With that, the sniper turned and took his time walking out of the church.

Sister Anne Marie felt herself breathing again. Her heart pounded with fear—and anger, which she knew was not an entirely Christian emotion. She took a moment to breathe deeply and compose herself.

"I'd like nothing better than to tell that Kraut to go to hell," Joey said. He flicked an apologetic glance at her. "Sorry, Sister. No offense."

"None taken." She had been thinking about telling the German the same thing, even if she hadn't spoken it aloud. "Now, let's see if we can share this among the others."

Very quickly, the supplies that she had brought were used up. Once again, she had been forced to let the German soldier take what he wanted, which further cut into her supplies. Her medical skills were inadequate to treat the more grievously injured soldiers, who suffered silently. Unless they received real medical care, some might die.

As she and the young soldier passed out the last of what she had brought, she said, "I may have to appeal to a higher authority than these guards."

"God?" he asked, puzzled.

"No, the German commanding officer."

CHAPTER THIRTEEN

HER MIND MADE UP, Sister Anne Marie hurried down the street, dodging glances from the German soldiers she passed. Reluctantly, she had come to the conclusion that she must see the German commanding officer. The prisoners were short on supplies, lacking everything from food to blankets to basic medical attention. Ultimately, the prisoners were his responsibility. Sister Anne Marie could not provide for them, but perhaps he could.

Before crossing the street, she had kept an eye out for the sniper who had harassed her at the church. Sister Anne Marie liked to believe that there was good in everyone, but she had serious doubts about that particular soldier. She spotted a group of soldiers smoking cigarettes, bouncing on the balls of their feet to stay warm in the cold, and approached them.

"I am looking for your commanding officer," she announced to one of the young soldiers who appeared more cordial than the others.

"He is in that big house there," said the soldier, pointing to what Anne Marie knew to be the mayor's home before he fled. A look of concern crossed the soldier's face. "Is everything all right, Sister?"

"I am going to see your commanding officer on behalf of the American prisoners," she said.

"Are you sure that you want to do that?"

Nearby, one of his companions guffawed. "You won't get very far with Colonel Lang. He doesn't like civilians—or nuns."

But she remained undeterred. "Why wouldn't I go to see him? He is in charge, isn't he? I must discuss the care of the prisoners with him."

"In that case, I wish you luck," the young soldier said, shaking his head. "But if I were you, I would not argue too hard on behalf of the Americans."

The young soldier's comments had not been encouraging, but she continued toward the mayor's house, apparently now occupied by the commanding officer. Looking more closely, she could see two soldiers standing guard beside the door.

The mayor, along with the priest and the two town constables, had fled ahead of the Germans, leaving the villagers to fend for themselves without their leaders. Considering that the house was the grandest in the village and centrally located, it made sense that the German commander had moved in.

She approached the guards, who had been slouching against the wall, but now stood up straight as she walked toward them.

"What is it sister?" one of the guards asked brusquely.

"I am here to see your commanding officer."

"Colonel Lang is busy."

"It is important."

The soldier stared at her for a long moment, but she did not lower her gaze. She suspected that if she had not been wearing a nun's habit, she would have been sent on her way—or worse. He had not lowered his weapon.

"Wait here."

"Bless you," she said.

The soldier glanced at his companion, as if silently warning him to keep an eye on her, then went inside. He was back a minute later.

"Colonel Lang said he can spare five minutes for you, and no more."

She followed him inside. Immediately, she was struck by the trans-formation of the mayor's house, which had once been a respectable middle-class home with fine furniture and carpets, and even a few oil painting on the walls, valuable old landscapes that had been handed down through the family. Much of the village's business had been conducted there in the home's comfortable atmosphere, usually in the mayor's study on the first floor.

Now, the mayor's house was a shambles. Snow and mud had been tracked across the floors and carpets. Equipment and even cartridge boxes covered the tables and chairs. Windows bristled with machine guns, some of the glass broken out. The oil paintings were all gone, stolen along with anything else of value.

She was ushered into the mayor's study, where some of the furniture had been broken up and was now burning in the fireplace in an attempt to keep the winter chill at bay. That wasn't an easy task, considering that one of the windows was open to the cold air, telephone lines snaking through it to a pair of field telephones on what had been the mayor's desk.

Colonel Lang turned out to be a tall man of no more than forty years of age. His thinning blond hair was slicked back against his scalp. His boots were covered in slush and like his men, he wore several days of stubble on his face. He looked cranky and exhausted.

He shouted one last order into a telephone as she entered and then turned his attention to her.

Sister Anne Marie noticed the other men in the room. There was a young officer holding some papers who might be an adjutant of some kind, along with a clerk. With a tiny gasp of recognition, she saw that the sniper was also present. The man seemed to be everywhere, like the Devil himself. He looked at her with an expressionless face.

"What is it, Sister?" the officer demanded. "I only have a few minutes. I have to admit, I would not see you at all except that you represent the church."

"Thank you, Colonel," she said. "I have come with concerns about the prisoners."

"The Americans?" His eyebrows raised in surprise.

"You are holding two hundred and fifty-two men in the church."

"That's a very exact number. How do you know?"

"I counted them."

"Ah. What about them?"

"Many are wounded and need medical care. They need medicine and bandages that I do not have. They need food and water. They need blankets. I am asking you to provide for their care."

"Why trouble yourself about them?"

"They are in my church!"

"Where is the priest? Perhaps he could talk some sense into you."

"The priest ran away."

"He did, eh? He's a smarter man than many."

"Sir, I am doing what I can to help them, but the prisoners are your responsibility."

The colonel glanced at the sniper, who stood near the fireplace, warming his hands. "Do you hear that, Hauer? This nun is telling me my job. Apparently, I am to care for *prisoners*. I thought my job was to fight the war."

So the Devil had a name, she thought. *Hauer*.

Hauer flexed his broad shoulders. "Do you want me to throw her out, sir?"

The colonel stared at her and seemed to think over Hauer's offer. "Not yet. Sister, I would like nothing better than to shoot these prisoners and be done with them."

"You cannot!"

"Who says? You? God?" He shook his head. "Don't worry, Sister. We are not monsters. Besides, the Americans are very sensitive after what happened at the Malmedy Crossroads. As ridiculous as it seems when we are in the middle of killing one another, there are rules in war. The lives of German POWs hang in the balance. So you see, no harm will come to the prisoners because of the repercussions to our own men being held by the Allies."

He moved to the open window and gestured for her to join him.

"Sir?"

"Look out the window, Sister. Do you see that warehouse across the street? It is filled with wounded. My men. Good men. They need bandages and medicine and food that I do not have to give them. If I cannot help my own men, how can I possibly help the prisoners?"

Sister Anne Marie was surprised. She had assumed that the Germans were well-supplied. "I did not know."

"Find what supplies you can in the village," he said. "I can't help you, but I won't stop you. That is all."

He reached for a ringing telephone, dismissing her with the gesture as he turned his attention elsewhere.

As she left the room, she felt Hauer's eyes on her, following her out.

* * *

SISTER ANNE MARIE left the German commanding officer's headquarters and made her way back up the street in the direction of the church. Suddenly, she felt so very tired. Each footstep in the snow and cold took an effort. It was no wonder. She had been working almost around the clock to do what she could for the POWs. When was the last time that she had eaten or slept? She could not remember when that had been. All of her efforts had been so focused upon helping the prisoners in the church.

The thought of a hot bowl of soup and a nap was suddenly quite appealing, but she forced herself to keep putting one foot in front of the other under the watchful eyes of the soldiers she passed. Tired and discouraged as she was, she kept going. Perhaps it was blasphemous, but she thought of all that Jesus had suffered. Her hardships were nothing in comparison.

She felt that she had not accomplished much in meeting with the commanding officer, but she had at least tried. That was something, wasn't it? Anyhow, where one door closed, another opened.

Sister Anne Marie busied her mind with all of the things still left to do. She would go door to door again, asking for blankets and food. In the houses that people had fled, she might look into the empty rooms in hopes of finding some forgotten scrap of food to feed the prisoners. The German soldiers had already gone through the houses, but perhaps they had overlooked a blanket or jar of jam.

Something penetrated her fog of exhaustion, some primitive warning sense, and she looked over her shoulder.

Trailing her like an ominous shadow was the German sniper.

* * *

HAUER WATCHED THE NUN LEAVE. The colonel was busy on the telephone, so Hauer had slipped out to follow her up the street. Her nun's dark habit fluttered around her in the winter wind. *Where are you going, little crow?*

Hauer did not care for nuns. Of course, outside of an overall sense of warmth toward the Reich itself, he did not care for much other than himself, but nuns were still toward the bottom of his list.

Why? He found them sanctimonious and cruel. As a boy, he had attended a Catholic school. Hauer had excelled at sports and schoolyard bullying, but he never had been keen on his lessons. Consequently, the nuns had cracked his knuckles with rulers, ridiculed him, even beaten him with a stick on more than one occasion. He had hated those nuns, yet as a boy, there was nothing he could do about it.

Or so he thought.

One of the cruelest of the nuns had been Sister Agnes. The fact that he remembered her name was a testament to the lasting impression she had made. Of all the nuns, she was the one who singled him out the most with her cruelty.

"You are stupid!" she had said, making him stand in front of the class as she diminished him in front of the others. "*Dummkopf!* You will never amount to more than a street sweeper!"

He had glared at her then, so much venom in his angry stare that she had looked away.

Hauer never had a clear plan in mind, but he knew that one day he would get even with this evil witch. His chance had come one day when he had glimpsed Sister Agnes headed for the stairs. It was an old building and the stairs were steep. She paused at the top and reached for the railing.

The halls were crowded with students, talking and hurrying to the next class, which gave Hauer the perfect camouflage. Quick as a cat, in the second before she had gotten a good grip on the railing, Hauer slipped up behind the old nun and shoved her with all his might. By the time she started to fall, he had already melted back into the mix of children looking on, horrified, as Sister Agnes tumbled down the stairs, her black habit flapping like the feathers of a bird tumbling from the sky. She landed in a heap at the bottom of the stairs, moaning, one of her legs twisted at a terrible angle.

The boy had smiled, thinking, *Not such a* dummkopf, *am I?*

None of the other children had seen him. Still, he had half-expected to be struck down by a bolt of lightning. Instead, that one moment of action had left him blissfully free from the nun's tyranny.

Hauer had embraced the fact that officially Hitler's Germany was agnostic—the only true church being the Third Reich. In the early days, Hitler and his minions had rounded up any meddlesome priests and nuns, then locked them inside the concentration camp at Dachau.

Hauer thought that it was a good place for them. He had long ago cast off whatever shreds remained of his upbringing in the church. After all, he had turned his back on religion many years ago, when he had shoved that witch down the stairs.

As for this nun, perhaps she needed to be taught a lesson as well.

SHE TRIED to pick up her pace, but it was no use. Hauer quickly caught up to her. Her heart hammered, recalling that he had attempted to drop a dead man on her head. She glanced at the soldiers on duty along the street, but they either watched in amusement or looked away, clearly with no intention of interfering with whatever Hauer had in mind. The sniper seemed to intimidate many of his fellow soldiers.

"Where are you going in such a hurry?" he asked, falling into step beside her.

"If I cannot get help from your commanding officer, then I have much to do," she replied without looking at him. "Besides, if you have not noticed, it is quite cold out."

"I don't know why you are bothering with those prisoners," he said. "Why don't you help our good German wounded?"

"You have your own medical personnel," she said. "What do the Americans have?"

"I would not worry about them too much," he said. "We might still shoot them. Who knows?"

"I pray that you are wrong."

She felt Hauer's eyes staring intently at her face.

"You are too pretty to be a nun," he said. "Why would God waste you this way?"

"Waste me, how?" Sister Anne Marie was taken aback.

"Turn a pretty girl into a crow."

"That was God's decision, not mine."

Hauer suddenly grabbed her by the arm. "I would like to get you alone and teach you a thing or two that you did not learn in the convent." He gave her a lewd, knowing smile. "Maybe you can do more while on your knees than pray."

"Get your hands off me!"

Hauer did not let go, but began pushing her toward the doorway of an empty house. "Come, come. The prisoners can wait. This won't take long."

Hauer's intentions were all too clear. She slapped at his hands, but he didn't let go, dragging her closer to the empty house. Only a small desire for dignity kept her from screaming for help.

"Hauer! That is enough!"

An older soldier came toward them.

"Never mind about me, Scholz," Hauer said.

But the soldier wasn't having any of that. He blocked their path, forcing Hauer to stop. "A nun, Hauer? Really? What kind of *Dummkopf* are you?"

At the word *Dummkopf*, Hauer let go of Sister Anne Marie and rounded on the sergeant, big fists clenched in his leather gloves, clearly enraged.

"What did you call me?"

Hauer was much larger than the sergeant, but the man looked tough as an old tree stump left to weather in a field. He was not the least bit cowed by the sniper. He set his feet, his own fists clenched. If it was a fight Hauer wanted, it was clear he was going to get one. "I will call you whatever I want, *Gefreiter* Hauer. Get back to your post. That is an order."

Hauer glared at the noncommissioned officer, but kept his mouth shut. He turned his attention back to Sister Anne Marie. She did not think that she had ever seen such a look of malevolence. Thankfully, he had released his grip on her.

"This is not over, Sister," he said. "All the prayers in the world will not help you now."

CHAPTER FOURTEEN

THE COMMANDER of the U.S. forces poised to attack Wingen sur Moder had called a truce. He wanted a parlay with the Germans in the village. In preparation for meeting with the Germans, Colonel Allen had gathered a team that included Lieutenant Mulholland, an Army medic, and Private Cole. Cole still felt weak from his bout with the flu, but his fever had finally broken. He felt some of his old strength return with each passing hour.

"Why Cole, sir?" Lieutenant Mulholland had asked when he was momentarily alone with the colonel.

"Because Cole and that rifle of his look scary as hell," the colonel said. "Maybe it will help put the fear of God in these Krauts. Besides, I don't entirely trust these Krauts and if any shooting breaks out, I want Cole to have my back."

"I'll be there too, sir."

"I know you will, Lieutenant." The colonel seemed to ponder that thought. "Come to think of it, give Cole a submachine gun, too."

"Are you going to ask the Germans to surrender, sir?" Lieutenant Mulholland asked.

"Son, as much as I would like to do that, what do you think the chances are that the Krauts would surrender?"

"Slim to none, sir."

"Right, so I'm not going to waste my breath," the officer said. "They're welcome to volunteer to surrender. Besides, for all I know they'll be expecting us to surrender to *them*. We're pretty evenly matched up, you know. This fight could go either way."

The lieutenant looked taken aback. "I hadn't thought about that, sir. *Ich ergebe mich!*"

"What's that mean?"

"It's German for *I surrender*, sir. I suppose it could work in either direction, depending on how things play out."

"Well, don't brush up on your German phrases just yet, son. What I really what to talk to the Krauts about would be these prisoners. The villagers said they've got more than two hundred of our boys held in the church. From their reports, it sounds like a lot of those boy are in bad shape. I want to see if we can get any supplies to them. Food, blankets, bandages—whatever they need."

"Do you think that will work?"

"I'm sure the Krauts will steal whatever they want first, but something will get to the prisoners."

A response came back to the colonel's messenger, who had been sent into the village under a white flag. It all seemed very gentlemanly, this business of white flags and truces, like something out of an earlier era. But the flag had worked. The Germans hadn't shot the colonel's messenger, and now word came back that the Germans would meet.

* * *

THE FIGHT that was taking place at Wingen sur Moder was being mirrored in a handful of other places throughout the rugged terrain as the German's Operation *Nordwind* continued. The advance was Hitler's version of a one-two punch. Truth be told, Hitler had hit them hard. However, the American forces were proving to be tough adversaries.

Some of the fighting took place in and around towns, while in other locations, the fighting was dictated by nothing more than the collision of troops from both sides. The much-feared German Panzers had managed to press deep into the Allied lines, creating yet another bulge known as the Colmar Pocket.

But the German advance encountered difficulties, bogging down before long. Even the heaviest Panzers struggled for traction on the steep, snowy roads through the mountain forests. There was also the matter of food and fuel. The men needed one; the tanks and trucks needed the other. The Germans simply didn't have the supply lines to supply the essentials of food and fuel. The whole situation was like a rubber band that kept stretching and stretching—at some point it was either going to break or snap back into place, its energy spent.

Meanwhile, massive Soviet forces pressed closer to Berlin. The Third Reich was fighting for its life on two fronts against determined adversaries, a situation that was impossible to sustain.

The maps were something for the generals to worry about, however. For every soldier on both sides, the only battle that really mattered was the one that he fought in. His war was often limited to his foxhole and the man fighting beside him.

So far, the Americans held the hills to the south and west, as well as the main road leading into town, the one that led to the railroad underpass where the disastrous first encounter with the Germans had taken place. The Germans still held the big hill almost due north, overlooking the town. Though their force was divided, their defensive strategy proved quite effective.

Holding that high ground, with the ability to put machine-gun fire or mortars on all of the approaches to town, gave the defenders a distinct advantage. It was assumed that the German troops on the hill maintained contact with the rest of the unit in the town through radio communication or telephone lines. If the Americans could cut that line at some point, it would give them an advantage.

Like the Americans, the Germans had laid down endless miles of wire as they advanced because the hills severely limited radio communication.

Unlike the Germans in the village, the Americans were roughing it in the woods and fields surrounding Wingen sur Moder. They didn't have the benefit of buildings to get out of the wind. Instead, the U.S. forces sheltered in cold foxholes.

They had enough to eat, if you could call combat rations enough. Everything was eaten half-frozen. The more fortunate soldiers warmed up their food on the engine block of a tank or truck to at least take the chill off. They didn't even have hot coffee because orders had come down against building any fires that might give away their positions to the enemy.

The men grumbled about that. It wasn't as if the Germans didn't know they were out here.

It would have been better if the snow and ice hadn't turned to slush in the bottom of the foxholes. The freezing slush soaked everybody and made them colder.

"I've had enough of this snow," Vaccaro said, his teeth chattering violently. "When I get back home, I swear I'm going to buy a place in Florida. Maybe New Mexico or Arizona."

"You'll be bitching about the heat come summer, City Boy," Cole pointed out.

"Hell no, Hillbilly. All that I'll need to do is think about this place and I'll cool right off. Better than air conditioning."

"I reckon I'd rather have it cold than hot all the time, like them fellas fighting in the Pacific. I hear tell the air is so swampy that they get jungle rot in places you don't even want to think about."

They thought about that anyway, and the images that came to mind made them cringe. "We've got frostbite and trench foot," Vaccaro pointed out. "I'm telling you—Florida."

Cole just shook his head. "Florida is way too flat for me. I need mountains."

"Yeah, then you should feel right at home in this place."

Cole was cleaning his rifle, working gun oil into the action, smoothing it over the barrel. The cold could make the oil gum up, so Cole had slipped out the bolt and put it inside his coat to stay warm. The rifle positively gleamed, which was something of an accomplishment in the grimy, slush-filled foxhole.

"I can tell that you're feeling better," Vaccaro said. "You were so sick before that you went a couple of days without cleaning that rifle—as if it even needed it."

"I had to get better," Cole said. "We're about to launch another attack. You need me around to make sure you don't get your ass shot off."

"Shot off? Well, that's a relief. For a while there, I was worried that I was going to *freeze* my ass off."

* * *

HAVING AGREED TO A TEMPORARY TRUCE, the two sides met on the road leading to the village. The snowy, ice-covered surface of the road had been packed as hard as asphalt by the passage of trucks and tanks. Cold wind blew through the valley, carrying a few flakes of snow. With sunset approaching, the sun dipped low toward the surrounding mountains, tinging the sky in yellow and purple tones, like a brilliant bruise.

The approaching sunset left Cole feeling wistful. Considering that the fight for the town would begin before first light tomorrow morning, it was unsettling to think about who might not be around to see the next evening's sunset.

Looking over the Germans, he recalled General Patton's words, "No bastard ever won a war by dying for his country. He won it by making the other poor dumb bastard die for his country."

Cole hefted the submachine gun draped across his chest, eager to help those other poor dumb bastards do their part. Cole was armed to the teeth. Along with the submachine gun, his rifle was slung within easy reach over his shoulder. He wore a .45 in a side holster. His wicked-looking Bowie knife, custom made for him by his old friend Hollis Bailey, was stuck in his belt, Indian-fighter style.

"Keep your eyes open, son," Colonel Allen had muttered to Cole, somewhat unnecessarily. "I wouldn't trust these Kraut bastards as far as I could throw them."

To Cole's surprise, it was clear that the colonel was nervous about this meeting. "Yes, sir."

The group going to parlay with the enemy consisted of the colonel, Lieutenant Mulholland, a medic, and Cole. Only Cole was armed. Mulholland carried a white rag tied to a stick, which made him look vaguely silly.

Of course, an entire company of GIs was ready to open up at long range with their M-1 rifles if the need should arise. But if that happened, there was a good chance that the colonel and all the rest would already be dead.

Similarly, by prior agreement, the German officers coming to meet them were not armed—with the exception of their pistols, Cole noticed. The pistols were tucked away into holders with a leather flap —not exactly a quick-draw weapon.

What was surprising was that the Germans had brought a civilian with them.

"What the hell?" the colonel said. "Is that a *nun?*"

Sure enough, a Catholic nun had accompanied the Germans to the parlay. Cole was struck by the fact that the nun was quite pretty, her youthful face framed by the nun's habit she wore.

Cole wasn't the only one was staring. With an effort, he flicked his eyes away from the nun to focus his attention on the one German who, like Cole himself, had come armed to this meeting. Like Cole, the man carried a submachine gun and a rifle. The German's rifle also had a telescopic sight. Another sniper, then.

Perhaps it shouldn't have been too surprising that the German officer had also chosen a sniper as a sort of bodyguard. In both armies, the snipers were not only the best all-around shots, but also the men who tended to be coolest under pressure. They wouldn't lose control and start shooting. And if they did have to shoot, they weren't going to miss.

As the other man came closer, Cole studied him. The details of the German's face became more evident.

Cole felt a current of shock go through him. He knew this man. It was the same sniper whom Cole had fought against at Ville sur Moselle. His presence here verified that Cole hadn't killed him, after all—that was a disappointment. This sniper had been a real bastard, murdering some villagers who had decided to play soldier. Their deaths had been cruel and unnecessary.

The enemy sniper seemed to recognize Cole as well. His eyes widened when he got a good look at Cole's face. But after that first glimmer of surprise, a smile played across his thick lips.

Quickly, the officers made brief introductions. The German officer saved the sniper for last. "That is Hauer. We call him The Butcher."

Colonel Allen nodded in Cole's direction. "That's Cole. We call him Hillbilly."

While the officers got on with the negotiations, Cole and the enemy sniper settled into trying to stare one another down, fingers resting gently on the triggers of their submachine guns.

The officers got down to brass tacks. No mention of surrender was made by either side.

"I understand that you are holding American prisoners in the village," Colonel Allen began.

"This is correct," the German officer responded. "Two hundred and fifty-two to be exact. Well, two hundred and fifty-one. I believe one died this morning. If I were you, Colonel, I would avoid using any heavy weapons against this village, or there may be even fewer prisoners."

The colonel bristled. "Is that a threat?"

"No, only a commentary on your poor aim. If a stray shell hits the church, you are the one responsible."

"You could let them go."

"Come now, Colonel," the German remarked, as if the American officer had just said something mildly amusing. "If you were in my shoes, would you let your prisoners go?"

"It was worth a try, I suppose."

The German turned to the nun, who had remained quiet, watching the exchange between the two men. "This is Sister Anne Marie. She has expressed special concern for the prisoners and has been caring for them. She can tell you what supplies are needed for them."

"Thank you, Sister," the colonel said. "How are the prisoners doing?"

Clearing her throat, the young nun spoke up. "They are doing as well as can be expected," she said. "However, some of them are wounded and need medical attention. They are hungry. I asked Colonel Lang for supplies, but he said that he had none to spare."

The German shrugged. "That is the truth. Anyhow, I have allowed the nun to help your men as best she can."

"Listen, what I want to do is send supplies to those prisoners. I've got blankets and rations ready. Corporal Gregory here is a medic who volunteered to go back with you and see to their medical needs."

The German acknowledged the medic with a nod. "Corporal Gregory, you are a brave man. Come back with us, then. No harm will come to you. Is that all, Colonel?"

"That is all. Thank you."

The two officers saluted. No mention of surrender had been made by either side.

The German sniper edged closer and to Cole's surprise whispered in heavily accented English, "I will see you later, Hillbilly."

Then the two groups went their separate ways, boots crunching on the snow-packed road. The medic went with the Germans, hauling a sled that was loaded with supplies. Cole noticed that the nun was the only one who wasn't wearing heavy winter gear or footwear. Cole thought she must be freezing, but she had not complained.

Out of earshot of the enemy soldiers, Colonel Allen remarked, "I think that went well. Best we could expect, under the circumstances. I just hope some of those supplies make it to our boys and that I didn't just hand over all that food to the Krauts."

* * *

As the German entourage returned to the village, Colonel Lang strode purposefully, forcing the others to keep up. Hauer practically trotted along beside him.

"Hauer, I thought you and that American sniper were going to shoot one another back there. Did you see the look he gave you?"

"He is nothing to worry about."

"You don't think so? Ha! If the Americans had another two hundred like him instead of those clerks in the church, we would not be the ones holding this village. The war would have been over already."

"Maybe I will have the chance to finish him off tomorrow when they attack us."

"I certainly hope so. Meanwhile, take half of the supplies they gave us to our own wounded. The nun and that medic can have the rest for the prisoners."

"Yes, sir."

"Do you know what else, Hauer? We just saw why the Americans are going to win the war."

Hauer was visibly taken aback. "Why is that, sir?"

"We are less than a hundred miles from Germany, and yet we have no supplies. The Americans are thousands of miles from their homeland, and yet they have supplies to spare."

"If you say so, sir. Just so long as we have enough bullets, that is enough."

The colonel shook his head. "Bullets don't always win wars, Hauer. You also need blankets and full bellies."

CHAPTER FIFTEEN

THE ATTACK WAS SET to begin in the coldest hours before dawn. The sky had cleared, leaving stars strewn across the void. In the distance, a fox barked, a sign that nature was oblivious to the soldiers at the edge of the forest.

"Cold enough for you?" Vaccaro muttered too loudly, his voice carrying in the winter air.

"Shut up, Vaccaro," Lieutenant Mulholland whispered harshly. He was as nervous as anyone. It was Mulholland who would be leading them right into those German machine guns when they opened up. The others just had to follow. "You want to let the Krauts know we're coming? Then keep it up."

Chastised, Vaccaro fell into a sullen silence. In the dark, Cole just shook his head. Vaccaro always talked too much when he got nervous.

They stood in a ring of men, breath steaming like smoke, stamping their feet for some warmth, nervously checking and re-checking weapons. One or two men fumbled with their heavy clothing to relieve themselves yet again, not even bothering to take more than a couple of steps away. The last thing anybody wanted was to have to go during a fight. Though craving nicotine, the men weren't allowed to light a cigarette, for fear that the sudden flare of a match would warn the enemy.

Given their concerns about being seen by the enemy, the starlight was a blessing and a curse. Reflected by the blanket of snow, the starlight provided the men preparing to attack with a little much-needed light. On the other hand, the light might reveal their movements to the Germans. Down the frozen road, across the valley, they could see the sleepy village, soon to be the target of their attack.

Like the others, Cole and Vaccaro had hardly slept, having been roused from their freezing foxholes as soon as they fell asleep, or so it seemed.

The captain came along, hurrying from squad to squad. "I need a couple of volunteers," he said.

"I'm guessing it's not to run down to Paris and bring back a case of champagne," Vaccaro muttered.

"Lucky you, Vaccaro," the lieutenant said. "You just volunteered."

Vaccaro groaned. "For what?"

"We need to cut the line of communication between the Germans in the village and the ones on the hill," the captain explained. He handed Vaccaro a pair of wire cutters. "They've got a telephone line running up there. See if you can find the damn thing and cut it."

"Sir, won't they just use their radio if that happens?"

"Sure they have radios, but if they're like ours they don't work right in these hills," the captain said. "Go cut that wire."

Orders given, the captain hurried off into the dark.

Mulholland spoke up. "Vaccaro, you heard the captain. Take Cole with you, if he's up to it. If Cole goes with you, there's at least a chance that you'll come back in one piece. We attack at oh six hundred, so get a move on."

"Yes, sir."

Vaccaro turned to Cole. "Aren't you glad that you're feeling better?"

Cole shook his head. He was feeling much better than he had been, but he wasn't eager for this mission to cut the German wires. "City Boy, what have you and your big mouth gone and gotten us into?"

"Good luck," Mulholland said. "Remember, the attack starts whether you're back here or not, so hustle."

Before they started out, Cole reached into his pack and brought out a white smock that he had taken off a dead German. For whatever reason, the U.S. Army had been slow in adapting to this simple form of camouflage that was so effective in the snow. Cole even had a helmet cover. It was for a German helmet, but it fit well enough. While the camouflage wasn't perfect, it went a long way toward helping him melt into the snowy backdrop.

"What about me?" Vaccaro asked.

"I took this off a prisoner," Cole said. "I guess you'll just have to capture a German."

"Or shoot one."

"Not if he shoots you first, which seems more likely, on account of how you make a right good target in all this snow. You stand out like a preacher at a whore house."

"Great."

The two moved off into the field. They were both exposed, but there was no helping it. Fortunately, some thin clouds were passing over the stars. If the moon had been out, a trip across the field would have been pure suicide.

They started across the snowy slope leading toward the hill north of town. While the Germans held the village, they also had troops on the hilltop, giving them the high ground above the entire valley. From up there, they had a clear field of fire to drop mortars or bring machine guns to bear on much of the ground surrounding the village. The troops themselves were hidden from view by the forest, but had a clear view out—almost like a one-way mirror in a funhouse.

You had to hand it to the Jerries, Cole thought. They knew their business, inside and out. Whoever controlled that hill could rain hellfire down on the approaches to the village, so the Germans had made sure that they were dug in up there.

What does that leave us? he wondered.

The Americans controlled the road leading toward the village. Unfortunately, to reach the village, they would have to go through the railroad underpass that had been the scene of the disastrous assault on the village earlier, before it was understood that the Germans were there in strength. The wrecked hulk of the Sherman tank still stood in the middle of the road, creating a barrier against further attack.

As the captain had noted, the success of the German defense also meant being able to coordinate between the forces in the village and those on the hill.

That was where Cole and Vaccaro came in.

"How in the hell are we ever going to find that wire?" Vaccaro wondered, speaking quietly. They were both well aware of being exposed, and how far sound carried in the still night air. With no choice, they climbed higher up the slope. The snow wasn't more than eight inches deep, but between the snow and last fall's deep grass, it was just enough to make crossing the slope difficult. Before long, they were both breathing hard. Cole realized that he could have used another day or two to recover from his bout with the flu.

"With any luck, we'll see the tracks where the German engineers laid that wire down," Cole said. "There ain't been much snow since then. Not more than a dusting, anyhow."

"If we see it, can't you just shoot the wire from here?"

"Yeah, that would be real smart. We'd have every German in those trees shooting back at us."

"I noticed that you didn't say you couldn't hit the wire. It was the noise you were worried about. I mean, I was talking about shooting a *wire*."

"Yep," Cole said.

Vaccaro waved the wire cutters. "I guess we'll have to do this the hard way."

They trudged through the field, glad for the clouds, but keeping a wary eye on the trees above them. The tree-line began a couple of hundred feet away. They couldn't see the Germans, but they were there, all right.

Finally, up ahead, they saw where the snow had been disturbed. In fact, a regular trail had been beaten through the snow, likely with men and supplies moving between the hill and village below.

"Give me the cutters," Cole said. "You stay here."

"What?"

"I'm the one with the camouflage, remember? If the Krauts have eyes on anything, they'll have them on that trail."

Cole unslung his rifle and moved on alone, taking his time. He wanted his motions to be slow and steady in order to attract less attention, just in case he was visible at all against the snowy backdrop. Although it was still dark, snow had a funny way of gathering what light there was.

He found the rubber-coated wire, half-buried in the snow. He had to take off his gloves to work the wire cutters, but soon found that the damn things were useless. Dull as a butterknife. The wire just kept getting hung up in the blades. Not only that, but his cold fingers couldn't seem to get enough leverage to cut through the wire, anyhow. Now what? Maybe Vaccaro was right. Maybe he'd have to shoot through the wire, after all.

But he had a better idea. Cole drew the big Bowie knife, placed the edge closest to the hilt against the wire, and started sliding the blade. After a moment of initial resistance, the knife cut right through the copper wire. Satisfied that the phone up on that hill had just gone dead, he started back toward Vaccaro.

He hadn't gone far before the shooting started. Down on the road below, the attack into the village had begun. Tracers flashed across the snow, with fire from the village answering. From the hill above them, a mortar fired, and then another. More flashes lit the night. It was quite a fireworks show.

Cole and Vaccaro found themselves caught out in the open.

"Now what are we supposed to do?" Vaccaro wondered, crouching in the snow, his rifle aimed toward the trees.

"Forget that," Cole said. "We're sitting duck out here. Run!"

No sooner had Cole spoken, then a burst of fire stitched across the snow nearby. Cole felt the ice crystals kicked up by the burst sting his face.

They both ran like hell.

* * *

ON THE ROAD, two Sherman tanks raced toward the village. Despite the dark, it was fairly easy for the drivers to follow the road. The lead tank charged ahead, engine roaring, spouting exhaust that was lost in the darkness, while the second tank moved along slightly to the left and behind the other.

Although the tanks didn't show any lights, their sound and fury were enough to give them away. Tracers from their machine guns lit the night.

Both tanks had crew manning the fifty-caliber machine guns on the turrets. Mounted in the mid-sections of the tanks, the thirty-caliber machine guns blazed away, making the tanks seem like gunfighters shooting from the hip.

However, the tanks were holding back their firepower, avoiding use of their main .75 millimeter guns. A few tank rounds would have gone a long way toward putting a dent in the defenses in the village. But if one of those rounds went astray and hit the church, every last one of the POWs inside might be killed. Consequently, the tanks had been ordered to use only their machine guns in leading the assault into the village.

Even without their main guns, the tanks possessed plenty of fire-power. The sight of those tracers sizzling through the cold and dark was dazzling.

Higher on the slope, Cole and Vaccaro skidded to a stop.

"Look at those tanks. Now that's a beautiful sight," panted Vaccaro. Both he and Cole paused long enough to watch the attack, using the time to catch their breath and get their bearings. "Give 'em hell, fellas!"

"Shout that a little louder," Cole said, breathing hard. "I don't think the Germans heard you."

"It doesn't matter, Hillbilly. Those tanks will put those Jerries on the run."

"I hope you're right," Cole said. "We'll see."

The Germans in the village had been expecting the attack, and they were prepared. Soon, the staccato *ratatatat* of "Hitler's Zipper" could be heard. The deadly German MG-42 machine guns had an incredible range. Although they were useless against the armored tanks themselves, the exposed gunners on the tanks were being targeted. Sparks flew and tracers bounced as a stream of enemy fire scored a hit on one of the tanks. The big fifty fell silent. It was all too easy to figure out what had happened to the machine gunner on the tank.

Suddenly, a rocket of fire shot from the German position, detonating against the lead tank. An explosion rocked the night, blinding everyone's night vision. Lying in wait, Kraut soldiers had just hit the lead tank with a *Panzerfaust*. Time and again, these shoulder-fired weapons had proved more than effective against a Sherman tank.

Cole held his breath, praying that the tank hadn't already been knocked out. They needed all the help they could get peeling open the village, and the tank made a pretty good can opener.

"They made it!" cried Vaccaro.

"Amen to that," Cole said.

Sure enough, they could see the tank forging ahead, fragments of burning debris clinging to its armored front. The *Panzerfaust* had scored only a glancing blow. For now, the nimble Sherman remained in the fight.

The tanks roared ahead, directly toward the underpass where the previous attack had bogged down. In the wake of the tanks, they could see dark shapes just visible against the snow. The infantry was advancing.

"Looks like we're late to the dance," Vaccaro said, also noticing the movement on the road.

"Oh, I reckon this party will go on for a while," Cole replied. "Let's go see if we can catch up."

Cole hadn't taken more than two steps when the guns opened up on the hillside above them. It was the two captured anti-tank guns, being used against the Americans. Although he and Vaccaro had cut the communication lines, it was clear that the Germans on the hillside knew well enough what their role was in this fight.

The muzzle blasts from the two big guns punched holes in the darkness, lighting up the trees on the hillside. In the sudden flash, they could see German troops advancing down the slope. The Jerries were counter-attacking.

Adding to their horror, it was evident to Cole and Vaccaro that the artillery must have been zeroed in ahead of the attack, with their sights set on the entrance to the railroad underpass. Just as the lead tank approached the tunnel, both shots from the German artillery struck in rapid succession.

Hit twice, the Sherman didn't stand a chance. A fireball engulfed the tank, gouts of flame shooting from the gash ripped into its armor and erupting from the open turret. Nobody could have survived that, Cole thought. The tank crew must have died instantly, the poor bastards.

Beside him, Vaccaro gasped in disbelief.

There was nothing so discouraging to an infantryman as seeing a tank destroyed. If a big can of armored whomp ass bought it, what chance did a guy with boots and a rifle have?

Seeing the fate of the lead tank, the second Sherman immediately began to reverse, getting itself out of the killing zone.

However, it wasn't quite fast enough. Another pair of shots came from the forest above the town, the flash of the guns again turning the valley into daylight in the way that a lightning bolt does.

The two shells struck with devastating force, obliterating what was left of the first Sherman. Luckily for the second tank, it had reversed just in time. The impact showered the tank with clods of frozen earth and burning debris, but the only casualty was the crew member manning the machine gun, killed instantly by shrapnel.

Rather than advance into certain death, the surviving Sherman took a different tact. Driving right into a roadside ditch to give the tank at least some protection, the Sherman finally brought its .75 millimeter gun into play. There weren't any American prisoners in the forested hillside above to worry about—but only German targets. The Sherman crew didn't need as long to aim as the artillery pieces above took to reposition. Less than a minute after running to ground in the ditch, the Sherman opened fire. On the hillside above, splintered trees flew. Direct hit or not, the tank had given the German gunners something to think about.

"Chew on that, Jerry!" Vaccaro shouted.

"Keep your head down, City Boy."

Now the Germans fired back, but far overshot the tank. Their shells crashed into a field, empty except for a small barn that was destroyed, sending chunks of stone and wood flying through the night.

The duel had begun.

However, the GIs were not sticking around to watch the duel play out. On foot, the American troops headed for the village kept their heads down, listening to shrapnel whistle through the darkness. Nobody could see a damn thing in the dark now that the explosions and muzzle flashes had wrecked their night vision.

The tanks hadn't succeeded in pushing into the village; now it was up to them.

The real fight for Wingen sur Moder was about to begin.

CHAPTER SIXTEEN

COLE AND VACCARO ran to join the assault, latching onto the troops moving toward the underpass. By some minor miracle, they found their squad and Lieutenant Mulholland.

"Cole, is that you? Damn, I thought you were Germans sneaking up on us."

"Sorry to disappoint you, sir."

"No disappointment there, believe me. We've got plenty of Germans as it is, right in front of us. Did you cut those telephone wires?"

"That we did, for all the good it did. Those Kraut guns are just getting warmed up. They didn't need anyone to tell them what to do. They already had their guns sighted in."

"You've got that right. They're tearing us up." Mulholland shouted orders, "Everyone, spread out and get ready to climb over those railroad tracks. We're not taking the tunnel. At this point, it would be like trying to run through a sausage grinder."

It went without saying that with the enemy artillery having targeted the underpass, trying to go through it would have been suicide. Not only that, but the burning hulk of the tank partially blocked the entrance to the tunnel. There was no way past it without being singed. A sickening smell of burning flesh drifted in the pre-dawn air.

Down in the roadside ditch, the surviving Sherman was still firing at the German position on the hilltop. Already, the plan of attack had gone to pieces and the officers were having to improvise.

The soldiers fanned out and began climbing the embankment and crossing the railroad tracks, then rushing pell-mell down the other side.

All the while, the German machine guns kept up their deadly *ratatatat*. As the tracer fire lit the scene with an eerie glow, Cole could see soldiers falling as the machine-gun took its toll. Some of the wounded or their companions called for a medic. Other crumpled forms lay still and silent.

"Follow me," Mulholland shouted.

The lieutenant led his men up and over the railroad embankment and they raced toward town. By now, dawn approached, tinging the horizon a deep shade of blood red. It was a warrior's dawn, if Cole had ever seen one. Despite the red dawn, the morning was cold as ever. The bright colors promised as much warmth as a can of paint.

They cut away from the road, getting out from the machine gun's line of fire. It was a feeling like stepping out of a downpour or hailstorm. Slowly, as the light grew, houses, outbuildings, even fences began to take shape as the squad advanced. With any luck, they could start to flank the German defenses, which had been set up to cover an attack from the road. That didn't mean the enemy didn't have defenses set up elsewhere.

"Keep your eyes open, everybody. If we can see them, they can see us."

In the murky pre-dawn light, six figures suddenly appeared from a ditch and charged at them, shouting as they ran. Rifle shots crackled.

"Krauts!"

Cole leveled his rifle and dropped one of the enemy, but they were too close to get off another shot. He reached for his Bowie knife, thinking that maybe he could stab one of the bastards.

But there was no need. A burst of machine-gun fire came from their left. The line of Germans went down. Not all of them were hit, however. Some had thrown themselves to the ground instinctively and managed to dodge the deadly burst. They began to get back up.

Cole had a new round loaded and started to aim.

But Mulholland had gotten in the way.

"Not so fast, Hans!" Mulholland grabbed a rifle away from one of the Germans, then dragged the soldier to his feet. Vaccaro grabbed another German. "Hands up! *Hände hoch!*"

The Germans did as ordered. Soon, they had three prisoners standing before them with their hands up. Three bodies lay inert in the snow. Vaccaro went over and poked at them, but they didn't move.

Mulholland made the prisoners get on their knees in the snow, hands on their heads.

Cole watched the Germans warily, keeping them in his sights. "We ain't got time for prisoners, Lieutenant. We ought to just shoot 'em. Stand back and I'll take care of it."

"Hold it, Cole! Battalion could use some intel. We'll send these three back to see what they can tell us."

Cole didn't lower his rifle. It was as if the weapon had a mind of its own. They were in the middle of an attack. Prisoners required guarding. He told himself that he was being practical, not cruel. He was a hard man, but not a monster.

But truth be told, he had seen too many good American boys killed. In his mind's eye, he could picture all the bodies in the snow from this bloody Battle of the Bulge. What a goddamn waste. He couldn't seem to take his finger off the trigger.

The Germans must have seen something in Cole's stance. He wasn't a captor, but a killer. Beneath the rim of his helmet, his eyes glittered in the light of the winter's dawn and the fires burning in town.

One of the prisoners began to plead quietly, *"Bitte, bitte, bitte."*

Mulholland looked over and saw Cole standing there as if frozen in place. "Cole, that's an order!"

"What about those poor bastards at Malmedy, Lieutenant? Do you reckon they ever had a chance?"

"Dammit, Cole! Don't make me say it again!"

Reluctantly, Cole lowered the rifle. "Have it your way, Lieutenant.

You want me and Vaccaro to take these Krauts to HQ? We'll be back here in no time."

"Hell, no. I'm not sure they would make it with you guarding them." Mulholland looked around. He turned to another soldier in the squad. The man had been wounded lightly in the arm. "Private, take these prisoners back to HQ. See to that arm while you're at it."

"Yes, sir," the private said. "C'mon, Hans. On your feet. Looks like it's your lucky day."

The lieutenant turned back to Cole and glared at him. Now that it was getting lighter, the anger in his face was clear. "If it's Germans you want to kill so badly, Cole, then follow me. There's plenty more of them in the village."

"Yes, sir."

Cole felt chastened. The lieutenant was right. What had he been thinking? He realized that he had been fighting this war too damn long.

* * *

WITH THE AMERICANS now entering the village, the narrow streets had been turned into a battleground. Some of the Germans were veterans of the fighting in the Soviet Union and were all too familiar with street fighting. Wingen sur Moder was no Stalingrad, but the battle for the town was becoming just as vicious.

Very efficiently, the Germans had placed machine-gun positions at the street corners, giving each machine-gun nest a clear line of fire in several directions. All that the attackers could do was scurry from house to house, trying to stay under cover until those machine guns could be knocked out.

"Every last one of these houses has been turned into a damned bunker," Vaccaro said. "They can hit us from any direction. What the hell are we supposed to do?"

"We take this village one house at a time, that's what," Cole replied. "Now, cover me."

Without waiting for a response, Cole dashed toward the nearest house. It was tall and narrow, offering a good vantage point up and down the street.

His movement was met with muzzle flashes from the windows, then bullets plucking at the snow around his feet, but he managed to reach the back corner of the house and hugged the wall. He stayed there for a moment, gasping for breath and realizing that he still felt pretty weak from the flu. Suddenly, he found himself having a terrible coughing fit. Hell, maybe he ought to still be in bed instead of being out here, fighting the war.

Inside the house, the Germans could hear him. He could definitely hear *them* inside, shouting excitedly to one another. The angle was all wrong for the Germans in the house to get a shot at him. However, he couldn't just hide out here all day. Vaccaro was right about every house being a bunker. At any moment, somebody might spot him and pick him off.

One of the Germans leaned out of an upstairs window, trying to get a glimpse of where the American had gone. Cole raised his rifle and fired, sending the enemy soldier tumbling to the snowy ground.

There was another open window on the ground floor, but none of the Krauts was dumb enough to stick his head out. Cole got down low and crawled under the window. Across the way, he spotted Vaccaro, giving him covering fire. Bullets smacked into the house. Cole just hoped to hell that Vaccaro didn't shoot him by accident.

From his position under the window, Cole pulled the pin on a grenade and lobbed it inside. The ear-splitting blast was almost instantaneous. He heard screams and curses despite his ringing ears. Leaping to his feet, he fired through the window at anything moving in the smoke.

There were still Germans upstairs, though, and they weren't too happy. He could hear them shouting angrily and rushing down the stairs. The interior of the house echoed with automatic fire. Cole ducked back down; his single-shot Springfield wasn't any match for that. Now what?

He needn't have worried. In the confusion, Vaccaro had scrambled across to the house. He emptied a clip from his semi-automatic M-1 into the interior of the house, and then for good measure, tossed in another grenade.

"Fire in the hole!"

Another blast tore through the downstairs, followed by more screams. The grenade had silenced the enemy within. This was going to be an ugly business, repeating the same process from house to house. Not all of the attacks on the houses were one-sided victories, like this one had been. The growing number of American bodies in the streets was evidence of that.

"You all right?" he shouted at Vaccaro, even though the City Boy was just a few yards away. Neither of them could hear a damn thing, thanks to the gunfire and grenades.

"I don't have any holes in me, if that's what you mean."

"All right, then. I'm going in."

Cole slung the rifle, put both hands on the windowsill, and levered himself inside. His boots came down on something soft. A dead Kraut. In the light from the window, he got a good look at the face. The dead German was young—maybe just a teenager—and quite handsome, blond, his blue eyes now staring. Cole felt a twinge of regret, and just as quickly snapped it off like a light switch. *Start thinking that way and it will get you killed*, he thought. A few minutes ago, this German lad had been trying to shoot him. Hell, not so long before that, Cole had been more than ready to shoot those German prisoners. What the hell had gotten into him? It seemed like sometimes he got in a killing mood and it was hard to shake.

Vaccaro came in through the other window. Cole unslung his rifle. Together, they made their way from room to room, making sure that there weren't any surprises. The air smelled heavily of cordite and fresh butchering. They found a handful of dead Krauts, killed either by the grenades or their rifle fire. One of the Germans was still moving, but he was badly wounded, barely even conscious. Cole finished him off with a mercy shot, then started upstairs.

Unlike the downstairs, the second floor was thankfully free of any dead Germans. The furniture was a jumble, everything having been dragged toward the windows and piled up—mattresses, bed frames, dressers, linen chests. Basically, anything that had a chance of stopping a bullet.

Cole peeked out one of the windows. Below, spread-eagled in the snow, he could see the body of the German he had shot. Beyond, the house offered a commanding view up the street toward the Catholic church, which wasn't more than two hundred feet distant.

"Hey, isn't that where the prisoners are being held?" Vaccaro asked, joining him at the window.

"That's what the lieutenant said," Cole replied.

"Do you think the two of us have a prayer of getting to that church?"

Cole thought about the machine-gun nests lining the streets, and the other well-defended houses between here and there. "Hell, no."

"Then what's our next move?"

Cole thought about that. "We're gonna stay right here and do what we do best."

"Yeah? What is that, by the way?"

Cole put a pillow across the windowsill to create a pad, then set his rifle across it. The window offered a perfect vista not only of the church, but of anything that moved on the street leading to it.

"Shoot Germans, that's what," Cole said, pulling the rifle tight against his shoulder. "You call out any targets you see. And keep an eye out for any Germans making a move on us. This is our house now."

CHAPTER SEVENTEEN

LIKE AN INCOMING TIDE, the U.S. troops worked their way deeper into the village. From the second-floor window of the house that they had captured from the enemy, Cole and Vaccaro watched the soldiers move up the street. It wasn't an easy task. Other houses were still held by the Germans, who peppered the attackers with fire. The Germans also held the street corner nearest the church, where a machine gun kept up a steady and withering fire. There were few sounds as sure to send a shiver up the spine of a GI as that.

However, it wasn't just the machine gun that the attackers had to worry about. Occasional rifle shots rang out with deadly accuracy, dropping Americans in their tracks. Cole had wondered what had become of The Butcher, and now he knew. He also had a good idea of where the sniper was located. Like Cole, he had chosen a high place with a good view of the streets below.

"That Kraut sniper is in the church steeple," Cole said.

"Can you see him?"

"Not yet."

"He picked a good spot," Vaccaro said, scanning the church. "He knows we can't take him out with a tank or a grenade launcher, not with that church full of our guys."

"He's also got himself a bird's eye view up there. He's higher than we are, anyhow."

Cole pressed his eye tight against the telescopic sight, focusing every bit of his concentration on the church steeple. He was hoping for a glimpse of movement that would provide him with a target.

It wasn't the first time that Cole had encountered a sniper in a church. A question occurred to him that he hadn't asked before.

"Vaccaro, are you Catholic?"

"Sure I am. Well, don't expect me to be carrying rosary beads or anything, but yeah, I'm Catholic."

"Huh."

"What are you?"

"God-fearing."

"Sounds about right. Just remember what the chaplain says—there's no such thing as an atheist in a foxhole. Did you want to discuss religion right now?"

"Hell, no. I was just thinking about that nun helping the prisoners in the church."

"I saw her. The young and pretty one. I've got to say, we didn't have any nuns like that growing up."

"What would lead a young woman like that to become a nun?"

"Faith."

Cole snorted, but Vaccaro wasn't done.

"Don't knock it. Some people have faith in God, Hillbilly, just the same as you've got faith in that rifle. That's what that nun has. Plenty of faith."

"I reckon I hadn't thought of it that way."

"Yeah? Well, there you go. Now, will you think about shooting that sniper, for God's sake?"

Cole didn't need to be told twice. The trouble was that he didn't have a clear target. The German had hidden himself so cleverly that Cole didn't have the slightest glimpse of him.

* * *

HE THOUGHT about what he would be doing if he were the one in that steeple, instead of Hauer. The entire structure could not have been more than eight feet wide on each side. There was a roof, covering a bell that was no longer there—the last time that the Germans had come through earlier in the war, they had taken the church bell to be melted down for the war effort. Brick walls, essentially solid railings, covered each side of the steeple, each about three feet high. There was no way for a bullet to punch through that brick.

Cole didn't see any sign of The Butcher using the top of the brick wall for a bench rest. That was what any ordinary sniper would have done, but of course, The Butcher was no ordinary sniper.

So where was the son of a bitch? He had to be up there somewhere.

His eye went to the bottom of the wall. All around the steeple, small arches ran along the base of the solid railing. They had been designed to drain water that blew in, similar to the scuppers on the deck of a ship.

That's where he is, Cole realized. *He's down on the floor of the steeple, looking out through one of those scuppers.*

Cole pushed the rim of the sight so hard against his eye that it pressed a ring into his flesh. Moving his gaze from scupper to scupper, he still saw no sign of the German sniper.

Again, Cole considered what he would do. If he didn't want to be seen, then he would have positioned himself more in the center of the space, where he could see from—and shoot out of—any of the scuppers.

Cole grinned, showing some teeth, but his smile was hidden behind the rifle.

If he could shoot through one of those scuppers, he had a good chance of shooting the German. Considering the distance, it was far from an easy shot to make.

Vaccaro interrupted him before he even started to aim. "Hey, something's happening."

All of Cole's attention had been focused on the church steeple, but Vaccaro had been keeping an eye on the bigger picture of what was happening in the street below.

"What?" Cole asked, annoyed. The last thing he wanted to do was break his sight picture.

"I think you'd better have a look."

Muttering a curse, Cole pulled his eye away from the scope and looked at the scene before them just in time to see the nun running out of the church door and into the street, toward the two fallen Krauts.

"What—"

"I think maybe those were the guards from the church," Vaccaro said. "They ran out to join the fight and got hit right away. She's going to help them."

"They're Germans."

"She's a nun, Cole. They don't take sides."

It was indeed apparent that Sister Anne Marie was running to the aid of the two Germans, both of whom were now fallen in the snowy street. One lay unmoving, but the other was holding his belly and rolling in the snow, clearly wounded.

"Is she trying to get herself killed?" Cole wondered.

"Nobody is going to shoot a nun. Not unless they want to burn in hell."

For the nun's sake, Cole hoped that Vaccaro was right. The fight for the village remained intense. Even with the machine gun knocked out, there was still fighting from house to house, brutal and vicious.

The young nun knelt in the snow beside the wounded German, seemingly oblivious to the bloody snow soaking into her cassock. She had a handful of bandages and tried to staunch his wound. However, he was badly hit and too far gone for her to be able to do much more than hold his hand and say a prayer. Sometimes, it was the best that could be hoped for.

Captivated by the scene, Cole's attention remained riveted on the nun. But out of the corner of his eye, he detected movement in the steeple. The Butcher had finally shown himself. Cole could see him above the brick railing of the steeple, aiming down at the street below, directly in front of the church.

Puzzled about what the sniper was up to, Cole was slow in bringing his rifle to bear. There was nobody down there but the nun and the dying soldier. Who was the German aiming at?

Cole saw the muzzle flash, even heard the crack of the rifle. Instantly, the nun collapsed in the street.

Cole's heart clenched. What the hell? That sniper had just shot the nun.

He and Vaccaro hadn't been the only ones to witness the shooting. A young American soldier with a bandage around his head ran from the open door of the church. Keeping his head down, he sprinted toward the still figure of the nun and sank to his knees beside her.

The rifle fired again. The young soldier crumpled, his body falling beside that of the nun.

Cole was still stunned, hoping that the nun or even the young soldier might stir. But the shots from above had been too precise and deadly.

Almost too late, he swung his rifle up at the steeple. He caught a glimpse of a head, maybe a shoulder, disappearing behind the brick wall. Dammit. The German was out of sight.

But he was still there in the steeple, likely crouched right behind that brick wall. *Several inches of brick wall*, he reminded himself. The sniper could hide behind that all day if he wanted to.

Through the scope, Cole studied the steeple, hoping for any sign of the sniper scurrying away like the rat that he was. But the sniper wasn't showing himself again.

If Cole could put a bullet through the gap at the bottom, right through the drainage scupper, he might have a chance of hitting the sniper.

He rested the rifle across the windowsill, forcing himself to breathe, to be calm. It wasn't easy. His heart hammered and he kept wanting to check on the nun, to see if the sniper's shot had been fatal.

Vaccaro's muttered curses told him all he needed to know in that regard.

He took a deep breath, held it, let it out again. He lined up the sights on the scupper. Not an easy shot—the target was essentially a half-circle, four inches across and four inches high.

A stray burst of machine-gun fire struck the house, but Cole ignored it.

Cole squeezed the trigger.

There was no puff of dust, no flying chips of mortar. The bullet had gone right in.

"Did you get the son of a bitch?" Vaccaro asked.

"Only one way to find out," Cole said. "Come on."

Cole didn't give Vaccaro any choice but to follow him down through the house and out into the street. The Americans were still mopping up, with the Germans shooting at anything that moved, which included Cole and Vaccaro.

"This is nuts, Hillbilly!" Vaccaro protested, one hand on his helmet and the other wrapped tightly around his M-1.

"Shut up and run."

They sprinted for the church, juking right and left as they ran to make themselves difficult targets. They passed the bodies out front, then ran right through the door of the church.

Inside, more than two hundred American soldiers were huddled down, waiting to see what happened next. They had been expecting to see their German guards return after running outside to join the fight. The prisoners recognized the U.S. uniforms worn by Cole and Vaccaro. Some whooped with joy, but most looked too cold and exhausted for much of any reaction.

It might have been expected that once the guards disappeared, that the soldiers might flee the church and join the fight. However, none of them had weapons and these mostly weren't combat troops. Running unarmed into the middle of a firefight was certain suicide.

"Boy, are we glad to see you guys," the nearest soldier said. "I hope there's more where you came from."

"They're right behind us, I can promise you that," Cole said. "The smart thing to do right now is stay put inside these brick walls."

A look of concern crossed the soldier's face. "What about Sister Anne Marie? What about that dumb kid who ran out after her? Did you see them out there? Is the sister all right?"

Cole shook his head.

The soldier slumped back down. "Dammit!"

"Yeah, I know. I'm going after the Kraut SOB who shot them. Now, which way to the steeple?"

The soldier pointed to the far end of the church, where a door to one side of the altar gave access to the steps leading up to the steeple. "Watch out. We saw that German sniper heading back there a while ago. From the look in his eye, we thought he was going to shoot a few of us."

Cole thought about that, then handed the soldier his pistol. "Take this. If any more Germans come through that door, shoot them."

"No problem."

Cole and Vaccaro headed toward the stairs leading up to the steeple. It wasn't the first time that he had gone after a sniper in a church steeple. The sniper might be trapped, but he had every defensive advantage. There was nothing more dangerous than a cornered animal. Cole half expected to hear a grenade come bouncing down the steps at them. He peered carefully up the stairs that spiraled into shadow.

"After you," Vaccaro said.

"Out of the way."

Cole pushed him aside and started up the steps. If that Kraut sniper was up there, he intended on nailing him, no matter what. He got as far as the first landing and stopped.

"Hold on, City Boy. I don't think he's up there anymore."

"What are you talking about?"

"Look at that blood."

Cole nodded toward a bloody footstep, just visible on the dusty stone landing. There was a brick arch there, more of a vent or even like a castle archer's slit than a window, intended to provide natural lighting for the stairs. The opening was just wide enough for someone to squeeze through. More blood was visible on the brick windowsill.

"The son of a bitch went out the window!" Vaccaro cried.

"Maybe. How high up are we, anyhow?"

Cautiously, Cole looked out the slit. The snow-covered ground was about ten feet below, with footprints in the snow leading away from the church. A few flecks of blood showed against the white snow.

"He's getting away!" Vaccaro said.

"I ain't about to jump out that window and twist an ankle. That frozen ground is about as hard as concrete. I'm surprised he made it. Come on."

With no other choice, they lost precious time making their way back through the church, out the front door, and around back again to the spot where the Kraut sniper had jumped out the window. Cole hated to admit it, but Vaccaro was right. The sniper was escaping.

Cole was a skilled tracker, but he didn't need any of those skills to follow the German. The tracks were plain as day. They followed the trail to the outskirts of town. Cole kept his rifle at the ready, hoping for a glimpse of their target, but the Kraut managed to keep out of sight.

"Be ready to hit the ground," Cole said. "He might be trying to get the drop on us, if he thinks we followed him."

"Why would he think that?"

"It's the same damn sniper I ran into back in Ville sur Moselle. There's some unfinished business between us."

"You're not the only one he's got unfinished business with. The whole village will be out to get him. He shot that poor nun."

"Just keep your eyes open."

They lost the trail in a jumble of other German tracks but managed to pick it up again on the other side when he saw another fleck of blood in the snow.

Soon, it became clear that Cole's worries about an ambush were unfounded.

The tracks struck out across the field, toward the hilltop where the German forces still held the high ground. Nearest the village, the slope was wide open, but closer to the forest, small trees and shrubs provided cover. The enemy sniper had simply disappeared.

Like a rat fleeing a sinking ship, the German had fled the fight in the village.

"Come on, let's go after him," Cole said.

Vaccaro grabbed Cole by the shoulder, but seeing the look in his eyes, quickly let go. "He's gone, Hillbilly. We both know that forest is full of Krauts. No way we can go after him."

"I can't let him get away with what he did. It ain't right."

"In case you haven't noticed, we're fighting a war. There's nothing right about it."

Deep down, he knew Vaccaro was correct, even if he wasn't happy about it. Cole gave one last look toward the German stronghold in the forested hilltop, then shook his head and turned away.

CHAPTER EIGHTEEN

SLOWLY, house by house, shop by shop, control of the village was wrested from the Germans.

The fighting remained bitter. One house would be cleared, only for more firing to open up from across the road. Then there would be another attack on the next house—more shooting, more grenades tossed through windows. The capture of each house was a battle in miniature.

At the same time, they tried to avoid shooting into basements or tossing grenades into houses, unless the Germans were in there shooting at them. Many of the villagers had taken refuge in their cellars and basements, trying to dodge the stray bullets and shrapnel. Most of the villagers who remained were older, or very young families. Flight for them had proved too difficult. Anyone who could do so had fled as soon as the Germans began to move in, knowing that a battle was coming.

Cole watched as Vaccaro emptied a clip at a tall stucco house. The firing from the house stopped.

"Why the hell won't these Krauts just give up?" Vaccaro wondered.

"Because they're Krauts, that's why. Besides, we're almost on their front porch. They're going to fight harder and harder now."

Like most of the American troops, Vaccaro looked like Cole felt—cold, exhausted, minor wounds wrapped with dirty bandages. Everybody was either wet or covered in snow, shivering.

The conditions and the prolonged fight wore on their patience. For some men, their pilot light of decency had gone out. Sometimes when German soldiers emerged from a house with their hands up, they were not taken prisoner. Instead, a few quick shots rang out. The officers looked the other way. Some might have called it murder or simple revenge, but often, the soldiers had half-frozen tears in their eyes—not for the Germans they shot down, but for their dead buddies, sprawled in the snow nearby.

It didn't help that the specter of Malmedy was on all their minds—helpless American POWs machine-gunned at a crossroads. These particular Germans might not have had anything to do with that, but they were the enemy all the same.

However, most of the Germans who did give up without a fight were treated well enough, herded into a courtyard, and put under guard. The GIs weren't taking any chances. Most of the battle-hardened veterans had preferred to die fighting rather than surrender. The guards soon realized that many of the prisoners were quite young, hungry, and shivering just as much as the Americans. As the sounds of combat faded and emotions calmed, it was hard to see the prisoners as anything but fellow soldiers. Many spoke passable English. Besides, it was no secret that the German soldiers at the tail end of this war didn't have much choice about putting on a uniform.

"They look as cold as we are, poor bastards," Vaccaro said, passing a group of prisoners being rounded up. "You still want to shoot them, Hillbilly?"

"Never mind about me. Anyhow, this fight ain't over yet."

Most of the shooting in the village had died down. Over by the railroad underpass carrying the road into the village, the tank still fired at its opponent up on the hilltop, where a German force remained dug in.

Another round from the tank shot toward the forest, bursting among the snow-covered trees. In response, a round struck the frozen ground near the Sherman, showering the tank with frozen clods of earth. The tank fired again. A tremendous explosion ripped through the trees this time, and the enemy gun finally fell silent.

"Got him," Cole said with satisfaction.

"Maybe the Jerries will clear out now."

Cole couldn't help thinking that The Butcher was somewhere up there on that hill, maybe trying to put a few Americans in his crosshairs. Hauer had been wounded, but it was too much to hope that the wound was incapacitating. The Germans still held that high ground, which could only mean one thing for the troops who had just taken the village.

"We're gonna have to go up there and take that hill," Cole said.

"Not until I warm up first, we're not."

Dotted around the streets, near where the machine-gun positions had been, the Germans had built warming fires in barrels. Now, it was the Americans who warmed themselves around these fires. Cole and Vaccaro joined the others in their squad, took off their gloves and mittens, and held their stiff fingers closer to the flames.

More villagers emerged. Some of the old folks had died of exposure from days and nights spent cowering in the cold cellars, and their bodies were carried out and laid in the streets. The sight of the dead brought a wave of fresh weeping from the villagers, who thought that they had already cried themselves out.

The villagers eyed the Americans warily. Some looked just plain shaken and haunted. The village had been occupied before by the Americans, but then lost. Would that happen again? So close to the German border, there were even more than a few villagers who didn't necessarily welcome the U.S. victory.

As always, the children seemed frightened but resilient. Cole gave a nearly frozen chocolate bar to a child, who smiled and said, "*Merci.*"

They counted more than forty enemy dead, with about as many enemy soldiers taken prisoner. The Germans looked worried, as if convinced Americans would shoot them like what had taken place at Malmedy. Some soldiers wanted to shoot the ones with American watches on, but Lieutenant Mulholland wouldn't let them.

Before dark, an assault was organized on the hilltop, with the tank leading the way. Cole and Vaccaro found themselves following in the wake of the tank, sucking in exhaust fumes.

"How come we got to take part in this?"

"Just lucky, I reckon."

The truth was that somebody wanted Cole and his rifle handy, and following the tank was the best way to make sure that he reached the hilltop in one piece—unless the Germans decided to ambush the tank with a *Panzerfaust*. Then all bets were off.

Cautiously, the assault team approached the forest, more exposed than they wanted to be, but without much choice given the bare, snowy slope leading up from the village. At any moment, they expected deadly fire to be unleashed against them.

But when they reached the tree line, all that they found were empty foxholes and the smoking wreckage of the German artillery.

The Germans had slipped away.

* * *

FINALLY, there remained one task for the survivors of the fight for Wingen sur Moder, and that was to bury the dead. The ground remained frozen hard beneath the snow and ice, so digging through the frost was backbreaking work. No one complained about this final chore. The soldiers mostly just had their trenching tools, but the able-bodied villagers arrived with picks and mattocks and soon joined the soldiers to work side by side with them.

Cole joined in and despite the bitter cold, soon found himself sweating. He hadn't grown up as a farmer, but he was no stranger to hard work. Taking turns and trading off whenever one person grew tired, the soldiers and villagers dug down. Some of the former prisoners who had been held in the church, the ones who weren't in bad shape, also turned out to help once they had gotten some food and something hot to drink.

It was easier to dig one large hole for a mass burial, rather than trying to cut several small graves through the frosted earth. This wasn't how things were normally done, but there was something that felt right about burying the victims of the fighting together. A separate grave was dug for the dead Germans.

One of the soldiers who had been held in the church knelt by the body of the private who had been shot dead when he ran to help the nun.

"Serra, what are you doing?"

"Hold it," he said to the soldiers who were about to finish wrapping the body in a blanket. He reached inside his shirt and produced a tiny crucifix on a thin chain, which he then slipped over his head. He laid it on his dead buddy's chest, mumbled a prayer, then wiped at his eyes with the back of his hands. "Go on, then."

The bodies of the dead young soldier and the nun were wrapped in blankets like the others, and then laid in the bottom of the hole. Soldiers and villagers gathered, hats and helmets off despite the snow. Some of the villagers sobbed. A few days ago, they had celebrated Christmas and all seemed right with their world as the end of the war seemed to be coming into sight. Now, not even a week into the new year, it seemed as if their whole world had shattered.

Prayers were said, and then began the slow work of refilling the grave. The fresh earth was one more scar in the village left by the fighting.

But not for long. More snow fell during the night, covering the landscape in a new blanket of white, as if giving the world a fresh start.

"All right, get ready to move out," Lieutenant Mulholland shouted. Enough gasoline had been found to keep the trucks running, and two more tanks joined them as the unit prepared to head down the mountain roads.

"Sir, are we going after those Germans?"

"No such luck. Division is sending us somewhere else. Besides, those guys are probably halfway back to Berlin by now. Chances are that we'll have to fight them again."

Cole listened, disappointed. Some officer, somewhere, was probably sending them to clean up someone else's mess. He had hoped that they would be going after the Germans who had escaped from Winger sur Moder. Then again, he agreed with Mulholland that too much time had elapsed. That unit could be anywhere in these mountains.

Truth be told, he wouldn't have minded another shot at that German sniper. After all, Hauer wasn't just another soldier. The way that Cole saw it, Hauer was a murderer. It also nagged at Cole that the enemy sniper had eluded him. Cole knew that he was the better shot. He just needed a chance to prove it.

As far as he was concerned, there was some unfinished business between them.

If not this time, he thought, then maybe another.

It seemed as if Vaccaro had more immediate concerns.

"Sir, can I ride up front? It's cold in the back and I think I'm starting to get whatever Cole had. My throat feels all scratchy."

"Shut up and get in the truck, Vaccaro. Nobody else can get sick. That's an order."

"Yes, sir."

"If we run into more Germans, things will get hot plenty fast. You know what's on the other side of these mountains, don't you? Germany, that's what."

Cole thought that sounded good to him, and reached for his rifle.

ALREADY MILES AWAY, what was left of the German forces retreating from Wingen sur Moder made their way along the snowy mountain roads.

Like a wave that had crashed against the shore in all its fury, only to have its foaming remains drawn back into the sea, the German advance of Operation *Nordwind* finally ebbed. Hitler had made a desperate gamble by gathering his remaining forces for one last push against the Allies poised to invade across the Rhine. Thousands of troops, hundreds of tanks and trucks, even the last of the Luftwaffe's aircraft, now lay shattered in the cold snow of the Ardennes Forest and Vosges Mountains.

In the end, the offensive had never been much more than a forlorn hope against well-supplied forces. The Allies had been delayed and thousands had died in what would come to be known as the biggest battle ever fought by the United States Army.

The Allies would now push on, with fewer and fewer enemy forces to stop them. From the East, the Red Army pushed ever-closer to Berlin. Caught in the middle, for the average German, all of this seemed impossible to grasp. The end of the Third Reich seemed all but certain. Now, it was only a matter of time. Their world was falling apart, but many weren't prepared to give in quite yet.

"Hurry, hurry!" shouted a German officer, riding past in a *Kübelwagen*. The agile vehicle threaded its way along the slick road. "*Hop, hop, hop!* If the Allied planes catch us in the open, there will be hell to pay!"

With the other soldiers, Hauer glanced at the sky, but he was not particularly worried. "Let them come," he said. "So what?"

"Maybe you will shoot them down for us with that fancy rifle of yours, eh, Hauer?" a nearby soldier asked.

"Maybe I will."

"I hope you do!" the soldier said cheerfully.

Not all of the others were as friendly toward Hauer. Some viewed snipers with something like disdain, thinking that they were like thieves of souls, shooting from concealment. Even if they tolerated snipers, some of them just didn't like Hauer. Others, like young Krauss, who had somehow survived the battle and was following along two steps behind him, seemed to regard him with something like awe.

What did he care, either way?

Hauer shook his head. He was cold; he could barely feel his feet. His left leg dragged, stiff from the wound he had suffered in the church steeple. In this case, he was glad of the temperature because it numbed the pain. He was sure that if he stopped moving, he would be captured, or simply die of the cold.

For many hours his stomach had rumbled, but then the sensation of hunger had gone away. Some of the younger soldiers ate snow to keep their bellies full, but he knew that only burned more energy than the temporary relief was worth. What he would give for a hot, sizzling sausage right now! The very idea of it made his mouth water. But for now, there was nothing to eat—no telling for how long.

He thought back to the fight in the village, satisfied that he had killed that meddling nun. He had been wounded while hidden in the church steeple, hit by an impossible shot that had come in through one of the small gaps in the brick wall that he had hidden behind. He was sure that it had been the American sniper whom he had encountered before. In fact, he had seen that sniper chasing him through the village.

Why hadn't he made a last stand against him? Hauer shrugged to himself. Sometimes, even The Butcher had done enough. He would live to fight another day. He had to hand it to that American sniper, though. He was an excellent shot. If they ever crossed paths again, Hauer would be sure to return the favor.

The cheerful soldier beside him started singing in a low voice. All around him, other soldiers began to pick up the tune. The song was *Panzierlied*, the "Tank Song" so popular with all the troops:

Was gilt denn unser Leben
Für unsres Reiches Heer?
Für Deutschland zu sterben
Ist uns höchste Ehr.

What do our lives matter
In serving the nation?
To die for Germany
Is our highest honor.

THE SNOWY FOREST rang with deep German voices, soldiers marching to make their final stand for the Fatherland.

PART III

CHAPTER NINETEEN

Autumn 1991, Munich

STANDING in the middle of the WWII museum, surrounded by the opening night crowd, Cole stared in disbelief at the German sniper that he had last seen that January day in 1945.

"I was hoping that I killed you," Cole said.

The Butcher shook his head and smiled. "Apparently not. Why, are you not glad to see me, Hillbilly?"

"No. And where do you get off calling me Hillbilly?"

"That is your nickname, is it not? This is what the exhibit here says. *The famed Hillbilly sniper.*"

Cole was embarrassed about it, but he had to admit this was just what the exhibit stated. "I reckon it does say that, but it wasn't my idea."

"Come now, Hillbilly. After all these years, surely we can put our differences aside?"

"Sorry, but it's hard to forget some things," Cole said.

Hans was looking from man to man, a worried expression on his face. "You two know each other?" he asked.

The Butcher held out a hand and introduced himself to Hans. "I am Karl Hauer. You are German, but you speak English with hardly any accent."

"Hans Neumann. As for my English, well, I was a POW during the war and was sent to America," Hans explained. "After the war, I stayed."

Hauer nodded, smiling as if pleased with his fellow German's answer. For all the American exceptionalism being celebrated here tonight, this was a club that the Americans could never be part of— two Germans who had fought for their country, rightly or wrongly.

"I will leave it up to your friend here to explain how we know one another," Hauer said.

"We ran into each other during the war," Cole explained. "We set our sights on each other, you might say. Why don't you go ahead and tell him, old buddy. Tell him all about how you got the nickname, *Das Schlachter.*"

"Of course," the Butcher said. He seemed pleased by the use of his nickname. "We first encountered one another at Ville sur Moselle. Then again at the second half of what the Americans called The Battle of the Bulge."

"You left out the part where you murdered those villagers at Ville sur Moselle," Cole said.

"Murder is a strong word. They had armed themselves. I am sure that they would have done the same to me, given the chance."

Cole snorted. "Villagers with some old shotguns and rusty hunting rifles? Not likely. What about those kids you killed? Had they *armed* themselves?"

The Butcher shook his head. "Sometimes, I cannot sleep at night thinking of what I have done. I remind myself that unfortunately, there is always needless killing in any war."

Cole stared at him in disbelief. The words had been delivered almost by rote, as if Hauer had been practicing them. He sounded so damn phony.

"Hauer, I don't believe you meant a word of what you just said about needless killing. Give me a damn break."

Hauer shrugged. "In your Gulf War, it is what you Americans called collateral damage."

If he'd had a gun in his hand, Cole would have taken The Butcher out then and there. "Collateral damage? That's when bombs go off target. You shot those villagers and those kids, you son of a bitch. I had to go back and make up some lie for that dead boy's sister."

"I am sure you did her a great kindness. Sometimes, a lie is better than the truth. As for what I did during the war, I am sure that I did what was required of me."

"There's being a soldier, and then there's being a murderer. Let's not forget Wingen sur Moder, where you shot that nun."

Hauer's polite mask seemed to slip, and his face darkened. "Do not forget that you yourself killed many Germans." The Butcher nodded at the exhibit displaying the old photograph of Cole in his sniper pose. "Because your side won, I can see how your actions are celebrated here. Did every soldier you killed deserve death? You and I are not so different in the end. We both have blood on our hands."

Cole had heard enough. He gave the German sniper one last glare, then turned and walked away. After a moment, Hans followed.

"What was that all about?" Hans asked. "Were those things you said about him true?"

"True, and then some. I need a drink, old buddy."

Cole approached the bar and ordered a bourbon. He was in luck that they had some on hand for their largely older, American crowd. He had been sticking with club soda, but running into Hauer again after so many years called for something stronger. He knocked it back in one gulp, welcoming the warm burn the liquor made going down.

Like Cole, Hans had been sipping a soft drink. He now ordered a schnapps. "Do you want another?" he asked Cole.

"No thanks. It might make me do something ornery."

"I am sorry that he upset you," Hans said.

"I guess it's to be expected. You can't open a museum like this without rubbing some salt in somebody's old wounds. I just wasn't expecting it to be *my* old wounds."

But Hauer wasn't ready to leave Cole alone just yet. He approached from the other side of the room, a contrite smile on his face, hands raised in a placating gesture.

"I must apologize," he said. "I did not mean to upset you."

Cole said nothing. He was glad that he had stopped at one drink, or there was no telling what might happen.

"You know, when the war ended, I found myself in East Germany," Hauer said. "Behind what you call the Iron Curtain. It is only recently that we have been able to experience any real freedom and I am enjoying every minute of it, believe me. Being trapped in a Communist country for so many years was its own form of punishment."

"The wall is down now," Hans said. "Germany has been reunited."

The Butcher brightened. "Yes, indeed. The wall is down and there is a new future, although it may be too late for me." He looked around and nodded in Danny's direction. "Hillbilly, I saw you come in with that young man. He looks like you."

"That's my grandson."

"Ah! I thought so. Is that his girlfriend?"

"My niece," Hans said.

Hauer smiled pleasantly. "I am glad that their future is more promising than ours when we were their age. Love is better than war, wouldn't you say?"

"I reckon," Cole said guardedly. He didn't trust a word that Hauer said.

"I have been thinking that this is more than a chance meeting," Hauer said. "Perhaps we have an opportunity to get to know one another better. Let me invite you to come hunting this weekend in the Vosges Mountains. Some old friends have a hunting club that gathers there. The food is excellent, real German food, in a comfortable lodge. No foxholes for us anymore."

"I don't think so."

Hauer smiled, not ready to give up. "Come now, I hope you will consider it. Last time, you almost bested me. This time, let me best you in hunting. It is a matter of honor."

"Honor? I didn't know you were familiar with the word."

Hauer shrugged. "Please, let us put our differences aside. The war is over. You will like these mountains. Fresh air. Boars and stags. We hunt with dogs, you know, and also with beaters who drive the game toward the hunters." Hauer looked at Hans. "Are you a hunter?"

"No, but I know that the Vosges are beautiful."

"Yes! Yes! It is so true. You and your niece must come also."

Hauer sounded so sincere and looked so eager that Hans seemed to waver. "Well—"

Hauer winked conspiratorially. "I knew you were an old hunter at heart. Most true Germans are. You will love this lodge and the fresh mountain air. Ah, the scenery! Hillbilly, what do you say?"

Cole surprised himself by responding not with a definite "no" as he had meant to, but with, "I'm not sure."

"Come now, what are you going to do, shop for cuckoo clocks and beer steins to take home as souvenirs?"

As much as Cole hated to admit it, Hauer had something of a point. They were scheduled to be in Germany for several more days, and after the museum opening, their calendar was clear to do some exploring. Hunting sounded better to him than shopping or visiting museums.

Hauer's invitation seemed genuine. Cole began to think that maybe he owed him the benefit of the doubt. The war had been a long time ago. He didn't think that he would ever come to like Hauer or under-stand him, but maybe they could agree upon a truce. Besides, Cole wouldn't mind showing him once and for all that he was the better shot.

"All right then," Cole said.

"Wonderful! Bring your grandson. He will have a great time. Don't worry—I have a shotgun that you can use."

"A shotgun, huh?"

"I'm not sure that I trust you with a rifle, ha!"

They exchanged information, with Hauer collecting the name of Cole's hotel and Hauer giving Cole a plain business card with just his name, an address in Berlin, and his telephone number.

After Hauer left, Hans studied the plain card that Hauer had also given him as if it contained far more information, perhaps hidden between the lines. "What does a man like that do in East Germany?" Hans wondered out loud. "So many are desperately poor who are coming out of there now, but he looked prosperous enough."

"I don't know," Cole said. "You tell me what he did. He seems like the type who sold used cars."

"Or maybe he worked for the *Stasi*. The East German Secret

Police." Hans rubbed his chin thoughtfully. "He has that look about him. You know, you do not have to go on this hunting trip."

"It's just two old men having a pissing contest," Cole said. "He's right that the war is over. Hell, Hans, it's been forty years. We'll hunt some boars and see which one of us can still shoot straight."

Hans rolled his eyes. "You're right. Two old snipers with grudges and guns, turned loose in the hills. What could go wrong?"

* * *

HANS BORROWED A CAR, a solid and comfortable new Volvo 740 that belonged to Angela's father, and they all drove down to the lodge together. The old German proved to be a good driver, but he drove the sedan in the steady, plodding way of a farmer—which he was back in Ohio. German drivers tended to be more aggressive, driving zippy Volkswagens and BMWs and Mercedes. These handled more nimbly than the Ford pickup trucks Hans was used to driving back home.

"The world just keeps moving faster and faster," Hans muttered as yet another sleek sedan zoomed past him.

"Uncle Hans, you need to speed up," Angela urged. "You are driving too slowly!"

The trip coincided with a fall break in Angela's school, so the timing was perfect. Ordinarily, Cole suspected, a hunting trip would not be something that the girl would want to go on, especially not with her aged uncle, but spending time with Danny seemed to be the main attraction. The two sat together in the back seat, deep in conversation.

Cole kept quiet and let Hans concentrate on the road.

Hans had turned out to be full of surprises. Not the least of which was that he had agreed to accompany Cole in the first place.

"I would have thought that you would want to spend time with your family, Hans."

"You know what Benjamin Franklin said about fish and company," Hans replied. "After three days, they both start to smell. So, I am giving them a break until I smell fresh again. Besides, I have Angela with me and she was excited about taking a trip."

Before leaving Munich, he had brought Cole around to the trunk of the car and quietly showed him a rifle case, which he opened to reveal a beautiful hunting rifle. Cole realized it was a "sporterized" version of a Model 1903A Springfield. Essentially, someone had customized the military surplus version of the rifle with which Cole was so familiar. Germany's gun laws allowed hunting rifles and shotguns, but not the private ownership of military weapons. As a result, many surplus rifles from WWI and WWII had been transformed into hunting rifles in order to skirt the law.

This rifle had been designed with more than function or legal loopholes in mind, because it was a pleasure to behold. The stock was made of burled walnut, intricately checkered, with end caps for the nose and grip done in a blond wood to create an interesting contrast. As a craftsman himself, Cole couldn't resist reaching down and running a finger along the beautiful grain of the stock. As a nod to comfort, the stock was fitted with a ventilated rubber Pachmayr recoil pad. His old battlefield Springfield had lacked any such niceties, and he'd often had the bruised shoulder to prove it.

The action and barrel were of polished bright steel rather than blued, which was a little showy for Cole's taste. Even the bolt had been upgraded to include a jeweled pattern rather than a plain knob. The rifle's receiver had been drilled and tapped to accommodate a high-powered Leica scope. Such expensive optics had never been in Cole's budget, but from his perusal of gun magazines, Cole knew that the scope alone must have cost as much as the down payment on this Volvo.

"She's a beauty," Cole said. "Where did you get her?"

"My nephew is a hunter. Angela's father," Hans explained. "He is a banker."

"Ah. Well, your nephew has good taste."

"I want you to use it for the hunt," Hans said. "I'm sorry, but I could not get another rifle for your grandson."

"I don't think Danny is so keen on hunting," Cole said. "But what about you? What are you going to hunt with?"

Hans shook his head. "What am I going to do, traipse up and down the hills? I am an old man. I have a bad heart. No, I am going to sit in front of the fire at the lodge, drink warm schnapps, and keep an eye on those two."

"Then why did you bring me the rifle? Hauer said that he would have a shotgun for me."

"I suspect that you are a better shot with a rifle," Hans said. "Which would you rather have in the woods?"

"No argument there."

"You know, if this was a duel, I suppose that I would be your second."

"It ain't a duel."

Hans shrugged. "If you say so."

As they left the city behind, Cole was struck by the beauty of the countryside. They passed through the heart of Bavaria with its rolling hills and neatly kept farms. When Cole had first seen Germany, it had been been a war-ravaged, defeated, muddy country in late winter. Now, although they had missed the best of the fall colors, he still spotted the pale fire of aspens in the hills. The autumn sunlight gave the landscape a crisp appearance.

The Vosges Mountains themselves rose to the south of the Ardennes region and straddled the border between Germany and France, in the region known as Alsace-Lorraine. Hans explained that the area had passed back and forth between Germany and France many times over the centuries. They crossed the Rhine into France, drove through the small city of Strasbourg, then continued into the Vosges.

Cole felt some small sense of relief at leaving Germany and entering France, although he knew that was foolishness in this day and age. But deep down, he had always liked the French and found them to be a welcoming people. After all, it was the French who had helped Americans win the Revolutionary War. Americans had returned the favor in 1944. Spending a few days in France was just fine by him.

Slowly, the road gained altitude as they climbed into the mountains. Cole felt right at home because these peaks felt more like the Appalachians, with rounded hilltops rising to elevations of around twelve hundred feet. The road grew narrower, following the valleys, with dense forests creeping closer. The afternoon grew darker. In the back seat, the conversation between Danny and Angela grew softer, then fell quiet. The grim mountains and woods seemed to demand silence.

"Where is this place?" Angela asked her uncle, sounding a bit nervous.

"It's just—"

At that moment, a stag came bounding out of the woods, directly into the path of the car. Hans stomped on the brakes. It wasn't the best reaction because the car began to skid on the damp fallen leaves littering the road. He fought for control of the wheel as the car slewed sideways.

From the backseat, Angela gasped. Danny swore.

Hans had braked, but it hadn't been enough to keep them from hitting the stag, which more or less ran right into the car. The big animal hit them with a solid *thud*, then bounced off the grill into a roadside ditch.

By some miracle, the car stopped skidding just before following the stag into the ditch.

"Well, I ain't had a ride like that since my rocking chair fell through the front porch last summer," Cole remarked. "Everybody all right?"

"All right," said Hans, whose hands still gripped the steering wheel with white knuckles.

Angela and Danny were fine. Like a good German, she had made them both follow the rules and buckle their seatbelts, even in the backseat.

"What about the poor stag?" she asked.

"You wait here. Let me go see about that," Cole said.

Cole got out, along with Danny. After a minute, Hans followed, although Angela had to help him—he was still shaky after hitting the stag. Cole had the worrisome thought that Hans had complained of heart trouble before.

The stag lay in the ditch, tangled in the ferns and bracken, still alive, but barely. When it saw Cole, the stag struggled pitifully to rise, but then gave up and lay there, its ribs heaving with labored breathing. Cole studied the animal with interest because he had never seen one up close. He recalled that a stag was more closely related to an elk than to a whitetail deer.

"Maybe there is an animal hospital nearby," Angela said, close to tears. "We can get help."

Cole and Hans exchanged a look. Cole was a hunter and Hans was a farmer. They both knew what needed to be done.

"I will get the rifle," Hans said.

Hans walked back to the trunk and got out the rifle, then returned and fed a single round into the chamber. Hans aimed down at the injured stag, then lowered the rifle. "I cannot do it," Hans said.

He held the rifle out to Cole, who took it, immediately enjoying the feel of the rifle in his hands. Damn, but he would never be too old for that.

"Danny, why don't you walk Angela down the road a ways," Cole said.

Danny did just that, putting an arm around her shoulders, which were shaking a little, and led her away.

Cole gave them a minute, then raised the rifle to his shoulder to put the animal out of its misery. His jaw fit tight against the rifle, with the stock fitting comfortably into his shoulder. He took a moment, just getting the feel of the rifle. Through the expensive scope, the stag's eye showed bright and clear.

He squeezed the trigger.

The sound of the single rifle shot echoed across the hills.

He ejected the shell and reached down to pocket the soft, warm brass.

"The lodge can't be far," Cole said. "When we get there, we'll let them know in case someone wants to come back here and get the meat."

"Good idea," Hans said meekly. He still looked pale after the accident. Cole thought about that weak heart again.

"You doin' OK?"

"OK."

"Why don't I drive the rest of the way," Cole said. "You can navigate. I thought trying to read German was bad enough, but these damn road signs are in French."

The car's hood wasn't even dented, with only some fur caught in the slats of the grill, and nothing mechanical had been affected. The car started right up. The Volvo seemed to be built like a tank. Cole backed it away from the edge of the ditch, got it pointed in the right direction, and headed for the lodge somewhere in the hills ahead.

Some might have seen the collision with the stag as a bad omen, but Cole wasn't so sure about that. He'd had the opportunity to fire the rifle and kill with it. He and the rifle were no longer strangers. They had made a bond by blood.

Tonight, he would dismantle the rifle and clean it carefully. He would get to know it that much better, inside and out.

Tomorrow, it would be time to hunt.

CHAPTER TWENTY

COLE DROVE them the rest of the way to the lodge, which turned out to be built of stone and timber, making it both stately and comfortable. Woodsmoke trailed from the chimneys, mixing with the scent of fallen leaves and fresh pine needles. Yellow lights glowed in the windows.

"Nice place," said Cole. "Where was this lodge forty years ago? I had to sleep in my foxhole back then. Damn near froze my ass off."

Hans laughed. After initially being shaken by the Volvo hitting the stag, he seemed to have recovered. "You can be sure some general stayed here, or at least a colonel," he said. "Meanwhile, you got the foxhole."

"Sounds about right," Cole agreed. "That's the way of the world, ain't it?"

Hauer greeted them as soon as they walked into the lodge. He looked like an outdoorsman in his thick corduroy trousers, chamois shirt, and sheepskin vest. The clothes looked expensive and new, as if purchased for the occasion. "You are here! I was sure that you would get lost in the dark. The roads are not well-marked."

"Hate to disappoint you," Cole said. Briefly, he explained about hitting the stag. The hotel sent two of its kitchen staff to fetch it—no point in letting good venison go to waste.

They found that all of the arrangements had been made, but there were only two rooms available in the lodge itself, with a single room with two beds available in a converted stable.

"The stable will be just fine for me and Danny," Cole said. It turned out that they were staying as guests of Hauer. Cole thought about insisting on paying, but then decided that if nothing else, he could hit Hauer in the wallet.

"Where did he get the money for this?" Hans muttered. "I am telling you, he was *Stasi*. Every last one of them lined their pockets at the expense of good Germans while they did the bidding of the Soviets."

As they gathered in the grand hall of the hunting lodge, Hans explained that he and his grand-niece would be sitting out the hunt. "Someone needs to stay here and keep the fire going," he said.

Hauer took the news in stride. It was clear that his only real concern was making sure that Cole was equipped for the hunt. Boots had been found, and warm hunting clothes.

"I have a shotgun for you," Hauer announced. "A very nice 12-gauge. It is a good weapon for boar, especially. At close range, you cannot miss! However, you do need some nerve to let them get that close when they are charging."

"I brought a rifle," Cole said. "I guess I won't need that shotgun, after all."

A scowl crossed Hauer's face, then disappeared so quickly that Cole thought he might have imagined it. "As you wish. Perhaps your grandson can use the shotgun."

"That's up to him." Cole turned to his grandson. "Danny?"

"I don't want to hunt tomorrow," he said. "I mean, I'll go, but I don't want to shoot anything."

Hauer appeared amused. "If you go into the woods, why would you not wish to join in the hunt?"

"I don't like killing," he said.

Hauer laughed. "I have to say, you Americans have gone soft in two generations. The boy doesn't like to hunt! If there is ever another war, you will be in trouble. Are you sure that he is really related to you?"

"Let the boy be," Cole said. He felt that Danny didn't appreciate being belittled in front of Angela, although, to the German girl's credit, she was glaring at Hauer. *If looks could kill.* She was clearly in Danny's camp. "If he don't like to hunt, so be it. It's a new world, in case you ain't noticed. Besides, he can help pack out whatever we shoot."

Hauer shook his head, still grinning, clearly amused by the thought that the grandson of none other than this famous hillbilly sniper did not like to hunt—or kill. "Suit yourselves," he said. "Get your rest. In the morning, the hunt begins."

Crossing to the accommodations, Danny said, "I don't like that guy Hauer, Pa Cole. It's not just what he said about me. There's something about him. I can't put my finger on it."

"You don't like him, huh? Join the club," Cole said. "I guess that just proves Hauer wrong about us not being related. You're a Cole, boy. That means you have good instincts."

"Pa Cole, if you don't like him, then why are we here?"

"I think Hans said it best," Cole responded. "I'm here to fight a duel."

Danny stopped walking. "What?"

"It's not the kind of duel where you count off twenty paces and shoot each other," Cole said. "I suppose we're here to show which one of us is still the best shot."

"In that case, I feel sorry for the deer and boars."

* * *

IN THE MORNING, Cole and Danny were up well before dawn, eating a hearty breakfast with the other hunters in the lodge. Hans and Angela were not there. Having opted out of the hunt itself, they had decided to sleep in.

This European form of hunting was unlike anything that Cole had experienced. He was used to heading off into the woods alone. As a boy, Cole had hunted for subsistence. Anything he shot that had meat on it, they ate—like as not in a stew if it was something like possum.

He still hunted deer to fill the freezer, but the truth of it was, they wouldn't starve anymore if he came home without a buck.

At most, Americans hunted in pairs or in a trio. Like as not, even then, they would split up to try their luck alone.

The hunt in the Vosges was nothing like that. In fact, it was more of a communal event, a group hunt carried out with help from dogs and drivers. This was the traditional way that hunting had been done for centuries.

An electric current of excitement seemed to fill the morning air and Cole felt caught up in it. The entire operation gathered just past dawn on the forest edge and received direction from the master of the hunt. Their quarry today would be stags and boars. Everyone wished each other luck, and then the "dog men" and drivers started out to get into position, with the hunters to follow. To Cole's surprise, many of the dogs were dachshunds. He didn't know how they covered so much ground on their short legs. He never would have considered them proper hounds, but they were eager hunters and he learned that the breed had been bred for just this purpose.

More than a dozen hunters had gathered. Cole had worried that they would all be Nazi fossils like Hauer, but to his surprise, they were a friendly, hale and hearty bunch. Some were French rather than German. Hauer was just the friend of a friend. Cole had been puzzled about how Hauer had landed an invitation, until he realized that the German had provided a case of premium Russian vodka and some bottles of rare schnapps. That alone seemed to be Hauer's ticket for admission.

The other hunters gladly welcomed Cole as a novelty. They had never hunted with an American.

"Let's see what Americans are made of, yes?" they kidded him.

"Where are your buckskins and coonskin cap?" another asked with a laugh.

The jibes were friendly and Cole could see that the other hunters were mostly beefy businessmen dressed up in new hunting clothes. "I'll see if I can keep up."

He soon saw that the kidding had not been idly spoken. To get into position, there was a great deal of hiking, mostly uphill, as they climbed from the lodge into the higher elevations. Cole wished that he was twenty years younger. Danny didn't seem to have any trouble, taking to the trails like a mountain goat. He spelled his grandfather by taking the rifle for a while and slinging it over his own shoulder. The rifle couldn't have weighed more than eight pounds, but after a couple of hours of hiking, Cole felt his shoulder sagging under the weight.

Although the fall morning was chill, Cole soon found himself sweating inside his hunting coat. The autumn woods proved to be a reward in itself for all of this exertion. The trail passed through heavy stands of pine and fir, making the air smell fresh and alive. Their feet scarcely made a sound on the matt of damp, fallen pine needles. A few deciduous trees blazed among the pines in vibrant tones of yellow and orange. With no roads nearby, the only sounds came from the foot-steps of the men, occasional guffaws at quiet jokes, the twitter of birds, and the rush of the streams they passed. As Cole fell into the rhythm of the march, his heart and legs pumping, he felt intensely alive. He was in his element.

By the time they were deep into the hills, it was already past noon. Sandwiches were handed out. After a few shy appearances, the sun had hidden itself for good. With the short fall days, they would only have a couple of hours to hunt before having to start back to the lodge.

Once they were in position, the hunters spread out into smaller groups. He and Danny found themselves stuck with Hauer. After all, this was to be an unofficial shooting competition, so it made sense that they were together, although Cole would have preferred the company of just about anyone else.

"Good luck," Hauer said. He had seemed amused before, but now there was another look evident on his face, as if he was enjoying some private joke.

"Just watch what you're shooting at today," Cole reminded him. "Make sure your targets have four legs."

Hauer just smiled.

After following a narrow trail, they were set up in a pretty little valley, or what Cole would have called a "bowl" back home, a low, open area facing the edge of the forest rising beyond. He, Danny, and Hauer seemed to have the valley to themselves. The baying of dogs came closer.

Through the trees, they caught a blur of movement. Cole felt a thrill of excitement as he realized that it was game. He looked more closely and saw a dark shape rushing through the trees toward them.

It was a boar. Cole had seen wild pigs before, but never anything this size. The boar must have weighed at least a couple of hundred pounds and was the size of a German Shepherd. It burst from the trees and ran right at him, lowered its head, and charged. He could see ivory tusks jutting in front of the boar's mean, dark eyes.

"Pa Cole, he's headed right for us," Danny remarked nervously. His grandson stood just behind him and hadn't brought along a gun.

"Hold tight," Cole said.

He raised the rifle to his shoulder and tracked the boar through the scope. That pig could move. The boar had already covered half the distance across the clearing. This morning with the hunting master, they had all agreed on zones of fire. This boar was squarely within Cole's zone. Out of the corner of his eye, he caught a glimpse of Hauer with his own rifle nestled in the crook of his elbow. If Cole missed his shot, that boar was going to plow right through him. It was clear that he wasn't getting any help from Hauer in stopping the boar.

A running shot from the side was one thing, but a running shot with an animal coming straight at you was far more difficult. First of all, it meant that the animal wasn't running away but charging at you. Each second that one waited required another instantaneous mental calculation about where to aim to adjust for the trajectory of the bullet. Also, the boar coming at them made a small target from the front.

"Pa Cole!" Danny said nervously.

This was the point where some men might have run for it. Others would have shot blindly in desperation, hoping against hope that one of their bullets would strike true, stopping the tusked nightmare steaming toward them at full speed.

But Cole stood his ground, his crosshairs steady. He waited until the charging boar's head filled the field the view, then squeezed the trigger.

The boar made a sound that was like a grunt of frustration and rage, then skidded to a stop, not twenty feet from where Cole stood. His ears ringing from the crack of the rifle, he finally allowed himself to take a deep breath. So much of this trip had reminded him of his age, especially the hike up into these hills, but he suddenly felt like a young man again.

"I'll be damned," Cole said, inspecting the boar. He felt adrenalin surging through him, making him feel twenty years younger. "He was an ornery critter."

"I thought for sure he was going to plow you over."

"Close," Cole agreed. "If I'd missed him, this would be a different story. Wouldn't that be a way to go?"

"But you don't miss."

"Not if I can help it, boy."

Cole looked in Hauer's direction. Hauer saw him and gave him a nod, but his attention was soon claimed by more movement among the trees. The dogs and drivers were still at it, and this time they saw the flash of a stag's white tail, like a flag in the woods.

The mountain stag was running far ahead of the hounds, right in their direction.

"Here he comes, Pa Cole!" Danny whispered intently. Caught up in the excitement, he seemed to have momentarily forgotten his opposition to hunting.

Danny was right. The stag seemed to be headed right at them.

Cole raised his rifle, lining up the shot. Unlike the boar, the stag had no intention of leaving the cover the woods and charging them, but ran along the treeline, presenting its flank to Cole. Although the stag was farther away, this running shot was easier in some regards. All he had to do was lead the target. The fine optics of the Leica scope made the stag spring closer, gathering all the light of the overcast day.

Then at the last moment, the stag broke to the left and into Hauer's quadrant. Cole lowered the rifle, leaving the stag to Hauer. Off to his left, Hauer's rifle cracked. He saw the stag stumble, but it kept right on going. Before Hauer could fire again, the stag disappeared deeper into the forest.

Hauer came walking over to them. "I hit him," he said. "I am sure there is a blood trail. I will give him a minute to settle, and then I will go into the forest after him. With any luck, he did not get far. It is going to be dark soon, after all."

"Need help?"

"I can manage," Hauer said. He looked down at the huge boar that Cole had brought down. Oddly enough, the German did not seem at all bitter that Cole had managed to bag the animal. "Congratulations on your boar. He is a monster!"

"You got that right," Cole agreed. The tusks were several inches long. They would have ripped him right open if the boar had gotten any closer.

"You stay here," Hauer said. He held up the walkie talkie. "I will let the others know where we are, and that we will need some help bringing out this game."

"Sounds good to me," Cole said.

Hauer nodded and headed off into the forest to track his wounded deer. Finding the animal wouldn't be easy in the dark, so Cole hoped that it hadn't gotten far. He was a little surprised that Hauer hadn't hit the stag harder, with a more accurate shot. Yes, it had been a running shot, but the quarry had been fairly close to Hauer.

Cole smiled to himself, thinking that the old German sniper was finally missing a step—maybe two. Cole had dropped his target while Hauer was having to chase after his stag.

Up on the ridge, the dogs had changed direction and were no longer running toward the valley. The barking faded, then disappeared altogether, as if the dogs were being called back for the day. Was the hunt ending?

Around them, the shadows grew deeper. Through the overcast haze, he watched the sun slip down over a big hill to the west, and it was as if a curtain had been pulled across a window. Dusk arrived instantly. With the last of the daylight fading, the temperature dropped quickly. Cole felt the chill creeping into his old bones.

"Might as well do something with this boar while we wait for

Hauer," Cole said. He took out his hunting knife and with Danny's help, expertly field dressed the boar. When some of the other hunters and beaters came along, they would be ready to drag the beast out. That alone wouldn't be an easy task. They were many miles from the lodge, deep in the mountains, and Cole did not look forward to hiking back in the dark, which was how things were shaping up. At least the others would know the way and hopefully, have a flashlight. Cole didn't have one. They had started out at first light, and now it was growing dark. He hadn't planned on a full day in the field.

He also had the nagging realization that he didn't have a map. Maybe Hauer had one? He didn't know how far these mountains went. He did know that this was a preserved area, essentially the equivalent of a national park, which meant that there were no towns or villages. The setting sun gave him a rough indication of the direction they had come from, but that was about it.

Meanwhile, they kept listening for a rifle shot that would indicate that Hauer had found his wounded stag and dispatched it, but there was nothing.

"That stag must have made a run for Paris," Cole said. "Either that, or it was already down."

Night was coming on fast. The valley had become eerily quiet.

"What's that?" Danny asked, pointing toward the tree line. "I think I see Herr Hauer."

Cole followed Danny's finger, saw a shape move among the trees in the last of the light. Definitely two-legged. Definitely making no effort to come toward them. The hair on the back of Cole's neck raised. They were being watched.

"It's Hauer, all right," Cole said.

All at once, realization crashed down on Cole. Hauer had the walkie talkie, which was the only means to let anyone know where they were. Maybe Hauer had a flashlight and a map, too.

What did he have? Nothing. He and Danny were totally unprepared. Hauer had made sure that he held all the cards. Cole wanted to kick himself for being so stupid.

Cole shook his head. A chill that had nothing to do with the temperature ran through him. This whole time he'd been thinking that the game between him and Hauer, which they were playing to settle old scores, had been to see who could shoot the most deer and boar in these mountains. But maybe that hadn't been the quarry that Hauer had in mind. Perhaps the stakes here were much higher than Cole had suspected. Cursing himself all over again, he realized that Hauer had played him for a fool and that he had walked right into a trap—dragging Danny along with him.

Then full-on darkness arrived, flowing through the valley like a tide, and the silhouette at the forest edge was lost among the shadows.

CHAPTER TWENTY-ONE

COLE DIDN'T LIKE the idea of staying put, but he liked the idea of trying to hike back in the dark even less. One wrong turn, or one fall, could spell disaster. They had no flashlight and no way of calling for help.

While he thought it over, Danny was full of questions.

"If nobody is coming back for us, what should we do?" Danny wondered. "What is Herr Hauer up to, anyhow?"

"I wish I knew what Hauer was up to," Cole said. "I'm beginning to think he has something planned for us, and it's nothing good."

"He's going to kill us, isn't he?"

"Not if I can help it," Cole said.

"We could try hiking back."

"Keep your voice down," Cole urged. "Let's not make it any easier for Hauer to keep track of us. As for hiking back, we don't know the way and we don't even have a flashlight. There's no moon and it's darker than a well-digger's ass out here."

"Huh?"

"If we go off the trail or fall into a ravine, we'd just end up in a worse pickle than we're already in," Cole said.

"Hans and Angela will wonder where we are," Danny said. "The other hunters will figure out that we're missing and come looking for us."

"Maybe," Cole said. "For now, we're on our own, and that's a fact. Our friends and family help us when they can, but in the end, the only person you can count on is yourself."

"And you, Pa Cole,"

"And me," Cole said with a grin. "I'll tell you another thing. We aren't going to sit here and wait for Hauer to creep up on us. We can at least move down the valley to a different spot. He'll never find us in the dark."

"Whatever you say," Danny replied, fear evident in his voice.

"Follow me and keep quiet," Cole whispered.

The cold and damp was like a curtain that he had to push through. Leaving the spot where they had butchered the boar, he followed the slope of the valley down, Danny on his heels. Moving across the open field wasn't so difficult, but Cole couldn't see more than a few feet ahead. He stopped when they reached the trees on the bottom half of the valley, moving quietly across a narrow stream that gurgled there. They took time to refill their canteens. He figured the water should be clean enough here in the mountains. As a soldier, he'd drank worse.

Cole felt pleased that Danny barely made a sound crossing the stream.

"Boy, you might not be a hunter, but you picked up a trick or two about the woods, didn't you? Now, let's see if we can get into those trees just as quietly."

Danny didn't respond, but Cole could almost feel him grinning with pride in the darkness.

They reached the trees and slipped several feet into the forest. He stopped when he felt the ground begin to rise for the forested slope that led up from the valley floor. He wanted some shelter, but at first light, he also wanted to be able to see Hauer moving across the valley.

The Butcher had a rifle, but so did Cole.

He thought about Hauer's barely concealed disappointment when Cole had announced that he had a rifle and would not need the shotgun that Hauer had planned on him carrying. Now, it all made more sense. If Cole had a shotgun out here and Hauer had a rifle that could pick him off at long range, then Cole would have been as good as defenseless.

That old Nazi bastard was full of tricks, wasn't he?

If he spotted Hauer first and shot him, maybe Cole could call it a hunting accident. He had a pretty good idea that this was just what Hauer planned to do to him and Danny. It wouldn't be the first time that a hunting trip had been used as cover for a murder.

Cole took stock, cursing himself for not being better prepared. They had nothing to eat. No blankets. Not even a match to light a campfire—then again, the last thing Cole wanted was a fire with Hauer out there. What he did have were the canteens, a knife, and a damn fine rifle. In the end, what more did he need? Maybe legs that were decades younger, for a start. For that, he might have to depend on his grandson.

"I'm sorry you got dragged into this, Danny," Cole said.

"What's this all about anyhow, Pa Cole? Why would he be trying to kill us? Is he some sort of madman?"

"He's a madman, all right, but there's more to it than that." Cole had not gone into his background with Hauer, in part to shelter Danny from some ugly stories. It was clear now how well that had worked out. It was time to come clean. "Herr Hauer and I have some history," he said. "You know that we crossed paths back in the war. Right near here, as a matter of fact, in the closing chapter of the Battle of the Bulge. The Germans were winning at first, and then the tables turned on them. You know how a cornered animal gets."

"Yeah, I suppose I do."

"Hauer did some pretty ugly things. To be fair, I reckon I did, too. That's war for you. What's happening now is what you might call a reckoning. Hauer wants revenge."

"What do you want, Pa Cole?"

"First of all, I want you to get out of here in one piece." Cole thought about it. "And the second thing, now that the gloves are off, is that I want some justice."

"Aren't you two a little old for all this?"

Cole grunted. "Tell that to Hauer."

"If you ask me, this is crazy."

Cole didn't disagree, but he had learned a long time ago to accept the reality of any situation rather than deny it.

Without any fire or blankets, it was going to be a long, cold night. Cole put his back against a fallen log, facing the direction from which they had come. He leaned the rifle against the log, within easy reach.

"Sit over here right up against me," Cole said. "Our body heat will help to keep us warm."

Danny soon nestled against Cole, almost like he had as a little boy. There was some necessity here because the only part of them that stayed warm was where their bodies touched. Their extremities felt cold and they both shivered. Nonetheless, to Cole's surprise, Danny's head sagged against Cole's shoulder and his grandson drifted off to sleep.

Cole willed his own warmth to flow out of him and into Danny. He'd been a hard man all his life and never one to show much emotion —except anger, maybe. There were times when he regretted that part of himself. But even Cole recognized that it wasn't just warmth he was letting flow into Danny, it was love.

While his grandson slept, he kept awake, every sense alert. He heard the gentle night wind stir the trees overhead, the hoot of an owl, the bark of a fox. He didn't hear any stealthy footsteps in the forest, creeping toward them. He stayed awake, keeping watch through the night, until just before what he judged to be dawn, when he drifted off.

* * *

COLE COULDN'T SAY what woke him up first. It might have been the smack of a bullet hitting the log next to his head, or the sharp crack of a rifle that followed a split second later. He was half asleep, but instinct took over.

"Danny, keep down! Get on the other side of the log."

Quickly, Cole shook off the last blurriness of sleep like he was throwing back a blanket. Scanning the woods, he guessed that the shot had come from the direction of the valley.

Hauer had managed to track them, probably following their trail through last night's frosty grass. Now, he was coming after them and his intentions were all too clear.

Cole crawled over the log, putting it between himself and Hauer. Danny was already crouched behind it.

Through the rifle scope, Cole scanned the forest and looked into the clearing, but there was no sign of Hauer. Through the high-powered scope, mostly what he saw was a confusing tangle of tree branches. He reminded himself that the man had been a sniper, after all. One of the best. He wouldn't be exposing himself needlessly to Cole's rifle sights.

"Where is he?" Danny asked.

"Somewhere close."

Cole had to admit that he was a little troubled. He had been asleep; Hauer could have crept right up on them. He also wondered how Hauer had managed to miss.

It had been like that stag. Hauer had been presented with a clear shot that he shouldn't have missed. What if Hauer had missed on purpose? Cole suspected that Hauer had taken the more masterful shot of intentionally wounding the stag, thus giving him an excuse to trail it into the forest. What if he had done the same thing just now and missed on purpose? If so, it meant that Hauer was toying with them.

Cole didn't like the situation at all. Hauer knew where they were, but he couldn't see Hauer.

"Let's get out of here," Cole said. "We're going to make a run for it, deeper into the trees. Keep low, and juke and weave. Whatever you do, don't run in a straight line."

"I can do it." Danny seemed to be reassuring himself.

"Go!"

They jumped out from behind the log and ran, willing themselves to present as small of a target as possible. Danny ran a lot faster than Cole, who struggled to keep up.

Another shot rang out, passing so close that Cole heard the supersonic crack of the bullet. The sound made his spine quiver.

If Hauer had been toying with them before, he wasn't anymore. Hauer was shooting to kill.

He glanced over his shoulder, rifle at the ready, hoping for some glimpse of their pursuer. All that Cole saw were trees and more trees.

"Hold up," he called out to Danny, who was getting too far ahead of him. The last thing they needed was to get separated. In this dense forest, they would never find each other again.

Danny stopped running, getting behind a massive old oak for cover. Cole slid in beside him, breathing hard. Not for the first time, he was glad that he had given up cigarettes back in 1944. So many of the old-timers he knew who smoked now had emphysema or even used oxygen—the ones who hadn't already died of lung cancer, in any case.

"Now what?" Danny asked. Racing through the trees had burned off some of the boy's initial fright and he seemed calmer. Cole was glad that the boy was thinking about strategy.

"He did have the upper hand," Cole said. "He had us dead to rights back there. But now, he's got to come to us."

"What do we do?"

"We wait for him."

The massive tree that they had sheltered behind offered good cover. The tree was old enough that some Gallic archer might have passed here, or more recently, a Wehrmacht soldier. One side of the gnarled trunk was festooned with green moss. *North*, Cole thought. He filed that information away.

Cole got down on the forest floor to one side of the tree trunk and Danny took the left side.

"You be my eyes," Cole said. They didn't have binoculars, but his grandson's youthful eyes would be almost as good. They were using scout-sniper tactics now. "If you see any movement, you let me know. I'm going to stay on this here scope."

Again, the scope amplified Cole's vision, but it limited his field of view. All that he could see was a tangle of trees and underbrush, albeit crystal clear. He would rely on Danny to see the big picture spread out before them.

Their noisy flight through the woods had driven all the forest creatures into hiding. Not so much as a bird flickered through the branches.

Any movement that they did see would be Hauer coming after them.

Time passed slowly, but Cole was patient. Hell, he had spent a lifetime getting to this moment. He could wait. It was Danny that he was worried about.

With autumn, enough litter and leaves covered the forest floor that Cole was confident they would hear Hauer coming. There were quite a few pine trees in places, however, creating essentially a smooth carpet of needles. Nonetheless, Cole was convinced that if they didn't hear *something*, then they weren't being pursued by a man at all, but by a ghost. Then again, a lifetime of shooting meant that Cole's hearing wasn't what it used to be. He hoped Danny's eyes and ears were sharper.

"There!" Danny whispered hoarsely. "I see him!"

Cole scanned the woods but saw only the tangle of branches.

"On a clock face, where would he be?"

Danny thought. "Two o'clock."

Cole moved the scope in that direction. Sure enough, he saw a flicker of motion. Not enough yet for a clear target, but it was Hauer, all right, and he was on the move toward them.

Hauer was an impressive tracker, but Cole remembered that about him from the war. Grudgingly, Cole had to admire the man's skill. Then again, they had been plowing through that woods, leaving a trail of broken branches and disturbed leaves. On the plus side, their trail was leading Hauer right into Cole's rifle sights.

He waited patiently. Hauer was moving cautiously so that he came closer ever so slowly. But as he did so, the screen of tree branches in front of him diminished, giving Cole a clear shot.

"He's getting closer!" Danny whispered urgently.

"I see him," Cole said calmly.

Still, he took his time, letting Hauer work his way in. Cole had the rifle balanced in his arms, his elbows locked into the forest floor, his legs spread out behind him. He felt the whole steadiness of the ground beneath him. Other than having the rifle placed across a log, this setup didn't get any better.

He let a breath out. Took in a deeper breath and held it.

Cole was a hunter through and through. He never missed a day in the woods. Even so, he was out of practice for shooting at two-legged prey. He hesitated for just a moment before pressing the trigger.

It wasn't any fit of conscience. Cole had to admit that some part of him was enjoying having Hauer in his rifle sights just a little too much. For a marksman, this was the ultimate prey: another sniper. The moment before he fired was like some forbidden, delicious pleasure.

"Pa Cole, what are you waiting for? Shoot!"

Danny's nervousness made his voice too loud. His voice carried through the quiet woods.

Through the scope, Cole saw Hauer crouch and freeze. He had heard Danny.

Hauer was searching the forest. Cole watched him through the scope as his gaze moved in their general direction. He was so close that Cole could see his face.

Then Hauer did something totally unpredictable. Instead of obliging Cole by holding still, he charged through the forest, closing the distance between them.

Cole did not hesitate any longer. His finger took up the last bit of pressure on the trigger.

However, this was like shooting at the charging boar. The target did not hold steady but danced in the crosshairs, juking right and left in a way that the boar had not. Cole couldn't get a fix on him.

The rifle fired. Instantly, Cole ran the bolt and kept his eye on the scope, hoping for a second shot. He caught a glimpse of movement and fired again.

Through the scope, Hauer was gone.

"Did you get him?" Danny asked.

"Hush now," Cole said sharply. Danny had already given them away once.

Seconds later, they had their answer. Cole's luck must have run out with that boar.

A rifle shot crashed through the trees. In the same instant, Cole felt a burning pain rip down the length of his right arm and shoulder.

That son of a bitch Hauer had just shot him.

Cole had the presence of mind to roll behind the tree before a second bullet passed through the space that he had occupied only an instant before.

He switched the rifle to his left hand. His right arm was just about useless and already going numb. He wouldn't be able to shoot back now.

Danny saw the blood on his grandfather. He stared at the crimson flow in shock. "Pa Cole, you've been shot!"

"Never mind that," Cole said, struggling to his feet. "We've got to run!"

CHAPTER TWENTY-TWO

THEY CRASHED THROUGH THE FOREST, not caring how much noise they made.

"Keep going," Cole panted, urging Danny on. "We need to put some space between us and him."

"You think he's coming after us?" Danny asked.

"I know he is."

The only way to go was up. Hauer had cut them off from the valley and the only familiar territory they knew, forcing them up the mountain. It was also the only path to help and safety that Cole was aware of. What was beyond this mountain they were climbing? Another mountain. And maybe another beyond that. That was a lot of territory to cover before they had any hope of coming across a village or a road. Hauer had them right where he wanted them.

Cole's breath grew more ragged. The pain in his arm and shoulder increased as the shock wore off. Hauer's bullet hadn't gotten him, but a heart attack might at this rate. Good thing he had kept in shape hiking through the hills back home. He might be old, but he was a tough old bird.

Even so, after a few minutes of pushing it as hard as they could, Cole had to stop. He bent over, hands on his knees, gasping for breath.

"I'm too old for this shit," he announced.

Danny managed to grin in spite of everything. "When we get home, don't let Gran hear you swear like that."

"Don't you go telling her." Cole liked the fact that Danny was making it sound like a given that they would be getting out of this mess. He handed the rifle to Danny. "Here now, take this and shoot down the hill."

"Do you see him?" There was nothing below them but trees.

"No, but he won't know that. He'll slow down and take his time coming after us."

Danny shouldered the rifle and fired. The rifle boomed and echoed through the hills. He started to hand back the rifle, but Cole stopped him.

"You hang onto that for now. I've only got one good arm."

Expending the shot in hopes of keeping Hauer's pursuit slow and cautious had been a calculated risk, considering that Cole had a limited supply of ammunition. When Hans had procured the hunting rifle, he had brought along two magazines. Ten rounds total. Although rifles and shotguns were legal in Germany for hunting, ammunition was very limited and expensive. Hans had supplied ammunition adequate for a casual hunting trip, not a firefight. In heading to the woods, Cole had taken just one magazine. That had been all that he had ever needed on a hunting trip. He was now down to a few rounds. He was sure that Hauer had much, much more than that.

He didn't share his concerns with Danny, but Cole was worried. From here on out, each shot must count. In the end, Cole only needed one bullet—the one that he would use to kill Hauer. Growing up, he'd often gone hunting with one bullet. He would make it count.

They kept climbing. The terrain grew increasingly rocky and rugged as they ascended the mountain slope. The slope increased, slowing their progress.

"If we can get to the top of this hill, we can move along the ridge up there and then try to come back down circle around Hauer," Cole said. "I'd like to get back to that valley if we can. If we can find that trail out of there, we can hoof it back to the lodge. With any luck, Hauer won't be any the wiser and he'll set up here, looking for us."

"We ought to see if we can make it look like we reached the top and went down the other side," Danny said. "He'll go that way, looking for us."

Cole nodded. "I always knew you were a Cole, through and through," he said. "I should have thought of that myself."

With their goal in mind, they pushed harder toward the summit. The trees thinned out and Cole worried about being exposed, but Danny's plan to make it look as if they had gone down the other side of the ridge was a good one. He just hoped that Hauer would fall for it —so far, the German had proved himself to be a good tracker.

The ground became more treacherous because fallen leaves covered the rocks and small boulders, making their footing slippery and hiding good footing. They hadn't gone more than another fifty feet when Danny suddenly cried out and fell. He lost his grip on the rifle, which clattered to the rocks.

"It's my ankle!" he said.

Cole went to help him. Sure enough, his grandson's foot had caught between two rocks that held it securely as a vise. With his left hand, he helped to work Danny's boot free.

"Can you put any weight on it?"

Danny stood and hobbled for a few feet, his face wincing in pain. "Wow, that hurts. Is it broken?"

"Let me see it a minute." Cole felt the ankle, which was already beginning to swell. As best he could, Cole tugged the boot laces tight.

"Ow! What are you doing? Shouldn't we take that boot off?"

"No, leave it on. Your ankle is sprained, most likely." Cole thought the ankle might be broken, but he didn't say that to Danny. Anyhow, a bad sprain was just as serious as a broken ankle. "The boot will give it some support. Sit down a minute and catch your breath."

Picking his way carefully over the rocks, he made his way to where the rifle had fallen. Thankfully, the costly Leica scope wasn't cracked. He checked to make sure that the muzzle was free of debris. The beautiful stock was now marred by a big scratch, but otherwise, the rifle seemed fine. This was a fancy customized version, but at its heart the Springfield was a tough nut to crack.

Next, he sat down next to Danny and used the hunting knife to cut some strips of cloth from the tail of his shirt. Some he used to bind up Danny's ankle. He handed the rest of the cloth strips to Danny and told him to bandage Cole's wounded arm. They both had a long drink of water from the canteen, and then Cole announced it was time to keep moving.

"I don't think I can walk on that ankle."

"You ain't got any choice," Cole said. "Here, grab hold of my shoulder."

The two of them hobbled up the hill, struggling for each step, with Danny keeping weight off his ankle and Cole nursing his arm.

"We're a fine pair," Cole said.

"Now what?"

"Let's get to the top of this ridge and see if we can put Hauer off the trail, then hoof it out of here as best we can." After that, Cole hated to admit it to Danny, but they were out of options. All that they could do was run and hide.

* * *

THEY MADE their play to put Hauer on a false trail. By the time the sun was starting to sink below the hills, they had made it back down the mountain, making a wide loop to dodge Hauer.

"Almost there," Cole said, encouraging Danny.

"Downhill isn't any easier." Danny grimaced. "Boy, this ankle hurts. Are you sure it's not broken? I don't know how much longer I can do this."

Cole cast about for some way to keep Danny distracted. Their predicament brought to mind the story of Cole's cousin, Deacon Cole. Like Cole, he had served in the war, but in the Pacific, fighting the Japanese.

"Did I ever tell you about Cousin Deacon?" Cole asked.

"Didn't I meet him?"

"Sure, once or twice when you were a young 'un. I'm surprised you remember."

"I remember him a little."

"Well now, Cousin Deacon was mauled by a bear when he was just a boy. He was trying to protect his sister and that bear chewed him up good. He had the scars to prove it. It's a wonder that bear didn't kill him. It took him months just to get around again."

"I remember the scars," Danny said. "They were hard to look at. I remember being scared of him."

"Cousin Deacon used to say that during the war he went through some hard times, all that fighting in the islands, but he kept going. He said that he figured if the bear hadn't killed him, then he sure as hell wasn't going to let the Japanese do it."

"That's a good story, Pa Cole, but I twisted my ankle. I didn't get attacked by a bear."

"The point is that Deacon Cole was tough. That bear made him that way. Who's to say this ordeal ain't your version of the bear?"

Danny fell silent, thinking it over. He didn't complain again about the pain in his ankle.

Cole thought it was too much to hope that Hauer had taken the bait and followed the false trail down the other side of the mountain. Under different circumstances, the majestic surroundings of the Vosges Mountains and the European forest in autumn would have been stunning in and of themselves. However, Cole and Danny were injured, hungry and cold, and hunted by a deadly opponent. By the time they reached the valley below, they felt exhausted.

For now, they were sheltering at the edge of the forest, keeping to the cover of the trees with the open valley visible. He hadn't wanted to spend another night in these hills, but here they were. They had not eaten anything in more than twenty-four hours, and with their injuries and the cool autumn weather, it was starting to take its toll.

"How much longer do you think we'll be out here?" Danny asked. "I'm starving."

"Me too," Cole said. "One way or another, I promise you that we won't be out here another night."

"What about Herr Hauer?"

"It's me that he's after," Cole said. While coming down the mountain, he had begun to slowly put a plan together that might mean at least one of them would survive this mess. The time had come to share his plan with Danny. "I've been thinking that I'll lead him off into the woods, and he and I will finish this, one way or another. While we're doing that, you can head down toward the neck of the valley and find the trail out of here. If we cut you a crutch, you should be fine."

Danny shook his head. "No way! With your arm and shoulder like that, there's no way you can shoot back at him."

"I can still shoot," Cole lied.

His grandson shook his head emphatically. "We are in this together, Pa Cole. There's no way I'm leaving you here by yourself."

If Danny was going to be stubborn, then so was Cole. Stubbornness was a family trait. "Boy, I've got to be honest with you. I don't know that I can beat Hauer at this game. At my age, I've lost a step or two. Hell, maybe I've lost three or four steps. The best that I can hope to do is buy you some time to get to safety. One of us needs to survive this."

Danny didn't say anything for a while, and Cole felt relieved. He was sure that Danny was going to agree to the plan. Considering the shape he was in—cold, hungry, and in pain—who wouldn't opt for a way out?

But Danny surprised him. The light was fading fast, but Cole could see that his grandson's eyes, which were normally a soft brown, had turned dark and hard. Those eyes reminded Cole of Norma Jean's when she was feeling determined.

The boy had plenty of fire in him, that was for sure. If their circumstances hadn't been so dire, Cole would have smiled.

"I'm not leaving," Danny said. "You're the one who said this might be *my* bear. I've got to face the bear, not run away from it. And listen to you, Pa Cole—it sounds as if you've given up."

"I managed to get you dragged into this, but it's not your fight. I should have known better than to walk right into Hauer's trap. I wanted one last chance to show him who was boss. Like the Bible says, *pride goeth before a fall.*"

"There's no point in blaming yourself," Danny said. "Listen, I know you never talked about the war, but I read that museum exhibit same as everyone else. You killed an awful lot of people."

"It was war, Danny. It's nothing to be proud of. I was doing my duty."

Danny fixed him with that hard stare, the one that showed he was determined to hear the truth. "Are you sure about that? I see how people who knew you then treat you, even Colonel Mulholland—like they're a little afraid of you. Even now. I don't care if you're old. I don't care if you're hurt—or that I'm hurt. You need to show that German sniper that you're the same old Caje Cole. He couldn't beat you then, and he's not going to beat you now. You're a Cole, remember?"

Oddly enough, Cole felt chastised. It was as if the roles had been reversed so that Danny was the old man and Cole was the foolish boy at his feet.

Cole took a deep breath, letting the cold mountain air fill his lungs. Deep within him, he felt the primitive critter start to stir, awakening in the cave where it had hidden away. Danny's words had been like poking the critter with a pointy stick, which was a dangerous thing to do.

Danny was right that he shouldn't give up. It was time to turn the tables on The Butcher. It was time to hunt.

"So that's how you feel, is it?" Cole said. "Your old Pa Cole has let you down?"

"You said it yourself. You're giving up."

"Not yet," Cole said. "If you want to stay and fight, I could use the help."

Danny nodded.

"But first, what do you say you and me get something to eat?"

"How are we going to do that?"

"I seem to recall that there's an entire boar not a quarter-mile from here. The one I shot yesterday. In this cold, the meat will still be good."

"What are we going to do, eat it raw? Won't Herr Hauer see the fire?"

"Let him," Cole said. "Let's show that son of a bitch that we're not afraid of him. The smell of that roasting meat will drive him crazy."

His grandson grinned. "Sounds good to me. Do you think there's any bacon on that boar?"

CHAPTER TWENTY-THREE

HAUER SCANNED THE FOREST AHEAD. He had the American and his grandson right where he wanted them. On the run. He knew it was only a matter of time now, with Cole wounded and his grandson being nothing more than a weak boy.

He smiled. The time had come for a reckoning. The American sniper would be losing this last fight.

His plan for revenge on Cole had been loosely conceived, and if Hauer had to admit it, it wasn't much of a plan at all. It was more how a sailor might experience favorable winds and smooth seas. Everything had simply fallen into place.

Back at the museum opening, he had invited Cole on the hunting trip on a whim. But the possibilities presented by getting Cole alone in the woods had soon presented themselves in his mind. Of course, he hadn't even been sure that they would end up hunting alone. He had taken a few small steps, such as making sure that he had the walkie talkie and flashlight. Hauer was no criminal mastermind, but he was an opportunist. He always had been, all the way back to the day that he had pushed that old witch of a nun down the school stairs. In this case, all the circumstances had been in his favor and had led to this moment.

He had managed to get himself and Cole assigned to the same
hunting spot. Then, he had deliberately wounded the stag that had run
his way. Hauer used the walkie-talkie to communicate with the larger
group of hunters. It had been a simple matter to relay that they were
not only heading back early on their own—but that they were
returning to Munich.

The other hunters wouldn't be expecting them back at the lodge.

Hauer had all the time in the world now to stalk his prey.

Eventually, he would emerge from the woods with some story
about getting lost and losing track of Cole and the boy. If and when
their bodies were ever found, it would be chalked up to a hunting
accident.

He had even gotten lucky and wounded Cole during their exchange
of fire. That shootout had been just like the old days! For once and for
all, Hauer was going to have a chance to settle the score against the
American sniper.

He looked up at the slope ahead of him, knowing that Cole was up
there somewhere. It was Cole that he was after. The boy posed no
threat, having made it clear that he did not care for hunting. The boy
did not even carry a weapon. When the time came, Hauer would
dispatch him along with his grandfather. *Collateral damage*. Hauer
grinned at the thought. There could be no witnesses.

"Run, little pigs, run," Hauer muttered, smiling to himself. "The
Butcher is coming to find you."

The Butcher. He had earned this nickname because Hauer really
had been a butcher, slaughtering goats and sheep and cattle, before
the German invasion of Poland. His previous vocation had proved
useful whenever the troops had a windfall of livestock to supplement
their rations. The choice cuts of meat he provided to officers ensured
their favor. And of course, Hauer's casual brutality, honed in the
slaughterhouse, had served him well as a soldier. His nickname had
come to take on a different meaning, a different sort of butchery.
Most of Hauer's fellow soldiers looked the other way. The few who
spoke up did not last long—war had a way of quickly winnowing out
honorable men, leaving the real business of war to soldiers such as
Hauer.

His only regret was that the war hadn't gone on for a while longer. Hauer had never quite gotten his fill.

He knew that Cole still held those incidents from the war against him, not only killing the villagers at Ville sur Moselle, but also the incident at Wingen sur Moder here in these very mountains at the end of what the Americans called the Battle of the Bulge.

In his mind's eye, Hauer could still see the nun that he had shot in his crosshairs. He could still hear the satisfying smack of the bullet hitting home. Some memories did not fade over time.

"If she chose to help the Americans, then she was the enemy," he said aloud to the trees. He shrugged. He had no regrets.

In East Germany, employed by the *Stasi*, he had managed to continue his share of killing. Even so, that had taken place quietly. It was not at all the same as the battles that had taken place in France and then in these hills.

Now that the wall had come down and the Iron Curtain had been swept aside, those days were over for good. The Butcher was just an ordinary citizen now. Fortunately, like most members of the *Stasi*, he had managed to line his pockets over the years in a way that enabled him to live in some comfort, if not exactly luxury. Mostly, he found himself bored, sometimes paying for the company of women—there was no shortage of prostitutes from places like Poland and Hungary—and drinking too much vodka. This game with Cole had been a pleasant diversion from the doldrums of retirement.

Hauer kept going up the hillside, moving cautiously. Just because he had gotten lucky so far didn't mean that his luck would continue. As long as Cole still had a rifle, he was dangerous.

A shot rang out and Hauer ducked. He held himself still for several minutes, worried that he had miscalculated his quarry. Was he in Cole's sights even now? He hadn't heard a bullet come anywhere near him. Maybe it had been a random shot intended to slow him down—which it had.

"Nice try," he admitted. "Very smart. But it is not enough to stop me."

Satisfied that Cole did not have him in his crosshairs, after all, Hauer continued up the slope. His breathing came heavily—drinking vodka and chasing whores were not exactly the best activities for staying in shape at his age. He took his time, reading the landscape as he went.

He had spent many of the intervening years hunting with other members of the *Stasi* and had sharpened his tracking skills as a result.

Here and there, the bed of leaves and pine needles was disturbed, indicating that his quarry had passed this way. He spotted broken twigs left in the wake of their passage.

Finally, he saw spots of blood, rich and dark. So, his bullet had found its mark.

He squatted down and touched a spot of blood, wetting his fingertip and then rubbing the blood between his fingers.

"I am coming to put you out of your misery, Hillbilly!" he shouted.

The hills echoed back his words, but there was no answer.

Hauer shrugged and kept moving. Slowly, laboriously, he followed the blood trail and the footsteps on the soft carpet of the forest. Where the ground grew rocky, he saw places where the rocks had been disturbed. A couple of hours passed. Hauer sat down and ate a candy bar, wished for a hot cup of coffee, rested for a few minutes, and then kept going.

Finally, he reached the summit.

The view was stunning. Even someone like The Butcher could admit to the natural beauty of the place. He saw deep forests, tall pines mixed with the fiery colors of autumn leaves. No buildings. No roads. No signs of civilization at all, in fact, except a single column of woodsmoke that appeared to be several miles distant. The days were so short this time of year that the sun was already slipping low in the sky. The mountain winter was just around the corner.

He studied the trail leading down the other side of the summit. What was down there? More rocks, more forest. Had Cole gone that way? Hauer was doubtful. The only real chance Cole had was to get down to the valley again and look for the trail out. That Hillbilly was clever—it would be just like him to have left a false trail, and then doubled back.

"Where have you gone, little pigs?" Hauer wondered aloud.

After another moment of thought, he turned and headed back

down the slope, returning toward the valley, confident that Cole was trying to give him the slip.

But not for long.

* * *

BACK AT THE LODGE, Hans was worried. When his new friend, Cole, and Cole's grandson had not returned with the other hunters at nightfall, he had expressed concern.

"They have gone back to Munich," the hunt master explained, holding up a walkie talkie by way of proof. "Hauer radioed me to say that they'd had enough and that he was driving the American and his grandson back to the city."

"They did not tell me," Hans said. "I'm the one who drove them here."

The hunt master shrugged. He looked toward his companions, gathered around a fire and drinking schnapps. He seemed eager to join them, rather than to debate with Hans. "What can I tell you? That is all I know."

"We should call the authorities."

The hunt master groaned. "Oh, we don't need them here! They will just have us answering questions all night, when we should be sitting by the fire drinking schnapps. If your friends were driving back to Munich, they won't get there until much later tonight. Why don't you wait until tomorrow morning and give them a call? I am sure that they will explain everything then."

The hunt master gave Hans a reassuring pat on the shoulder, then moved toward the ring of celebratory hunters. Someone passed him a glass of schnapps.

Angela had been nearby, listening in. "Do you think they really went back to Munich."

"No, I do not."

"Neither do I," she said. "We should go have a look at their room."

The limited accommodations at the lodge had required that the grandfather and grandson share a room in the converted stable. However, calling it a stable was something of a misnomer because the building had been completely renovated to match the lodge in comforts. The door to the Americans' guest room was not even locked. Not that there was anything of value in it, other than clothes. Pajama bottoms, two scattered socks, and some underwear lay on the floor near Danny's unmade bed, evidence that he had dressed in a hurry to go hunting, and a suitcase full of disheveled clothing lay open on top of the covers. Cole's side of the room had a military precision about it, with the bed neatly made.

"Your boyfriend is a slob," Hans said, smiling. The situation might be serious, but he could not resist teasing his grand-niece.

"Uncle Hans, he is not my boyfriend!"

"Hmm," he said. "Are you so sure about that?"

Angela made an exasperated sound in response.

"All their things are here," Hans said. "It does not make sense that they left. I don't trust that Hauer one bit. He is up to something."

"We need to go look for them," Angela said. "Maybe they need help. Maybe they are hurt. We need to go right now."

Hans shook his head. "It is dark out. What would you and I do, an old man and a city girl?"

Angela pouted. "We must do something! I am worried about Danny!"

"I already expressed my concerns to the hunt master. Whatever else we do will have to wait for morning."

"We can't wait that long!"

Hans thought about it, knowing his grand-niece was right. The question was, what could they do?

Then he remembered the business card in his billfold. He took it out. On it was the telephone number for the retired American officer who had helped to organize the WWII museum.

"Angela, we must find a phone. We will call Colonel Mulholland. He will know what to do."

*　*　*

MILES AWAY, Cole and Danny were preparing for another night in the forest. It was clear and cold. Through a gap in the treetops, Cole could see the stars overhead, sparkling bright. He had spent a lifetime looking at those stars. They felt like old friends.

Danny surprised him by saying, "Look, there's Orion." He pointed up at the three stars that made up The Hunter's belt.

"Huh, I reckon somebody was paying attention when I taught him the stars, after all."

"Sure, Pa Cole. I know all the stars." He pointed. "There's Pegasus. There's Taurus. The Bull."

While their situation remained desperate, they were both in better spirits. They had built a small fire and roasted some of the pork, and both of them had eaten their fill.

While the fire had been a way of thumbing his nose at Hauer, Cole wasn't foolish enough to sleep right beside it. Instead, they had made their makeshift camp about one hundred feet away. They had left a couple of bundles of branches on the ground near the fire so that from a distance the bundles would resemble sleeping bodies.

Cole was close enough that he would see Hauer if The Butcher entered the circle of firelight. If that was the case, then Cole planned to shoot him. In part, Cole had broken every rule for stealth and built the fire because he now suspected that it wouldn't be Hauer's style to ambush them in the night, or even to pick them off from the darkness. That was outside the rules of the strange game that they were playing. No, he suspected that Hauer would want Cole to see what was coming. He would want to savor his final victory. Hauer would want to gloat. With no sign that help was on its way, Hauer wasn't in any rush to finish them off.

Cole felt confident that Hauer would wait for daylight. When daylight came, Cole had a surprise of his own planned for his old enemy.

With a full belly, Cole felt new energy coursing through him. Whatever came tomorrow, he would be ready to finish this business with Hauer for once and for all. This was going to be the finish to a fight that had started forty years before.

"Get some sleep," he said to Danny. "I'll keep watch."

Danny didn't argue. They were both exhausted after a day spent trudging up and down the mountain, trying to stay ahead of Hauer.

Danny's injured ankle and Cole's own wounds had also drained their energy.

His grandson tugged his coat tighter and rolled over in the leaves to get some sleep.

Cole had no plans of his own to sleep. He smiled to himself. What did an old man need sleep for, anyhow? He had an eternity to rest, and that eternity was coming on fast. No, sleep was for the young. He glanced down at the resting young man, wishing that he could walk with him through life and guide him, but knowing that we each have to make our own way. The best that any parent or grandparent could hope for was to set younger folks on the right path.

He wanted Danny to live and have a chance to follow that path, wherever that might take him. For that to happen, Cole was going to have to kill Hauer.

Instead of sleeping, he took out the hunting knife that he had used to butcher the boar and began to sharpen it. He had no proper sharpening stone with him, of course, but he had found a reasonably flat, smooth stone, speckled with flint, that would serve the same purpose. He spat on the stone and got to work. He worked gently and patiently, so that the sound of steel on stone wouldn't carry through the woods.

The knife itself was a Böker lock-blade, made in Germany. He hadn't brought any of his own hand-made knives with him on the trip, but he had to admit that the German knife was a quality product. After a while, he tested the edge with his thumb. The steel took an edge well and held it.

When he was finished with the knife, he moved on to the rifle. Back in his military days, it had always been a source of ribbing—as much as anyone kidded with someone as serious as Cole—that he had the cleanest rifle in the army.

Old habits died hard. He didn't have any proper cleaning tools to speak of out here in the woods, but he made due. Earlier, he had cut yet another strip from his tattered shirt and soaked it in some of the pork fat from supper. He used the rag to rub down every part of the action that he could reach, along with the exterior metal surfaces to protect them from the nighttime dew.

"It ain't gun oil," he muttered. "But grease from that boar will have to do."

He unloaded the magazine and reloaded it. Two rounds left. It would have to be enough.

Cole ran his hands over the bright, smooth steel and the burnished walnut stock, enjoying the feel of the checkering under his fingertips. The sporterized Springfield was indeed a beautiful rifle. He just hoped that he had an opportunity to return it to Hans once this business was finished.

With the knife sharpened and the rifle ready to go, Cole leaned back against the fallen tree and gazed up at the stars. Danny slept, but Cole had Orion to keep him company. Some distance away, the dying flames of their campfire flickered through the empty woods. Hauer might be watching the fire, but he hadn't shown himself. Cole stayed awake, keeping his own vigil.

CHAPTER TWENTY-FOUR

DAWN ARRIVED SLOWLY, the sun touching the mountaintops first, then creeping into the valleys. Cole stood and stretched, but didn't feel the least bit cold. It was as if he could sense the heat of the coming action in his blood. One way or another, the final confrontation with Hauer would be this morning.

With any luck, Hauer had been drawn by the firelight and had spent the night watching the dying coals, anticipating his revenge. He would be as cold and exhausted as his quarry this morning.

Cole had spent those wakeful hours planning his trap. His plan was simple, but it was going to rely on Danny. The question was, would the boy be up to the task?

"You awake?" he asked, by way of waking Danny up.

Groggily, Danny opened his eyes. "Darn, I was hoping that all this was going to be a bad dream when I woke up, but I guess it wasn't."

"No such luck," Cole said.

Quickly, he outlined his plan to Danny. Cole would walk out into the open, heading back to where he had butchered the boar yesterday, as if planning to carve off more meat for breakfast. He would leave the rifle with Danny, who would be hidden at the forest edge. Once Hauer showed himself, or if he took a shot at Cole, it would be up to Danny to put Hauer in his crosshairs and finish him.

Just as Cole had feared, Danny didn't like the idea one bit.

"I can't do it," Danny protested. "You want me to *shoot* him?"

"You've got to," Cole said. "My arm and shoulder are too stiff to shoot that rifle. It's up to you."

Danny shook his head emphatically. "I can't. Pa Cole, you know I couldn't even shoot a deer when you took me hunting back home. I just couldn't. I sure can't shoot a human being."

"Even if that human being is trying to kill us?" Cole grumped. He had no such compunctions about defending himself from a threat, but he had to remind himself again that Danny was still young enough to trust that people were essentially good. Cole had learned otherwise a long time ago.

"You know what I mean. It's not right."

"Danny, Hauer doesn't have any human decency. Put it out of your head that you're shooting at a person. He's just a target. Instead, remember all the basics of shooting that I taught you. You're a good shot, Danny. You can do this."

"How am I even going to see Hauer if he's still in the trees?"

Cole had thought about that. "The thing with Hauer is, he'll want to gloat. He ain't gonna shoot me from a distance if he can avoid it. If he does, he'll wound me and then come closer to finish me off. He'll want to make sure that he's the last thing I see."

"So you're using yourself for bait?"

Cole didn't comment on that, but only handed Danny the rifle. "You've got two shots," he said. "Don't miss."

"Easy for you to say."

They crept closer to the edge of the forest, where it opened up to the valley. Cole got Danny set up with the rifle across a log, Cole's cap stuffed under it to steady his grandson's aim.

"Are you sure about this, Pa Cole?"

"You just remember everything I've taught you," Cole said. "You may not be a hunter, but you know how to shoot. Just take your time and be sure of your target. You'll do fine."

Danny nodded, but he didn't look convinced.

* * *

HAUER HAD them right where he wanted them. Cole was wounded, and that grandson didn't pose any threat. They had tried to give him the slip on the ridge by laying the false trail, but Hauer felt confident that they had moved back down the mountain.

His instincts had been correct and he soon found their trail. All that he had to do was follow them. A wounded man and a teenaged boy had no hope of escape from The Butcher.

He made his way back down the mountain, taking his time. It would not do to be overconfident. Cole still had a rifle and could set up an ambush. The American might be wounded, Hauer thought, but he still posed a danger.

He thought back all those years to the war. The Hillbilly sniper acted as if Hauer should feel some remorse, but did the wolf regret the sheep that he had killed?

There had been no real rules, not when the officers felt inclined to look the other way when there was dirty work to be done. If Cole kept a grudge against him, then the feeling was mutual. The American sniper could act as righteous as he liked, but the truth was that he had caused the demise of many German soldiers. His hands were not free of blood.

Hauer grinned, wondering how the final act would play out. He preferred not to shoot Cole from a distance. He wanted the American to *see* that the end was coming for him. Hauer wanted to savor that moment.

Already, it was starting to get dark. He wanted to make sure that they did not somehow give him the slip during the night. Who knew, but if the opportunity presented itself during the night, he might even finish this business with a knife—up close and personal.

Down below, Hauer spotted something flickering in the deepening shadows of the forest. To his surprise, he realized that he was seeing a campfire. As he crept closer, he even smelled grilling meat. They must have returned to the boar that Cole had killed. Hauer's belly rumbled. It had been a while since he had eaten any real food.

Reassured that his quarry wasn't going anywhere, he sat down to eat his rations, which consisted of half a sandwich that he had saved. He took a pull or two from the flask of vodka that he had brought along on the hunt. Most of his fellow Germans preferred schnapps, but the Soviet influence had long ago gotten him into the habit of drinking vodka, which was cheaper and far more plentiful in East Germany. He just hoped that this hunt wrapped up before his flask ran dry.

"Let me see how the hares are doing," he said.

With the edge taken off his hunger, he continued down the mountain. Near the fire, he moved cautiously, concerned that Cole might have set some sort of trap for him. He crept closer to the circle of firelight.

Already, the Hillbilly and his grandson must have gone to sleep. He could see the dark outlines of their bodies, stretched out on the ground near the fire. The two must be exhausted. Still, building the fire had been a risk and he was surprised that Cole had taken it. It would have been a simple matter to put a bullet into each one of their sleeping forms and be done it it, but that wasn't Hauer's way. If anything, he would slip closer during the night and end this business with a knife. However, the thought that Cole still had a rifle held him back.

Hauer watched from the forest, a little envious of the warmth those two must surely have enjoyed from the fire. But something wasn't right. The sleeping forms didn't so much as stir.

After another hour of keeping watch, Hauer realized that he had been duped. The shapes that he had thought were sleeping forms were surely no more than bundles of sticks.

Hauer considered approaching the fire, just to make sure, but then decided against it. If Cole had set a trap, then this was it. Once Hauer walked into the ring of firelight, then Cole could pick him off from the shadows. Clever, clever. He had to admire the resourcefulness of the American, who must be hidden nearby.

Hauer did not stir from his vantage point, even once he realized that he had been tricked.

In the morning, when it was light enough to see their trail and possibly spot them in the forest, he would find Cole and the teenager —then finish this business for good.

* * *

COLE WAS MORE than ready for the day to begin, but he had to wait for the daylight to crystallize. Dark shapes became bushes. Blurs became trees. Now that it was light enough to see his way, it was time to set his plan in motion.

Leaving Danny behind with the rifle, Cole moved out of the cover of the forest and into the open valley. He paused to take a deep breath, letting the mountain air fill his lungs. He was struck again by the beauty of the place. The cold mountaintops stood indifferent against the backdrop of the sky, tinged with pinkish clouds from the rising sun. It had been damp and cold in the lower elevations during the night, resulting in a heavy frost that coated the brown grass, so that the ankle-high grass crackled like glass under his boots. He could see the tracks through the grass that he'd left last night, going out to collect meat from the boar, and then back again. He didn't see evidence of any other tracks, which meant that Hauer must not have ventured out here during the night. Surely, however, Hauer was watching even now from some vantage point. He would have been waiting for this moment.

The spot between Cole's shoulder blades itched fiercely as he imagined Hauer's crosshairs there. He was gambling that The Butcher would not kill him outright, but would want to take some measure of pleasure in drawing out Cole's death, like a cat toying with a mouse.

Cole was not disappointed. He heard a shout behind him, and turned to see Hauer emerging from the woods, rifle pointed at Cole. He stopped and waiting for Hauer to approach, heart hammering. If Hauer sensed a trap, then all that he had to do was pull the trigger and it was all over.

"There you are!" Hauer called, crossing the grass more confidently now.

"You son of a bitch!" Cole shouted back.

Hauer stopped. "Where is your rifle?"

"Out of ammo."

Hauer made a *tsk, tsk* sound. "Too bad for you."

Cole held up the hunting knife. "Come a little closer and see how you like it."

Hauer did come closer, but stopped well short of knife range, wary of Cole's blade. He lowered the rifle but kept it pointed in Cole's direction, looking him up and down. Cole worried that Hauer sensed a trap.

"I imagine that wound hurts," Hauer said.

"It's a mite sore," Cole allowed.

Hauer cocked his head. "I do not think that you are out of ammunition," he finally said. "What I think is that your grandson is at the edge of the forest, intending to shoot me, and that you have put yourself out here as bait."

Cole's heart sank, but he kept a poker face. Hauer was no fool. But why had he exposed himself out here in the field if he knew better? "Is that what you think?" Cole said.

"I am not concerned about the boy," Hauer said. "*Der Junge ist ein Weichei.* He is a soft egg. He would not even bring along a rifle or shotgun on this hunting trip because he doesn't like to kill animals."

Hauer raised the rifle, lining up the sights on Cole, and a chill went through him. This was it. It was all up to Danny now. Silently, he urged his grandson to shoot. *Do it now.*

Smiling at Cole, Hauer suddenly turned and fired two quick shots at the tree line, in two different directions. To Cole's relief, the bullets were nowhere near where Danny was hidden, but that wasn't Hauer's intention. He'd meant to rattle Danny. He turned back to Cole.

"Right about now, your grandson is probably shaking like a leaf and pissing himself," Hauer said with a laugh. "We both know what it's like to have someone shoot at you for the first time."

"You are a piece of work, Hauer," Cole said, desperate to buy some time. *Come on, Danny. You got this.*

From the woods, a single shot rang out. They both heard the bullet sing through the crisp air. It might have passed right between them.

Neither man so much as flinched.

Hauer turned his back to the forest, as if dismissing the threat there. "Do you see what I mean? I could stand out here all day without fear of being shot. Like I said, your grandson *ist ein Weichei*."

Cole ignored the insult. *One bullet left, Danny,* Cole was thinking. *Breathe, aim, squeeze that trigger. Just like I taught you. Take your time—well, maybe not too much time.*

"Get it over with," Cole said, his voice raised, hoping that his grandson could hear him. It was a message for Danny more than Hauer.

"You should have killed me during the war," Hauer said. "After I shoot you, I will track down the boy and take care of him as well."

Hauer raised the rifle again. This time, he put it to his shoulder and aimed carefully at Cole.

"Where would you like me to shoot you?" Hauer asked. "Through the heart? Through the head?"

"Just get it over with."

Another shot came from the forest.

There was no snap of a bullet going past. Instead, there was the solid *whunk* of a hollow-point bullet hitting flesh and bone.

Hauer reacted as if someone had just slapped him hard between the shoulder blades. Intended to bring down big game like wild boar and stags by shredding lungs and internal organs, the mushrooming slug was equally effective on human targets.

Hauer stumbled forward a couple of steps, a look of disbelief in his eyes. The rifle drooped in his hands. Slowly, he sank to his knees. Then he slumped over sideways.

But he wasn't dead yet. Hauer's hands still grasped the rifle. He struggled to find the strength to point it at Cole.

Cole walked over and took hold of the rifle, wresting it from Hauer's hands. His right side hurt like fire and his shoulder felt stiff, but not much effort was involved as he aimed the muzzle down at Hauer.

"Hauer, there's something I've been meaning to ask you. Why the hell did you shoot that nun all those years ago? Hell, she was just trying to help one of your own men."

"I never liked nuns. Isn't that reason enough?"

"No."

"Look at the two of us, all shot to pieces," Hauer said softly. It was an effort for him to speak. A bubble of pink froth appeared at the corner of his lips. "For us, the war is finally over."

"I reckon," Cole said. "I've got to say, this has been a long time coming."

Then he pulled the trigger.

CHAPTER TWENTY-FIVE

IN THE AFTERMATH of the final gunshot, a stillness settled over the valley, the forest, and the surrounding mountains. It was a peaceful quiet for a change, rather than a menacing silence. Cole breathed in the crisp morning air, saying a silent prayer of thanks that he and Danny were still alive.

Hauer had been a goner, lung shot by Danny's bullet, but Cole made sure that he was the one who finished him off. When the authorities asked, he could say with a straight face that he had been the one who killed Hauer.

He turned his attention to the edge of the forest, where Danny was emerging, rifle at his side. Cole stood, smiling, waiting for him.

"Good shooting," Cole said.

Danny looked shaken. "I shot him," he said. "I just killed a man."

"You did what you had to do. It was self-defense—him or us," Cole said. He reached for the rifle and took it in his good left hand. "Listen up now. We both know you did the right thing. I'm the one who did all the shooting, if anyone asks."

A thought seemed to occur to Danny. "You mean the police?"

"I reckon someone might wonder how Hauer ended up dead.

Considering that he's shot in the back and all, they ain't going to buy that it was suicide."

Danny looked down at the body. Hauer had been an imposing man in life, but in death he seemed to have shrunken.

"He tried to kill us," Danny stated, as if still trying to convince himself.

"He surely tried, but that didn't work out so well for him, now did it?" Cole took Danny by the elbow, steering him away from the body. "I'm proud of you, Danny. I know it's not easy, but you can hold your head high. You did the right thing."

Danny nodded.

"C'mon, now that Hauer's not here to stop us anymore, let's go see if we can find that trail out of this valley. I could use some coffee."

The thought of food seemed to snap Danny out of his trance. "And pancakes," Danny said.

"Hmm. Bacon, too."

"And some orange juice! My stomach is rumbling now, Pa Cole."

"All right then, let's get out of here."

Together, they started toward the western neck of the valley.

They were not alone for long.

The stillness of the morning air was interrupted by the steady *thup, thup, thup* of an approaching helicopter. Soon enough, the aircraft came into sight, flying low.

"You think they're looking for us?" Danny asked.

"Only one way to find out. Give 'em a wave."

Danny did just that, using a big howdy motion that they called a hillbilly wave back home. Instead of continuing on its route, the heli-copter flew lower and circled overhead.

"I reckon they were looking for us, after all," Cole said.

Further confirmation arrived a few minutes later, when a couple of official-looking off-road vehicles came bouncing up the rough road into the valley. Several men and a couple of women got out, all wearing the bright red jackets of the mountain rescue team, known as *le Peloton Gendarmerie de Haute Montagne*. They gave Cole and Danny water, put new bandages on Cole's arm, and much to Cole's embarrassment, wrapped him in a shiny emergency blanket that looked as if it came off a spaceship.

Another blanket was used to cover Hauer's remains, which Cole had managed to point out to the team.

But there was no return to the lodge just yet. They waited for an hour until yet another vehicle arrived, this one carrying two uniformed gendarmes and two plainclothes men who appeared to be detectives.

The detectives clearly had not expected to be called into the forest that morning, because both wore dress shoes, overcoats, and suits, one with a tie and one without. It was not gear for the outdoors, and neither one seemed too inclined to venture very far from the vehicle. They lifted the blanket long enough to get a good look at Hauer, then one of them put on some gloves and picked up Hauer's rifle. Eventually, they came back and asked Cole and Danny some questions. Soon, they left Danny alone and focused their attention on Cole.

Cole had already made up his mind that he wasn't going to try and explain that Hauer had tried to kill them. How could Cole ever prove that? Who would ever believe him?

"I reckon I got confused," Cole explained, trying somewhat unsuccessfully to come across as a feeble senior citizen. He hunched his shoulders under the blanket to seem more convincing. Never mind the fact that he resembled a rangy old wolf. "The light wasn't good and I thought he was a stag. My eyes ain't what they used to be."

Cole told the detectives that they had gotten lost after being separated from the group of hunters. Cole kept his explanation short, which was easy for him, being naturally a man of few words.

The French gendarmes spoke English fluently. The two detectives, in addition to fluency in English, also had eyes like sharks. They seemed to see right through him, as if they had heard it all before, which they probably had. *It was all an accident.* One thing for certain— these men were not fools. They asked a lot of questions.

"Did he shoot himself also?"

Cole shrugged. "Maybe when he fell?"

Leaving Cole, the two detectives moved off to one side and conferred, smoking cigarettes and speaking French in low tones, glancing in Cole's direction from time to time. One of them had taken

Hauer's ID along with Cole's, then sat in one of the vehicles, relaying the information.

"Are they going to arrest us?" Danny whispered.

"They seem a little hung up on the fact that he's shot in the back and in the front with two different rifles," Cole said. "It's a mite confusing."

After a while, the detectives tossed away their cigarettes and marched purposefully toward Cole.

"Did you know this man was former *Stasi*?" they asked. "The German authorities wanted to ask him some questions, it seems. He was a Nazi, perhaps a war criminal, and then a member of the East German Secret Police. He was not what you Americans would call a Boy Scout."

"News to me, son."

"We know about you, too. Some important people are very concerned about you. You were here during the war. You helped fight to free France. A war hero."

"Long time ago," Cole said.

"Some of us have long memories." The one who seemed to be the senior detective pointed at Hauer's body, then looked Cole right in the eye and announced, "Hunting accident."

Once that was settled, everybody seemed to relax. The senior detective produced a flask and they all had a nip—even Danny.

"Don't tell your gran," Cole muttered, already feeling better as the alcohol and the shiny blanket warmed him.

Then the people in the red jackets loaded up Hauer's body and everybody bundled into the vehicles and drove slowly out of the valley.

Cole glanced back once at the mountain peaks, oddly saddened to see them go.

* * *

AN AMBULANCE WAITED to transport Cole to the hospital to be treated for his wounds. The rescue team had bandaged him up, but his arm and shoulder needed more expert medical attention. First, they had some other business to attend to. They gathered in the lodge lobby, near the big fire in the hearth, which helped to warm their chilled bones.

Danny got a hug from Angela, and even a kiss right there in the middle of the lobby. Judging from the red blush that spread across his grandson's face, Angela had warmed him up plenty.

Hans was also waiting.

"Hans, I'm sorry your rifle got a little banged up," Cole said.

"My friend, that is the least of anyone's worries. I am glad that you are all right."

Hans explained how he had called Colonel Mulholland, who had pulled some strings so that a search-and-rescue operation was finally set into motion.

"I have to thank you, Hans," Cole said. "It would have been a long walk back from that valley."

"What in the world happened?"

Cole told the actual story, which was definitely not what he had related to the French police. Hans listened quietly. When Cole had finished, all that Hans said was, "I never trusted that Hauer."

"I should have listened to you," Cole admitted. "But it's all done now. He ain't going to cause any more trouble."

"Now, you need to go to the hospital and see to that arm."

"Oh, it can wait," Cole said. "Let's all have some breakfast first."

* * *

ONCE COLE WAS BACK from the hospital and had recuperated for a couple of days, the two old soldiers had one last mission together. They made it alone, leaving Danny and Angela to their own devices. Cole felt that Danny needed some time just to be a kid and forget about what had happened.

Danny had been quieter than usual as the enormity of what he had done sank in. Taking a life was never easy, even in self-defense. When Danny had retreated to his room to watch MTV and eat pizza, Cole had let him be, not sure what else he could say or do for his grandson. Cole was thankful that the upcoming day with Angela had snapped him out of his brooding.

"Are you sure those two don't need a chaperone?" Cole asked Hans. "Are you comfortable leaving your niece alone with my grandson? He is a teenage boy, after all."

Hans shrugged. "They are young," he said. "Let them do what young people do. Besides, your grandson is a gentleman. The business we are attending to concerns the past. Let them enjoy the present."

"Amen to that," Cole agreed.

At the wheel of the Volvo again, Hans drove them down winding mountain roads to the village called Wingen sur Moder. The place was too far off the beaten path to be much of a tourist destination. Cole had been there forty years ago, but none of the modern roads approaching the village looked familiar. Nonetheless, it was a lovely village, set among the hills, with one of every shop that the villagers might need in this remote location. It was also small enough that the arrival of an automobile with German registration plates did not go unnoticed. A couple of old-timers scowled in their direction.

"They noticed the car's *Nummernschilder*," Hans said, using the German slang for vehicle tags. "I do not think they like Germans very much."

"They'd be a lot less friendly if we had driven up in a Panzer."

"Good point," Hans agreed.

The looks that the foreign car received were in part because this village had not been so peaceful back in the winter of 1945. In January, German forces had pushed deep through this countryside as Operation *Nordwind* drove further into the Allied lines just as the Allies thought that the Battle of the Bulge had been won. Although it had little strategic value, this village had found itself caught in the middle of a battle that raged all around them. The battle had moved from the hills, to the narrow streets, and even into the houses themselves. The roar of tank engines, machine-gun fire, and individual rifle shots had shattered the mountain quiet. In addition to the soldiers on both sides, many villagers had died. Others had lost their homes and shops. It had taken the villagers many years to recover from the war's devastation.

At the village center, Hans parked the Volvo and got out with Cole. The village itself looked much as Cole remembered it. Several more trees had been planted, however, softening the street. The cobblestones were gone, replaced by modern paving with parking spaces marked in bright paint.

A few of the older villagers noticed them, and now that Cole and Hans had left the car with German tags behind, nodded in grim acknowledgment. They knew well enough why two old strangers were here. These aging villagers still remembered that day many years before.

The smell of woodsmoke transported him to another time and place. Cole stood thoughtfully, remembering the fight that had taken place there. He was lost for a moment in the sounds of battle, rifles firing, the *ratatatat* of machine guns, even the deep boom of tanks and mortars.

He glanced up at the church steeple, seeing what a clear shot Hauer must have had. It all seemed like yesterday.

With an effort, he shook his head to clear it and return to the present. The flashback had been so intense that he was startled to find the village so quiet and calm. A few people strolled the sidewalks, bundled against the chill autumn air, chatting quietly.

Hans had been watching him, but the old German soldier made no comment. Perhaps he had been lost in his own memories as well. Both men realized that as their generation faded, so would the last living memories of that war vanish.

They made their way to the small stone monument near the church that marked the graves of those who had died during the battle. Years before, a marker had been placed with the names engraved on it of the U.S. soldiers who had given their lives there. Cole didn't know the name of the young soldier who had died at the side of the nun, but surely his name was included. Cole had brought along a small American flag, which he now placed at the foot of the marker.

Then he moved on to the second marker, on which the names of villagers who had died in the fight were written. He had left his cheaters in the damn car, so he had to get on his knees to read the names. He quickly spotted Sister Anne Marie's name among the fallen.

Of course, Cole hadn't known her beyond that brief meeting all those years ago. But she had clearly been a selfless young woman, called to serve a greater good by helping the American prisoners. One more life lost among many. Hauer had murdered her, plain and simple. A few days ago, Cole had finally been able to deliver his final sniper's justice.

Still kneeling, he placed a single rose into the cold ground. *For you, Sister.*

Cole got to his feet, feeling the ache in his arm from that last fight. Hans stood a few feet away, his eyes closed, evidently offering a silent prayer. When he was finished, he crossed himself.

"For the nun?" Cole asked.

"For us all, my friend."

The two old soldiers headed back to the car, their mission done. They drove back without saying much, both lost in thought.

After Hans dropped him at the hotel, Cole was still in the lobby when Danny came through the revolving doors. He was alone but smiling, apple-cheeked from the crisp air. It was hard to believe this was the same young man who, just days before, had been hungry and haggard, fighting for his life. The young were so resilient. Cole felt proud just at the sight of his grandson.

"I thought you'd be out with Angela," Cole said.

"We had a great time," he said. "We went ice skating and had the best hot chocolate you ever tasted. Germans make the best hot chocolate. It's not like that powdered stuff back home, that's for sure. Angela has to go back home to her family tomorrow. And she's got school. I might not see her again for a while. Maybe I'll come back this summer, if I can save up some money."

"Maybe," Cole agreed. "Well, what do you want to do next?"

"Pa Cole, this has been a great trip, but I think it's time to get back."

Cole gripped Danny's shoulder with his good hand and grinned. "You know what? I'm thinking the same thing. I reckon we ought to get back home and see how Gran is doing."

-The End-

ABOUT THE AUTHOR

David Healey lives in Maryland where he worked as a journalist for more than twenty years. He is a member of the International Thriller Writers and a contributing editor to The Big Thrill magazine. Join his newsletter list at:

www.davidhealeyauthor.com
or
www.facebook.com/david.healey.books

Made in the USA
Columbia, SC
15 September 2023

22946456R00138